HEY LADIES!

HEY LADIES!

THE STORY OF 8 BEST FRIENDS, 1 YEAR, AND WAY, WAY TOO MANY EMAILS

Michelle Markowitz and Caroline Moss

Abrams Image, New York

introduction

"Hey Ladies!"

How is it possible that those two tiny words at the beginning of an email can bring on an onslaught of feelings: anxiety, stress, agita, and underneath all of that—the palpable excitement that lies in the possibility of having fun and making memories.

We're not exactly sure who sent the first email beginning "Hey Ladies," but we imagine it was an innocent salutation for a birthday or a shower of some kind. We imagine this poor woman probably realized all of a sudden that she had to brainstorm, organize, and host an event that appealed to a cross-section of women, while properly conveying how excited she was to perform this thankless, unpaid work. And we imagine the women receiving that first email had the following thoughts: 1) Why are there so many logistics that need to be worked out for a night that is ostensibly about having fun? 2) Wow, this is probably going to cost me more than I first anticipated! and 3) I want everyone to know how excited I also am for my friend's blessed upcoming marriage/graduation/baby shower/brunch so I will respond in kind with way too many exclamation points!!!

Why do we send Hey Ladies emails? The answer is, quite simply, like most things that drive us a little bit crazy: We do it out of love. We love our friends and family (even if our second cousin did plan her shower for the one weekend we mentioned we have a conflicting event!).

In the summer of 2013, we started chatting for the first time on Twitter and bonded right away over our shared experience of being on what seemed like hundreds (if not thousands) of Hey Ladies planning emails at the time.

And so, "Hey Ladies!" was born.

A question we want to answer before you ask: No! We're not making fun of you or your friends or women in general. We're making fun of ourselves, and how mass emails to big groups seem to bring out the "OMG SO EXCITED!!!!!!!!!" in all of us.

Now, we offer you a book. We hope it resonates with you, we hope it's cathartic, and we hope it makes you laugh. Remember: We're all in this together.

Enjoy.

Katie   Ali   Gracie   Ashley

Morgan   Nicole   Caitlin   Jen

january

To: Katie, Jen, Ashley, Morgan, Gracie, Caitlin, Nicole
From: Ali
Date: January 1 at 8:00 a.m.
Subject: New Year = New Us

Hey Ladies!

Rabbit rabbit. Happy New Year!!! I know this is going to be our best year yet! I had such a great time last night -- maybe *too* much fun. Which reminds me, can everyone send me their NYE photos this morning? I'll edit them to make us all look more fierce and collected and less like a drunk mess who spent twenty minutes comforting our crying friend in the bathroom because that guy she has been hooking up with didn't show up. (For the record -- I'm going into this new year letting go of bad habits and negativity and focusing on attracting positivity and good feelings into my life, but, Nicole, I *hate* that guy!)

These are my resolutions for the new year:
1. I will cultivate mature relationships with men in which I am recognized and valued for the person I am.
2. I will be the best friend that I can be, and I will use my god-given skills to plan fun activities for all of us so we can all enjoy this carefree time in our lives. (Should we plan an MLK weekend to Iceland? Or Greenland? I can never remember which one is cold!)
3. I will work out every day and lose twenty pounds. The weight loss will be a happy by-product of all my spinning and not the reason for it.
4. I will lean in to my career.
5. ???? TBD!

These resolutions are making me feel so centered and excited already! I can feel myself and my tribe (that's what I heard my yoga teacher call her group of friends -- so cute, right??) becoming healthier already!

Can you please email me all of your resolutions by EOD. This is so fun!

Also, I am writing this while Ben (my new boyfriend????) is sleeping next to me!!!! We'll probably spend the day building snowmen in Central Park and having sex by a fireplace. Jen -- if I go into his bathroom and take photos of what's in his medicine cabinet, can you text your doctor friend really quick and tell me what his prescriptions mean/what medical issues our potential children might have??

We're so #blessed.

Love,
Ali

"What would you do if you weren't afraid?" —Anyone who's ever given a TED Talk

To: Ali, Jen, Ashley, Morgan, Gracie, Caitlin, Nicole
From: Katie
Date: January 1 at 8:20 a.m.
Subject: Re: New Year = New Us

Ladiessssssss <3

Happy New Year! Ali, does Ben know you were making out with Teddy last night at Brother Jimmy's? Don't ask me how I know, but you did end up on the New York City New Year's Snapchat Story so...that's how I knew. LOL! Don't worry. Apps like Snapchat are so ephemeral. It will be gone within 24 hours.

Thought about my rezzies, and here they are:
1. Work promotion. I have told you guys before, so you def don't need reminding, so this is really for me: I am more than the freelance listicle journalist and girl who tags the stories on the *Times*' website with the categories that they belong to. I want to be an investigative reporter (maybe for a Euro bureau?), and I want that to happen by next year. This is like a 6-level promotion, but I did take 4 journo classes in undergrad, so I think I have an edge.
2. Find my phone. Wanted to check and see if my phone ended up with any of you last night. I can't find it, and I have no idea if I left it in the Uber, the Lyft, or at the bar. :(I want to kill myself. I feel like I have an unfair advantage because I know like everything that's happening 24/7, and in this case, maybe it's too much stimulation, because now I'm freaking out about someone stealing my phone. I know everyone says they can't live without their phones, but for me it's true because I am a (soon-to-be) journalist.

I think it's great for those of you who are focused on love, but I am very career-oriented and I understand that means love takes a backseat. We all saw what happened to Bethenny Frankel.

Are any of you awake yet?????? I know we didn't have brunch plans, but I am thinking about trying to get a table at that new upscale "diner" place on the West Side. I think it's called Diner, but I can't remember the name for sure. Thoughts? Can someone google? I feel like we could do it if everyone could be there at 9 a.m. (40 mins from now?) Jen, can you drive in from Jersey or take the "Path"?

OK, greatttttt, I'll make a rez. I can't summon an Uber though, because I don't have my phone so not really sure how to get there....subway???? Maybe I'll do Zipcar.

iMessage me (I have it on desktop) if you *can't* go. Otherwise I'll see you there. Sorry in advance for def being in a bitchy mood. I WANT MY PHONE BACKKKKKKKK.

Smooch,
Katie

To: Ali, Katie, Ashley, Morgan, Gracie, Caitlin, Nicole
From: Jen
Date: January 1 at 8:25 a.m.
Subject: Re: New Year = New Us

Hey Ladies!

Last night was so much fun! I can't even remember the last time Brad and I stayed out past midnight, lol! #PracticallyMarried

Sorry I had to leave right after the ball drop -- did I miss anything??

The new year is upon us, and while it's time to look forward, I think it's important to look back as well, and as Oprah says, "express your gratitude." So:

I am most grateful this year for my family (except my cousin Kayla, who's just so jealous of me and my life with Brad, it's sad), my friends (esp you ladies!!), and most of all, the love of my life, my hero, my Prince -- my boyfriend, Brad.

I can't believe this year we'll be celebrating 6 years together (if you don't count the 2 non-consecutive years we weren't together, and I do not). It feels like I've known him for a lifetime. ;) Brad is the most remarkable person I've ever met. Just this morning, I opened my eyes, and do you know what he said to me? "Happy New Year." How cute is that??? He's made me happier than I ever thought possible!!! I'll never forget the time we went to the top of the Empire State Building (I've been into spicing it up with *Sleepless in Seattle* role-playing) and I said, "This view is amazing!" and he was looking right at me and then he goes -- seriously I can't even make this up -- he said: "Yeah, it is. And I'm not talking about the skyline." SWOON!!!! That being said, if he doesn't propose this year I will likely be forced to break up with him. Sorry I am "old-school" and don't believe in long-term partnerships without forward momentum. Put a ring on it! Luckily he loves when I send him subtle hints, like leaving photos around our apartment of the exact ring he better buy soon.

I just keep falling more and more in love with him every day. Like right now? I love him more than I did when I started this email. I'm so lucky my soulmate danced into my life. I'm so #blessed. Here's hoping he pops the Q soon, because finding someone else on short notice would be difficult for me, and my plan has always been to get pregnant by 31.

With that in mind, here are my resolutions:
1) To get Brad to propose to me via a cycle of being warm (to show him what I'd be like as a wife!) and being distant (to show him what it would be like to not have me in his life!).
2) Begin the stressful process of shopping for a condo. (Tribeca?? Near the park?? Terrace space? There are so many things to think about!)
3) Lose 15 lbs, but only for health reasons and *not* for vanity reasons. I will cut out carbs, work out 7 times a week, and not eat anything after 7 p.m. each night as a long-term lifestyle change, rather than a short-term diet.

Anyway, can't make brunch! I'm going to make Cheerios for Brad, then we'll cozy up on the couch :) Can you please send me text updates though, and take lots of pictures??? I don't want to miss anything juicy!

Love,
Jen

p.s. I love Brad even more now than I did halfway through this email!

To: Ali, Jen, Ashley, Morgan, Gracie, Caitlin, Nicole
From: Katie
Date: January 1 at 8:47 a.m.
Subject: Re: New Year = New Us

Hey girls,

Great goals, Jen. So stoked for you :) But, as I mentioned re: Bethenny, women rarely get it all. So maybe there's like a backup plan you could work on (you'll never need to use it though!!!). Have you thought about exploring real estate as a full-time option? You could get your own Bravo show!

Katie

PS. Does that mean everyone else is in for brunch? Assuming yes!

To: Ali, Jen, Katie, Morgan, Gracie, Caitlin, Nicole
From: Ashley
Date: January 1 at 8:51 a.m.
Subject: Re: New Year = New Us

Hey ladies!

Happy New Year! I am so excited to report -- before I tell anyone, even the Yale Alumni Association -- that I have accepted a job teaching English at Choate Rosemary Hall! The news came in right before Christmas. Apparently, I am a mid-year replacement for a teacher that left Choate due to "personal reasons." I am so excited, and thank you so much in advance for your congratulations! I've been working hard for this, and I think that it's going to be amazing. I'll be coaching JV field hockey as well, which is my legacy there. It's so amazing to give back to a community that gave me so much.

So I guess my resolutions are:

1. KICK A** at this job!
2. More expensive, staple luxury pieces for my closet. Thinking: Lilly, Alice + Olivia, Badgley, and vintage Ralph Lauren.
3. Find love!!!!!! Obviously women can't have it all, Katie, but I'm not trying to! I think I'll do this job for 2 years tops, move back to Manhattan to find the love of my life, get married, have babies, and then buy a place in CT or Manhattan. Or maybe Brooklyn. Does anyone know if Cobble Hill (Brooklyn) is safe at night? Does anyone wanna look at real estate there with me this weekend? I know it's early but I'd like to get a sense of the market. Jen, maybe I can be your first client!

I was thinking I could come back into the city next week to celebrate. Thinking Fig & Olive? I want to make it a theme night. Ali, can you send some ideas for that?

PS -- can't make brunch, sorry!

kisses and love,
Ashley

To: Katie, Jen, Ashley, Morgan, Gracie, Caitlin, Nicole
From: Ali
Date: January 1 at 9:22 a.m.
Subject: Re: New Year = New Us

Congrats on the new job!!! I could never cut myself off from society and move to Connecticut even for 2 years (especially during our peak hotness years!) at this point in my life, but I love that you're so fearless! And teaching!! I wonder what kind of people you'll meet there! This is so *The Children's Hour* with a dash of *Dead Poets Society*!

I'd love to help with themes, but I am just crazed, and I'm trying to align how I spend my time with my greater goals and objectives in life!! Please follow up with me next week, and I'll see if one of the interns can help source some options.

Ben wants to spend the day getting work done. So driven!! I love it. We're meeting at Diner in Tribeca right? Does anyone have a new toothbrush + undies (preferably new with tags on) they can lend me??

See you soon!
Ali

"Say no now, so you can say yes later." —Basically this is how French women think about food, but this is how I want you guys to think about life

To: Ali, Katie, Jen, Ashley, Gracie, Caitlin, Nicole
From: Morgan
Date: January 1 at 10:12 a.m.
Subject: Re: New Year = New Us

Wait, I just got to Diner on the UWS.

Katie, which one is it?? I texted her but she's not responding. Oh wait, she doesn't have her phone. Wait...Okay I am going to walk around to every table and see if anyone is Katie. Brb.

Morgs

To: Ali, Katie, Jen, Ashley, Gracie, Caitlin, Nicole
From: Morgan
Date: January 1 at 10:30 a.m.
Subject: Re: New Year = New Us

No one here is Katie. I seriously don't get Manhattan. What's the difference between the UWS and the UES again? You guys should move to Brooklyn so I don't have to keep coming into the concrete jungle.

Ali, should I meet you at TriBeCa? Is it "at TriBeCa" or "in TriBeCa"?

Morgs

To: Ali, Katie, Jen, Morgan, Gracie, Caitlin, Nicole
From: Ashley
Date: January 1 at 11:41 a.m.
Subject: Re: New Year = New Us

Hey ladies,

Thanks for the supportive words, Ali! The thing about CT is it's just a lot of NYC ex-pats who wanted more estate lifestyles. NYC life is so cramped! Just feel like the $ per sq. ft. in CT is really amazing especially near Choate.

Should I buy a cute little New England cottage? What do you guys think? I'll bring some listings to dinner next week. Would be great to get your interns to come up with ideas, Ali. Appreciate the hard work you do for me. You're an excellent publicist!

Also, Jen, you know I love your love story with Brad. It's sooo Meg Ryan/Tom Hanks <3
Do you think you could help me make a good Pinterest for my future NYC home? Thinking
5+ years down the line, so no super current trends. Like, remember chevron? I had to toss
so many good monthly planners thanks to that being uncool. :(

XO,
Ashley

To: Ali, Katie, Jen, Ashley, Morgan, Gracie, Caitlin
From: Nicole
Date: January 1 at 11:52 a.m.
Subject: Re: New Year = New Us

You guys, I would be so freaked out if I were Katie!! How can we get in touch with her if she
doesn't have her phone?? Do you think she's okay?? Should we post on her Facebook or
Instagram to get in touch?? How can we find her??????

This must be what life was like for our grandparents :(

xx,
Nicole

To: Ali, Katie, Jen, Ashley, Gracie, Caitlin, Nicole
From: Morgan
Date: January 1 at 11:57 a.m.
Subject: Re: New Year = New Us

Hey ladies,

Nicole, I know Katie doesn't have her phone but you can still answer yours! Which Diner
did you go to??? I have no idea where I am in this city lmao. Brooklyn is easier, you guys!
Seriously, can someone's resolution be to visit Brooklyn, like, ever? It's very safe!

Morgs

To: Ali, Katie, Jen, Ashley, Morgan, Gracie, Caitlin
From: Nicole
Date: January 1 at 12:02 p.m.
Subject: Re: New Year = New Us

Ok, I'm just pulling up now -- I'm not sure the exact address, but I'm looking outside and there's a Starbucks and a huge pile of snow right next to the entrance...

An old man just walked by with the cutest dog that looks exactly like Jake Gyllenhaal's German shepherd Atticus (cutest dog name ever!).

My resolutions:
1) Stop taking cabs
2) ???
3) Make a profit doing something in business

I'm waving, do you guys see me?? Katie -- can you reimburse me for the cab since you lost your phone and we're meeting just to comfort you? I am so there for you, but it just seems fair.

x,
Nicole

To: Ali, Katie, Ashley, Morgan, Gracie, Caitlin, Nicole
From: Jen
Date: January 1 at 12:30 p.m.
Subject: Re: New Year = New Us

Hey ladies,

Can you take me off this thread (for now?)? One of my other resolutions as of the last hour is to really be present in my life and to keep my eyes open to the beauty all around me, and the constant dinging of my phone is sort of getting in the way of that.

Re: my last email with hints of fertility wishes, do you think getting pregnant "by accident" would help move the proposal plan along? I got the IUD, but I bet there's a YouTube video on how to take it out yourself. Or maybe one of you can come over and help?

Circle back with me post-brunch! Brad wants to watch football so we agreed on 2 hours of "me time screen time" around 4 p.m. EST. Thinking about rewatching *Real Housewives of New Jersey*. So inspiring! Hope you find your phone, Katie. Enjoy brunch! And email me when you're done!

Jen

To: Ali, Katie, Jen, Ashley, Gracie, Caitlin, Nicole
From: Morgan
Date: January 1 at 1:00 p.m.
Subject: Re: New Year = New Us

Hey gals,

Where are you??? I was at Diner UWS but now I am in a Duane Reade (not sure which one). Something about Duane Reade just feels so safe to me because we have them in Brooklyn. Please let me know.

In the meantime, I want to share my thoughts on a new year:

1. Be a better investor: since the fall of bitcoin, I have been smarter about my investments and more savvy about the state of the tech bubble.
2. Fewer Seamless orders and more cooking at home
3. Be better at going to the gym (maybe)
4. Drink more water
5. Always have a good manicure
6. Unfollow haters from my past on all social media channels
7. Watch *The Wire* (have any of you seen *The Wire*?): everyone in Williamsburg is obsessed.

I can't find anyone??? I might just cab home, you guys...this feels like a bad omen for the new year.

Love,
Morgs

To: Ali, Katie, Jen, Ashley, Gracie, Caitlin, Nicole
From: Morgan
Date: January 1 at 1:05 p.m.
Subject: Re: New Year = New Us

I think I'm stuck in the Duane Reade elevator :(This is why I only visit the mom and pop pharmacy in Brooklyn.

Love,
Morgs

To: Ali, Katie, Jen, Ashley, Gracie, Morgan, Nicole
From: Caitlin
Date: January 1 at 1:10 p.m.
Subject: Re: New Year = New Us

Hey Ladies,

Namaste! I'm writing this perched on a windowsill high above the Catskill Mountains. I'm putting my Caitlin's Green Tea Matcha Wellness Drink™ up to my lips and feeling truly at peace. Breathing out the old year, and breathing in the new.

I regret I had to miss the festivities last night, but I wish you girls could have made it up to the ashram with me. At midnight we howled at the moon, and I sent a gift of peace and positive energy to each of you <3 There's something so primal in being with a group of strong and powerful women up here -- the female energy is palpable, and our goddess spirits recognize and salute one another. It's truly profound. Also, all 40 of us have synced up menstrually, which is just so amazing. There's nothing like 40 women PMSing at the exact same time, so things have been a little tense, but ultimately healing.

I don't like to do resolutions (see my Instagram post from 12/31), but I will take this moment to state my INTENTIONS FOR MANIFESTATION™:

1) This year I will remember to listen to what my tattoo says in Sanskrit, which is: Just. Breathe.
2) I will greet each new day with gratitude.
3) I'll fully accept my own amazingness, which in turn, will allow others to accept their own amazingness, therefore I will change my community through loving myself.
4) I'll fully surrender to the fact that the Universe has my best interests at heart, and in turn, will let Her guide me.
5) Increase Instagram followers from 200,000+ to 1M by the next year. If I dream it, anything is possible.

Last year was incredible -- going from partying all the time and working in PR at a job that was just so...meaningless, to finding my true passion in life and building a community of people who are truth-seekers to the point where I can support myself (and make even more money than anyone I know!) from my CaitlinYourLife™ lifestyle business -- is just beyond my wildest dreams. It's really true what they say -- without ME it's just AWESO. I saw that on a t-shirt, but our guidance can come from anywhere.

The spirit in me salutes the spirit in you.

Wishing you peace,
Caitlin

Soon to be seen on: *The Doctor Oz Show*, Oprah's *SuperSoul Sunday*, the *New York Times*, and *Forbes* 30 Under 30 (I will manifest this goal, therefore it will come true.)

To: Ali, Jen, Ashley, Morgan, Gracie, Caitlin, Nicole
From: Katie
Date: January 1 at 1:12 p.m.
Subject: Re: New Year = New Us

Hi Caitlin + friends,

I am responding to this email on your friend's phone. I found it in the back of a cab this morning and it did not have a passcode on it. I tried calling the ICE number, but I only got the operator at the *New York Times*. I am hoping one of you can help me get this phone back to her. I live downtown in the Financial District at 2 Gold. I can leave it in an envelope with the doorman and someone can pick it up.

Let me know if there's a convenient time that works.

Thanks,
Topher Campbell

To: Ali, Katie, Jen, Ashley, Gracie, Caitlin, Nicole
From: Morgan
Date: January 1 at 1:20 p.m.
Subject: Re: New Year = New Us

Hello Topher,

Pleased to e-meet you. I'm in a cab en route to you now. I have long hair, and I am carrying a Duane Reade bag.

Very best,
Morgan (Morgs)

Jan 1, 1:22 PM

Ali

Hey! Great news! I'm literally in the neighborhood of whoever has Katie's phone, so I can just pick it up now. LOL this guy is prob a weirdo, but I'll take one for the team! :)

BTW is Sephora open today?

Morgan

Once I get out of the Duane Reade elevator I can go pick it up, no worries.

UWS is closer to the FiDi.

Plus I just bought pepper spray here, haha, so I'll be prepared if he's like the Craigslist Killer.

Nicole

I'll go! Can someone reimburse me for the metrocard to get there? Maybe Katie will.

Ashley

Sorry I'm OOO. Picking up new decor at CB2. Going lime green and pink for my bathroom. Cute or not cute? IMO it's cute.

Ali

Honestly I am pretty much there, just popped into Drybar really quick. This guy might be a murderer, and I took Krav Maga Yogalates once, so I should go since I'm the most prepared.

Morgan

Ok I am out of the elevator! Taking cab to FiDi. Be there soon.

Nicole

OMG I just googled him and he has dimples bigger than my apartment!!!!! I am on my way!

Ali

Don't bother ladies! I'm on it

Morgan

I'm on it!

To: Katie, Jen, Ashley, Morgan, Gracie, Caitlin, Nicole
From: Ali
Date: January 1 at 1:27 p.m.
Subject: Re: New Year = New Us

Hey Topher,

It is so sweet that you found Katie's phone and emailed all of us! You'll have to let me make it up to you ;)

I'm actually a block away from your apartment now -- I can meet you in the lobby. :)

People actually say I look like --this is so embarrassing -- a mix of Scarlett Johansson and Selena Gomez lol. It might be easier if you follow me on Instagram so you know what I look like? I can text you my handle if you email me back (not reply all) your number :)

See you in 5!

Ali

PR Executive

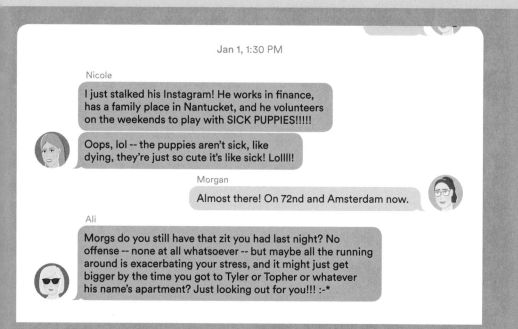

Jan 1, 1:30 PM

Nicole
I just stalked his Instagram! He works in finance, has a family place in Nantucket, and he volunteers on the weekends to play with SICK PUPPIES!!!!!

Oops, lol -- the puppies aren't sick, like dying, they're just so cute it's like sick! Lollll!

Morgan
Almost there! On 72nd and Amsterdam now.

Ali
Morgs do you still have that zit you had last night? No offense -- none at all whatsoever -- but maybe all the running around is exacerbating your stress, and it might just get bigger by the time you got to Tyler or Topher or whatever his name's apartment? Just looking out for you!!! :-*

SoulCycle
#therapy

Shake Shack
So fun, but the only meal of the day! ~1400 cals

DryBar
Best $50 you can spend if you have an important first date or meeting!

Bloomingdale's, Barney's, Bergdorf Goodman
The Trifecta

Museum of Modern Art
They have a great restaurant here!

The Metropolitan Museum of Art
There's no good food here :/

TriBeCa Equinox
HQ for finance bros, but you have to get there before 7am on weekdays. #Investment

Forever 21
The perfect place to find a last-minute outfit before work instead of doing the Walk of Shame into the office. Also, it's where your intern shops

Central Park
Great for autumnal photoshoots and summer days drinking rosé

The Highline
Cute spot to take your visiting aunt

Trump Tower
Where Ali got dumped by her college BF (don't ask)

New York Public Library
Where Big stood up Carrie on their wedding day :/

Grand Central Station
#30sCommutingGoals

Lincoln Center
Recommendation: See *The Nutcracker!*

Nobu
Great place to meet bankers!

Morgan

Oh you're right. Does anyone know if pepper spray could burn off a zit?

Nicole

 You guys, he is so cute!!!!!!!!!!!! Ali & Morgan, did you already google him?

Morgan

On 67th and Columbus now. Be there in 2!

Ali

 Oh he is? That's so funny. Maybe it was an old pic you saw? I'm sure he's some total weirdo! BTW, are beachy waves still in?? Or is it too anachronistic since it's January?

To: Ali, Katie, Jen, Ashley, Gracie, Caitlin, Nicole
From: Morgan
Date: January 1 at 1:30 p.m.
Subject: Re: New Year = New Us

Hi ladies and Topher,

Thank you Alexandra, but that won't be necessary. I am very close to the FiDi in my cab, and I will absolutely pick up the phone.

Topher, feel free to FaceTime me directly to coordinate. I am at 917-555-8978.

See you soon!!

Thanks,
Morgan

Brooklyn resident.

Jan 1, 1:32 PM

Ali

I'm one block from Topher's apartment. Just give up. I'm here. And this is so hard for me to say -- but you're kinda going through a lot right now -- the holidays can be "tough" -- and I'm just in a better place and ready for a loving relationship (my therapist/SoulCycle instructor Kayla agrees!). Topher and I belong together. Don't stand in my way. I didn't come here to make friends.

Morgan

I'm on 60th and Columbus, and you can't stop me.

Ali

Oh are you near the Sephora at Columbus Circle? I'm out of bronzer!

Morgan

No time to stop, Ali, I'm on a mission. Now excuse me. I'm going into airplane mode.

Ali

Morgs!!!!!!!! Is your phone still on airplane mode????

Morgan

Yeah

To: Ali, Katie, Ashley, Morgan, Gracie, Caitlin, Nicole
From: Jen
Date: January 1 at 1:41 p.m.
Subject: Re: New Year = New Us

Can you all please take me off this thread!!!!!!! My phone keeps vibrating and Brad is napping (and looks like an angel!). It's seriously annoying.

Love,
Jen

To: Ali, Katie, Jen, Ashley, Morgan, Gracie, Nicole
From: Caitlin
Date: January 1 at 2:00 p.m.
Subject: Re: New Year = New Us

Hi Topher,

Returning Katie's phone is really great karma.

I'm actually very interested in the karma/dharma/farm-to-table lifestyle, and I think you would really enjoy exploring my 15-part system, CaitlinYourLife™.

I will go ahead and add you to my newsletter list if you just email me back from your email. I think you'll really enjoy it :)

Namaste,
Caitlin

p.s. We should meet up for a matcha tea sometime and talk about our intentions!

CaitlinYourLife Online Store
Soon to be seen on: *The Doctor Oz Show*, Oprah's *SuperSoul Sunday*, the *New York Times*, and *Forbes* 30 Under 30 (I will manifest this goal, therefore it will come true.)

To: Ali, Jen, Ashley, Morgan, Gracie, Caitlin, Nicole
From: Katie
Date: January 1 at 2:30 p.m.
Subject: Re: New Year = New Us

Hey girls,

Katie here. Ali/Morgs not sure where you are on your journeys but I am at Diner, and Topher was already here, and I have my phone back! He's really...great.

I know I said all of that stuff about love and women not having it all but...we just had a really nice brunch, and I am feeling so good about it that I will forgive all of you for not getting your act together and showing up when you all said you would. I was *obviously* at this Diner location, lol! Why would I have gone to the others?

But maybe it's fate.

Just consider: I was at Diner for 4 hours, without my phone, and without my friends. This amazing, 6'2"–6'3", blue-eyed man, wearing a very nice coat and very nice shoes, comes into the restaurant. I'm already into him, but then he holds up a phone (my phone!) and asks: "Is there a Katie here? I have your phone." I'm Katie! I am sitting alone at a table, looking confident my friends will show up and meet me and not lonely, and I invite him to sit with me and we talk for 45 minutes before he says he has to go MEET. HIS. FAMILY. FOR. A. WALK. which he says is a Campbell family tradition on New Year's Day! I think he would have invited me, but I told him I had plans. (Duh.)

I have never been so glad to have you guys mess up and bail on brunch. This is gonna be the best year ever.

Katie Campbell (HAHA JK) (Sounds good though, right?)

To: Ali, Katie, Jen, Ashley, Morgan, Caitlin, Nicole
From: Gracie
Date: January 1 at 10:02 p.m.
Subject: Re: New Year = New Us

Hey Ladies!

Hope everyone had fun last night! My book club and I got together for some board games, and it was pretty great!

The BF and I spent today binge-watching Star Wars. I just realized my phone was on silent, oops! Everyone's night sounds fun though! Can't wait to hear more about Topher!!

Happy New Year, everyone!

xo,
Gracie

To: Ali, Katie, Ashley, Morgan, Gracie, Caitlin, Nicole
From: Jen
Date: January 5 at 1:15 p.m.
Subject: Re: New Year = New Us

Hey ladies,

Wow, Katie! SO fun! Some personal me news: since we last emailed, I've decided to start a lifestyle blog! I want it to be like *Cosmo* meets a mommy blog meets DIY (even though I don't do DIY -- it's just an aesthetic).

Caitlin, do you have any tips/can you show me how to do it/teach me how to brand? I definitely want to monetize right away so I can do it full-time and make my own money once my future kids start private preschool. Katie, do you think Topher could help market me to investors? Or ask him to ask his friends? LMK I can also reach out on LinkedIn. Is it cool to say you said it was okay to email him? I just did, so I hope so! Lol!

Thinking about domain names and color palettes if anyone wants to join my Pinterest board! Here are some names I am considering. Will put out a Twitter poll later!
• TheJenLife (like "The Zen Life" but me)
• MyPerfectLife
• JenYourself

Into grays, blacks, neutrals. Want it to be chic, cool, and viral. Katie, I know you want to be a journalist so maybe you can blog for us? I don't think I'll have enough time to actually write blogs between possibly trying to get "accidentally" pregnant and trying to get Brad to lock it down, but I know you do!! Let's try to work something out!

LMK, girls. I am excited about starting off the new year with a personal project :) And congrats, Katie, on a good first date! Did he pay? Brad still pays for literally everything we do. Whenever anyone says chivalry is dead, I'm like, lol...it's just in bed with me! Do you think that's a blog I could put on my new site?

Love,
Brad's Jen (omg maybe that's a name for the blog site????)

To: Ali, Katie, Jen, Ashley, Gracie, Morgan, Nicole
From: Caitlin
Date: January 9 at 3:39 p.m.
Subject: Re: New Year = New Us

Namaste!

Katie, I'm so happy for you! Sometimes we need to just let go and breathe, and the Universe will put us exactly where we're supposed to be. I did a Savasana this afternoon in which I sent you peaceful thoughts. Did you feel it? It was around 2:45 EST. I also sent peaceful thoughts to our friends in war-torn countries, but you should have still felt a little something as well.

And Jen, I think it's a very worthwhile plan for you to find meaning in your life! I've often wished that for you. That said, I'm not sure if your Brad's Jen (BJ for short?) blog is the way to go. While I'm sure you have a lot of BJ-oriented ideas, I don't know if your true calling is maintaining a ~lifestyle~ brand, which I've always said is the hardest job there is. Inner city schoolteachers? They can clock out. Firefighter? I'm assuming they get a lot of down time in between all the fires. But a lifestyle guru? That's a job that never ends. And when I say job, I mean higher calling. It's not something you can just pick up and do. You don't choose it, it chooses you.

If this is your heart's desire though, I truly encourage you to pursue it!

The spirit in me recognizes the spirit in you,
Caitlin

CaitlinYourLife Online Store
Soon to be seen on: *The Doctor Oz Show*, Oprah's *SuperSoul Sunday*, the *New York Times*, and *Forbes* 30 Under 30

P.S. Here's some annoying legal babble from my attorney/uncle lol:

Caitlin owns the rights to the phrases "CaitlinYourLife," "Your Life According to Caitlin," "Caitlin," and "Life"™. All rights reserved. No part of those phrases may be reproduced, distributed, or transmitted in any form or by any means, and legal action will be taken if anyone attempts to use any of her proprietary ideas such as: photographing healthy food, using interesting fonts for inspirational quotes, and photographing sunsets with a photo of yourself stretching or doing a yoga pose right next to it. Any similarities to anything listed above will be punishable by prison or severe fines. Namaste.

To: Katie, Jen, Ashley, Morgan, Gracie, Caitlin, Nicole
From: Ali
Date: January 13 at 4:07 p.m.
Subject: Re: New Year = New Us

Wow, Katie, I'm so happy for you!!!!!

He sounds so great!!!

I'm so incredibly excited for you!!! Sorry for not emailing back sooner! I was just overwhelmed with happiness for you!

Do you think it's a red flag that he hangs out with his parents? Is he too close with his mom maybe? You can tell a lot about a man by how he treats his mother. I'm just saying I've watched a lot of Lifetime.

Have you checked his Instagram/Facebook/Snapchat? What's his ex like??

What's his middle name and birthday? Wanna run a quick credit/sex offender search? I'm sure he'll pass with flying colors, but you can never be too safe!

Did he mention that I was on my way to his apartment? Did you guys talk about me?

YAY!!!!! This new year is off to such a great start already!!!!!

Love,
Ali

"Take all your big plans, and break 'em." —John Mayer, "Your Body Is a Wonderland"

"A woman without a man is like a fish without a bicycle." —Gloria Steinem via a poster in my dentist's office

To: Ali, Jen, Ashley, Morgan, Gracie, Caitlin, Nicole
From: Katie
Date: January 15 at 5:00 p.m.
Subject: Re: New Year = New Us

Hey Ladies!

Ahh, thanks for all of the emails about Topher. I agree, it really sounds promising, and while I can't say for sure that I am in love yet, it does feel like it will get there pretty soon (EOW?). It's already been two weeks and he has texted me first all three times we've talked so... promising start for sure!

Thanks for all of your inquiries, Ali! I feel like I don't want to do the whole like, background google just because I feel like there's such a lack of mystery surrounding love lately with all of these like, apps, and I just don't want anything to get ruined for me (esp if he's a sex offender!). That would suck (for me). Also, remember what happened when you back-googled Brandon from Yoga in the Park? If you had left it a mystery, you might have been able to score more free theater tickets from him before finding out he was just trying to date your male coworker. ANYWAY, neither here nor there now :) hahah.

Jen, re: your personal branding journey, maybe you could take this off thread? Just want to make sure we don't lose focus on me :)

Is anyone down for a SoulCycle tonight? I feel inspired. This year is going to be amazing.

Katie

To: Katie, Jen, Ashley, Morgan, Gracie, Caitlin, Nicole
From: Ali
Date: January 15 at 6:34 p.m.
Subject: Re: New Year = New Us

Hey Ladies!

I think I'm out for SoulCycle tonight. I'm just gonna nap at my place, and I bet Ben will text me to come over tonight so he can make me dinner. Or maybe we'll order in, Netflix it, and sit by the fire? Can't waste this blowout on SoulCycle, lol.

Happy New Year ladies!!! This is gonna be our best year yet!!!!!

Love,
Ali

"It's gonna be a happy new year!" —*RENT* ('90s-era *Hamilton*)

february

To: Ali, Jen, Ashley, Morgan, Gracie, Caitlin, Nicole
From: Katie
Date: February 1 at 11:07 a.m.
Subject: Gal-entine's Day annual plan!!

Hey ladies,

Happy February! Winter sucks so far, huh? I feel like no one is going outside this winter!!!!!
:) I am really hitting the therapy lamp hard these days. I know, you're probably like, what's
there to be depressed about, your life is so great! But honestly, there's a lot, and it's pretty
insensitive to ask a depressed person why they can't just be happy, you guys.

Anyway, in two weeks is the (dun dun dun) dreaded V-Day, which, I have to admit, I am...
not dreading this year? I know we usually do a Gal-entine's Day event (for those of us
not in long-term relationships), but what if...this year we did, like, a group date? Topher
mentioned some of his boys from Villanova are in town that weekend (V-Day is a Sat this
year, btw), and I thought this could be a great way to both hang out with my boyfriend AND
my friends at once. Just because I have a bf (ahh!!!) doesn't mean I am not down-to-earth.
Hoes before bros! Or, in this case, hoes at the same time as bros, and no one is before or
after! Gender equality, y'all! And really, isn't that what feminism is all about? Can someone
actually google that?

Does this sound fun to you guys? I don't have many details on these guys, and I am unsure if
any of them are remotely available, dateable, fuckable, etc., so you guys let me know if, off
the bat, the idea sounds fun, and then I'll get more intel? Jen, since it's a girls' night PLUS a
boys' night, you and Brad are welcome to join (hence why I put you on this email).

XO,
Katie

To: Ali, Katie, Jen, Ashley, Morgan, Gracie, Nicole
From: Caitlin
Date: February 1 at 2:39 p.m.
Subject: Re: Gal-entine's day annual plan!!

Hey ladies,

I am okay with a group date, but I am putting it out there now that even if all of the guys are
interested in me, I am really not looking right now. I have so much self-care and me time
scheduled for this year that it would be like a tsunami to my gcal if I try to add a man to the
mix. So these dudes are all yours!

Can we do the dinner or drinks or wherever we are going on the West Side? I am giving a CaitlinTalk (it's like TED Talk but me, Caitlin) at the Javits Center called "Feed Your Stomach with Gluten-Free and Dairy-Free Meals and Ultimately Feed Your Soul," and I imagine crosstown traffic will be crazy. If anyone wants to go, it's $40 a ticket! I'll send you the e-vite after I hit send on this.

XO,
Caitlin

CaitlinYourLife™
Ask me about my CaitlinTalk on 2/14!
"Live your truth." —As seen on a box of gluten-free cereal in Whole Foods last Tuesday

---

To: Ali, Katie, Jen, Ashley, Caitlin, Gracie, Nicole
From: Morgan
Date: February 1 at 3:04 p.m.
Subject: Re: Gal-entine's day annual plan!!

Hey gals,

I am in for Gal-entine's + Topher's Friends Day event, but I am going to skip the CaitlinTalk (sorry, C!). I am on this all-carb, all-sugar diet right now because my doctor said I need to gain three pounds by EOM to aid in boosting my immune system. Did you know the thin are most likely to catch the common cold in the winter months? I am literally eating a donut ice cream sandwich right now. I miss kale.

I am also down for any guys. Casting a wide net is en vogue for me this year.

Morgs

To: Ali, Katie, Ashley, Morgan, Gracie, Caitlin, Nicole
From: Jen
Date: February 1 at 3:26 p.m.
Subject: Re: Gal-entine's day annual plan!!

Hey girls,

Let me check in with Brad for his plans, and I'll let you know if we can make it. TBH I think he's planning something huge this year (!!!) so don't get your hopes up! ;)

Love, Jen

To: Ali, Katie, Jen, Morgan, Ashley, Gracie, Caitlin
From: Nicole
Date: February 2 at 1:15 a.m.
Subject: Re: Gal-entine's day annual plan!!

Hey ladies,

Down for both Gal-entine's Day and your CaitlinTalk, Caitlin! But since I am going to support you, do you think you could get me a comp ticket? I don't think I can make $40 work this month :(

Nicole

P.S. Did anyone get anything at the Madewell sale?

P.P.S. Happy Groundhog Day!!!! Should we try to see some groundhogs today?? Do they have groundhogs in Central Park?? But I seriously can't get rabies again. (Still sorry about how cray I got last time!! I am still going to pay you back, Jen, for that vase I broke at your grandma's country house. Love youuuuu!) I'll google!

"Sometimes you just have to annoy your way to the top." —A life lesson I learned from reading Andy Cohen's books

---

To: Katie, Jen, Ashley, Morgan, Gracie, Caitlin, Nicole
From: Ali
Date: February 2 at 8:45 a.m.
Subject: Re: Gal-entine's day annual plan!!

Hey Ladies!

Thanks for taking the lead on Gal-entine's Day this year, Katie! You are too cute.

Ben and I are at a critical moment right now. Since we met during the holidays, I can't tell if this is a winter relationship of convenience only, or if we're in it for the long haul and will spend the crucial, most romantic Judeo-Christian holidays together: Easter and Passover. Only time will tell! But everything is going great! We see each other about once a week, which I'm soo fine with because sometimes a slow build just really helps create trust. Speaking of...I just found out Ben's going to some conference this month for work, so DO WE KNOW ANYONE GOING TO SAN FRANCISCO ALSO who can spy on him?? Should I look into hiring a TaskRabbit?? It's so frustrating dating someone who isn't active on Instagram and Facebook. Obviously he's hiding something, and it's just so beneath me to have to find out IRL like we're in the eighties or something.

That said, I'm feeling super optimistic! #blessed. Sometimes you just know, right, Katie? :) Should I invite Ben to Gal-entine's, or test him to see if he's planning something himself? Or should I just say I'm unavailable that day and be super aloof??

I'm gonna say I'm in for Gal-entine's Day! For now. This is gonna be so fun and special!

Ideas:
Katie: Can you please price out some venues that would have cute drink and food options? Maybe tapas? That could be fun! "You take the last one!" "No, you!" LOL. Should we do a Facebook invite? Please find out exactly which of Topher's friends might be coming!!

Morgs: Can you see if one of your Brooklyn hipster friends could do our makeup? It might be fun to experiment with a downtown Kylie Jenner look! See if your friend can do it for free! We will Instagram our makeup, and since *some* of us are influencers (sorry, Nic!) I'm sure we can deliver tens of thousands of social media impressions!

Jen: If Topher's friends live in Philadelphia, that's a huge red flag, but we might be able to make an LDR work, and we can meet in the middle for romantic weekends in New Jersey! Can you google some romantic NJ options??

Nicole: I think we should do matchy Gal-entine's Day outfits! Do we wanna go with low-key tank tops with a TBD hashtag? Or matching dresses? Should we Rent the Runway? Please put together some looks, and I can approve or veto them! This is gonna be so fun!!!

Caitlin: I'm DYING to go to your CaitlinTalk! Can you reschedule it for when we can all go though??

This is going to be so fun!!!!! #LoveMyGirls

xx,
Ali <3

"You're beautiful." —Ben to me this morning!!!!

To: Ali, Katie, Jen, Ashley, Morgan, Caitlin, Nicole
From: Gracie
Date: February 2 at 12:35 p.m.
Subject: Re: Gal-entine's day annual plan!!

Hi!

I'd love to attend your CaitlinTalk! Let me check with Ryan. I'm pretty sure he hasn't planned anything for that night -- for Valentine's we usually end up just ordering in Thai and binge-watching something...which is also how we spend almost every Saturday, now that I think about it...

A big group hang does sound fun though! Could we do something chill? Maybe a wine bar and grab some apps? Or somewhere we can watch the game also? I'm happy to come up with some places if this sounds fun!

Are you guys totally freaked out about the Supreme Court verdict coming out today?? I am seriously stressed out and can't stop refreshing Twitter. I feel like we're witnessing history being made here!

Talk soon,
Gracie

To: Ali, Katie, Jen, Ashley, Morgan, Gracie, Caitlin
From: Nicole
Date: February 2 at 2:19 p.m.
Subject: Re: Gal-entine's day annual plan!!

I lost my Twitter password, what's going on in the Supreme Court??? Should I call my congressman???

Lol you're so great at planning, Ali! I actually looked into it, and I found this really great startup featuring a woman entrepreneur at its helm that can provide all of us with amazing outfit options for the big day!!! It's called Nicole The Runway (TM pending), and rentals start at $100. Basically how it works is people can look through my photos on Insta and Facebook, and if they like what I'm wearing, they can come to my place and borrow my clothes. It's $100 for a 24-hour rental.

Does anyone know any of the Sharks?? If Mark Cuban and I started dating, would it be weird if he's also technically my boss? Or would that just be kinda hot??

LMK!!!! Nic

To: Ali, Katie, Ashley, Morgan, Gracie, Caitlin, Nicole
From: Jen
Date: February 2 at 6:47 p.m.
Subject: Re: Gal-entine's day annual plan!!

LADIES. I just spoke to Brad, who told me he will be OUT OF TOWN on VALENTINE'S DAY this year!!!! Which is on a Saturday. For "work."

I honestly don't even care at this point. I can't be the only person making an effort in our relationship. I mean, I moved to *New Jersey* for him!!! I'm over this relationship. Fuck Brad.

I'm taking my push-up bra out of my bottom drawer, and I am fully prepared to get f'ed up and make some mistakes.

Let's do this, girls!!!! Should we go somewhere in the Meatpacking?? Should we all get a hotel for after?? Should I download hookup apps????

I'm so excited!!! If you need me, I'll be freezing out Brad here in the fucking suburbs.

Love,
Jen

"Well, you know what? Maybe I don't care about being polite, ok? 'Cause it's a Wednesday night, baby, and I'm alive!!!!" —Hannah Horvath, *Girls*

To: Ali, Katie, Jen, Ashley, Morgan, Gracie, Caitlin
From: Nicole
Date: February 2 at 7:10 p.m.
Subject: Re: Gal-entine's day annual plan!!

Jen, I am upset about what you just said, but really quick....

Caitlin, I forgot to ask -- do you know if any investors will be at your CaitlinTalk? If so I'd love some intros! Would like to get a seed round before Q2. I know it might be awk to do biz intros, but remember that time I let you book a yoga class on my account but didn't ask for you to pay me back? Now we can be even. LMK! This is so Silicon Valley!

Nic

To: Ali, Jen, Ashley, Morgan, Gracie, Caitlin, Nicole
From: Katie
Date: February 2 at 7:12 p.m.
Subject: Re: Gal-entine's day annual plan!!

Ladies,

Did we just read the words "push-up bra" in an email from Miss Pinterest New Jersey herself??

Katie

To: Ali, Katie, Jen, Morgan, Gracie, Caitlin, Nicole
From: Ashley
Date: February 2 at 10:09 p.m.
Subject: Re: Gal-entine's day annual plan!!

Sorry for my silence, my wifi situation in New England sucks. Did you know T-Mobile barely works outside of the city? WTF? Anyway! I am all caught up on this thread....

Does this mean... SLUTTY JEN IS BACK?????????????????

xo,
Ashley

To: Ali, Katie, Ashley, Morgan, Gracie, Caitlin, Nicole
From: Jen
Date: February 2 at 10:25 p.m.
Subject: Re: Gal-entine's day annual plan!!

For one night only, yes. Slutty Jen is back and she's a big fucking skank.

Can we please forget Topher and his bro buddies for V-Day and make it a real, true girls night? No offense, Katie, but I am so fucking fired up over Brad bouncing on what is literally the most important day of the year that I will literally murder someone for the cocaine under their nails and 5 hours on a Meatpacking dance floor just to forget my pathetic life for ONE NIGHT.

I do not want to sit around eating calamari with a bunch of Villanova grads wearing Vineyard Vines (no offense, Ash, I know you're into that). I want to get fucked up for Valentine's Day. Ali, please help.

Jen

WWSJD: What Would Samantha Jones Do? —Me

To: Ali, Katie, Jen, Ashley, Gracie, Caitlin, Nicole
From: Morgan
Date: February 2 at 10:46 p.m.
Subject: Re: Gal-entine's day annual plan!!

Jen, Jen, Jen, breathe it out.

You know Brad would never do anything to intentionally hurt you. He probably had no choice but to go to this work thing. You know how men can be with their jobs. Brad is a people-pleaser! Of course he's going to step in for his boss on this trip.

What if we kept our plans with Topher and the Villanova boys on V-Day night, but spent the day just us girls, getting blowouts, pedicures, manicures...

Ladies, thoughts?
Morgs

To: Ali, Katie, Jen, Ashley, Morgan, Caitlin, Nicole
From: Gracie
Date: February 3 at 7:02 a.m.
Subject: Re: Gal-entine's day annual plan!!

Hey gals!

That's a really fun idea, Morgan! I am trying to save some money right now (ugh, new year's resolutions, right?) but I will definitely opt in for a manicure and then head to Caitlin's talk. I am going to bring my friend Laura from work, Caitlin. She's the one I told you about -- she loves your blog and your tweets :)

Let me know what salon/spa you guys decide on!

Best,
Gracie

To: Ali, Katie, Jen, Ashley, Morgan, Gracie, Nicole
From: Caitlin
Date: February 3 at 10:31 a.m.
Subject: Re: Gal-entine's day annual plan!!

Omg! Aw! I love my fans!

If she buys my e-book tell her to bring her Amazon receipt (a screenshot of the email is fine!). Once I verify that she purchased, we can take a selfie! I'll make sure my intern sends her to the front of the line.

Caitlin

CEO of CaitlinTalk
CaitlinYourDestiny, Inc. (TM Pending)

To: Katie, Jen, Ashley, Morgan, Gracie, Caitlin, Nicole
From: Ali
Date: February 3 at 6:11 p.m.
Subject: Re: Gal-entine's day annual plan!!

Hi Ladies!!

Wow, Jen. I'm so so sorry you're going through this. But honestly? And I'm sure I speak for everyone here, you can do wayyyy better than Brad! I mean, he's always been nice and seemed to treat you well, but I've always secretly thought...he's just so totally boring and tbh, not even that cute. He always reminded me of Zach Galifianakis with a better body! But with a worse face :(

Anyway it feels so good to finally say it!!! Literally the only thing we liked about Brad was that he seemed devoted to you. But if he's not even taking you out for VALENTINE'S DAY -- which is the only day of the year that actually matters -- then I say we forget him!

Also...and I was never going to say anything but it's all coming out here since you guys are clearly done...wtf was up with the living together first?? It's so unfair of him to have been drinking gallons of your milk for free, without even putting a down payment on the cow! Not saying you're a cow, just wanted to make the metaphor. I mean, maybe if you were engaged and already put a deposit on a wedding venue and needed a bigger apartment to hold all the wedding gifts, then fine, I'm all for living together. But moving in together before he's even put a ring on it?? What is this, *Brooklyn*??? (No offense, Morgs. And I'm still dying to visit Williamsburg and try rainbow bagels or maybe Molly (??) and have a hipster night with you!)

So! G-Day is gonna slay this year! Jen, you are gonna look so hot!!! I will stop eating carbs until the big night in solidarity!!! We will take so many photos of you next to hotties and post immediately and Brad will be all "I've made a huge mistake!!" Do you wanna move out by the time he's back from his trip?? I think we should conduct this breakup in the style of Katie Holmes divorcing Tom Cruise -- I'll be your Martin Holmes and help you change your phone number, find a new place, everything! This will be awesome!!! You'll meet someone way better than Brad!!! It's all happening!!

Katie, please handle the logistics. Do Topher's friends wanna get bottle service somewhere for all of us?

Maybe we should do a night of clubbing? Nicole, can you rent a car and be our designated driver? If we pay you $50 for the night, is that cool?

So excited!!! We finally have you back!!!!

xo,
Ali

To: Ali, Jen, Ashley, Morgan, Gracie, Caitlin, Nicole
From: Katie
Date: February 3 at 9:04 p.m.
Subject: Re: Gal-entine's day annual plan!!

Hey Jen + ladies,

I can't realllllly back out of this plan -- Topher already invited his friends, we made reservations at Dallas BBQ (their choice lol, tourists are so cute!), and then maybe we'll go catch the game somewhere? I was kind of hoping it would be a low-key night...plus, are you sure one business trip is a valid reason to get back into drugs? You've come so far! I'm just saying.

In other news, I did get some deets on the guys that will be there. Ladies' choice!

Barrett: 31, finance, does securities trading in Chicago. He was Topher's roommate at 'Nova junior year and senior year. His parents have a house on Nantucket, and he was born and raised in Richmond, VA. He looks like a GAP ad! Wears khakis. Has a dad bod. 6'2". No word on last relationship, but his Twitter bio has a Bible quote.

Kent: 30, finance, does securities trading in DC. Played on all-county lax with Topher in HS so they go way back. Was engaged but found out his fiancée was cheating on him WITH HIS BROTHER. Apparently both families were horrified, and the whole thing is super hush-hush according to Topher. I promised T I wouldn't mention it to you girls, so no one can say anything okay? If it comes up, act surprised!!! Owns an apartment in Alexandria, VA, which is a very cute up-and-coming town. Like the Park Slope of Virginia!

Layton: 32, finance, works at a bank in Stamford. WANTS TO LIVE IN GREENWICH (ASHLEY, ARE YOU READING THIS) eventually. Topher and Layton were freshman year roommates. T says he's the hopeless romantic one of the bunch. He has a dog named Chance.

Griff: 30, finance, I forgot to find out exactly what he does and where because I was too consumed by the fact that he volunteers at a hospice home on weekends. SO CUTE! He graduated from 'Nova the year after Topher. He has 5 sisters (amazing), and he's the oldest (so protective!). He wears glasses, so he's a total hipster (Morgs, interested?) LOL.

Anyway, as you can see the night is already sort of figured out....so...maybe we can do a slutty Jen comeback another time? How about a weeknight or before-work coffee? I'll prob be coming from Topher's apt in FiDi, so can meet anywhere downtown (not too west though!).

LMK by EOD,
Katie

To: Katie, Jen, Ashley, Morgan, Gracie, Caitlin, Nicole
From: Ali
Date: February 4 at 11:01 a.m.
Subject: Re: Gal-entine's day annual plan!!

This is great intel, Katie!!!

I'll just say what everyone's thinking: Kent sounds perfect for me!! Since I've dabbled in the therapeutic arts -- I own *The Secret*, *The 4-Hour Workweek*, AND *The South Beach Diet* -- (sometimes mental health begins from the outside in), I think I can help him process his last relationship! Besides Ben hasn't responded to my text from last night, and it's already 11 a.m.!!! So over him!!!!

Nicole: You can take Barrett! You love Nantucket, are cool with dad bods, and since you are experimenting with your career/don't have anything tying you down, you can up and move to Chicago if things go well!

Ash: Layton is all yours! Get that uptight, country-club, squash-playing, bimonthly sex-having Connecticut D! You should definitely wear your Lilly P sweater dress -- it's like catnip for sexually repressed dudes.

Griff: Morgs! Glasses!!!!! Get it!!!!! You guys can carry matching tote bags and listen to vinyl!!!

I decided to split the diff and have a 'Nova boys night along with a Meatpacking Slutty Jen comeback night and just made a rez at Le Bain!! It's non-refundable, so everyone owes me $250 if they don't show up! So excited!!!!!

xo,
Ali

To: Ali, Jen, Ashley, Morgan, Gracie, Caitlin, Nicole
From: Katie
Date: February 4 at 2:41 p.m.
Subject: Re: Gal-entine's day annual plan!!

Hey, I thought we had decided we'd do Dallas BBQ with the guys, and then you guys could pick whatever club after?

Katie

To: Ali, Katie, Jen, Ashley, Morgan, Gracie, Caitlin
From: Nicole
Date: February 5 at 1:07 a.m.
Subject: Re: Gal-entine's day annual plan!!

Ladies,

Can someone spot me the $250? It'll be like your first investment in Nicole The Runway (CEOs have to eat, you know)!

If more than one of you wants to invest we can work it out. Just Venmo my share to Ali, and I'll make a note in my notes app for tax season.

Thanks!
Nic

CEO, Nicole The Runway

To: Ali, Katie, Jen, Ashley, Morgan, Gracie, Nicole
From: Caitlin
Date: February 5 at 11:19 a.m.
Subject: Re: Gal-entine's day annual plan!!

Hey ladies,

Thanks for divvying up the dudes, Ali! I've changed my mind about my availability. I initially thought my blog would be activating its paid subscription model this year, but my mentor says it's not the time for digital media to start getting greedy. That clears up a lot of my time that was previously scheduled for business-related travel. That being said, Katie, do you think Topher has one more guy friend he can bring?

Preferably tall, non-blond, non-American. Should work in finance but maintain strong interest in the creative arts. Should be comfortable with women who make their own money. He should not want kids for 7 years (if he says more like 5 years, I can work with that, but 7 is preferable). No food allergies but should voluntarily steer clear of dairy, processed sugars, and red meat. Easier that way for both of us.

Thank you!
Caitlin

CaitlinYourLife™
Ask me about my CaitlinTalk on 2/14!

To: Ali, Jen, Ashley, Morgan, Gracie, Caitlin, Nicole
From: Katie
Date: February 6 at 4:16 p.m.
Subject: Re: Gal-entine's day annual plan!!

Ladies,

Ali can you cancel Le Bain? It doesn't really make sense at this juncture....

Katie

"FEMINIST" —Enamel pin I just bought on Etsy

To: Katie, Jen, Ashley, Morgan, Gracie, Caitlin, Nicole
From: Ali
Date: February 6 at 4:17 p.m.
Subject: Re: Gal-entine's day annual plan!!

No. Per my email above, it's non-refundable.

Sincerely,
Ali

"There's a special place in hell for women who don't help each other." —Madeleine Albright

To: Ali, Jen, Ashley, Morgan, Gracie, Caitlin, Nicole
From: Katie
Date: February 6 at 10:40 p.m.
Subject: Re: Gal-entine's day annual plan!!

K. I'll just let the guys know we're having dinner prior and then we'll meet them out.

No problem. It's totally fine.

Katie.

To: Ali, Katie, Ashley, Morgan, Gracie, Caitlin, Nicole
From: Jen
Date: February 6 at 10:45 p.m.
Subject: Re: Gal-entine's day annual plan!!

Ladies, do you guys think this? Or this? For V-Day? Are we thinking of something more in the key of Net-a-Porter or Bebe?

lmk,
Jen

Feb 6, 11:07 PM

Morgan

FYI, Brad just called me and told me he is planning on PROPOSING to Jen on V-Day in front of all of us!!!!

Ali

Fuckkkkkkkkk.

Now Jen knows what I really think of him! This is so like Brad to make Gal-entine's Day all about himself!

Gonna fix this!!!!!!

Just realized: he's proposing at Dallas BBQ?!?!?!?!?! Ughhhhhh

---

To: Katie, Jen, Ashley, Morgan, Gracie, Katie, Caitlin, Nicole
From: Ali
Date: February 7 at 10:16 a.m.
Subject: Re: Gal-entine's day annual plan!!

Hey Ladies!

Guess what?? After much deliberation, I think we should go with the original plan! See, I listen to you guys! ;) Just an FYI, unfortunately the deposit was still non-refundable.

Katie, please organize it, and I'll just show up! Easy and mad breezy! Jen, it might be fun to get blowouts together, but dress really pretty in a classy way -- like something in the key of Carolyn Bessette-Kennedy (reading a book about her now! #MarriageGoals) or Blake Lively after she married Ryan R. Maybe like an LBD?

Btw, I was totally jk about Brad, hahahah lol. He's so great. Big fan.

Can't wait!
xox, Ali

p.s. Katie -- what did you mean by: "K." Are you mad at me??? If there's something you want to discuss, just come out and say it -- you don't need to be so passive!!! You know my *Five Love Languages* type is "words of affirmation" with a touch of "acts of service." Are we okay???

To: Ali, Jen, Ashley, Nicole, Gracie, Caitlin, Morgan
From: Katie
Date: February 7 at 1:14 p.m.
Subject: Re: Gal-entine's day annual plan!!

ok, here's the plan:

7:30 p.m. dallas bbq
after dinner drinks at bar nearby, tbd.

see you there,
Katie

Sent from my iPhone

To: Ali, Katie, Jen, Ashley, Morgan, Gracie, Caitlin
From: Nicole
Date: February 14 at 7:02 p.m.
Subject: Re: Gal-entine's day annual plan!!

Hey Ladies!

I'm so confused lol. I'm on my way to the Meatpacking club right now -- is anyone there yet??

BTW, when you see me you might notice that I am 3 lbs lighter!!!! My body transformation is due to the AMAZING shakes I've been drinking! I just drink one for breakfast, 1/2 of one for lunch, have seven almonds, 1 oz. of fish (I usually sub in a fish oil vitamin for this one), a shake for dinner, and that's it! The shakes are seriously so delicious and filling! They come in a ton of different options, like chocolate and vanilla!!! Like you, I've been trying different diets for years -- the Kate Middleton Dukan diet, waist training, only eating while I'm on the elliptical, the pirate scurvy diet, the infamous tapeworm diet of 2009 -- and it's so nice to not be dieting for once! It's just a lifestyle choice. Plus, The Shake Company™ is so amazing -- if you all try this for 365 days, then I can go to a conference in Omaha where Frank Robbins (Tony Robbins's step-brother!) will be a featured speaker!!!

Sign up here: The Shake Diet (disclosure: sponsored affiliate link attached)

Ok, I'm waiting outside, and I'm freezing, where are you girls????

x,
Nic

Human Ambassador Associate, The Shake Company

To: Ali, Katie, Jen, Ashley, Morgan, Gracie, Nicole
From: Caitlin
Date: February 14 at 8:40 p.m.
Subject: Re: Gal-entine's day annual plan!!

We're at Dallas BBQ, silly! Come meet us!! But first can you please swing by Whole Foods and pick me up some kale?? There's seriously nothing to eat here, lol!

Are you close by?? I want to tell you all about how my CaitlinTalk went!!! Spoiler: it went AMAZING!!!! I'll send you all the link for the video version of it (you can access it on my site for only $9.99. A steal!). Also, if you're at Whole Foods, can you please pick me up some alkaline water? They only have tap here, for some reason.

Caitlin

CaitlinYourLife™

To: Ali, Katie, Jen, Ashley, Morgan, Gracie, Caitlin
From: Nicole
Date: February 14 at 9:02 p.m.
Subject: Re: Gal-entine's day annual plan!!

Hey! If you tried to text me, I'm not getting texts since I'm over my text limit this month, LOL.

On my way now! Can someone email me the address?? I just told the Uber driver to start driving to different Dallas BBQs till I find you guys! Is it fun so far?? I'm so tired, my body is just burning tons of energy these days eliminating toxins and adjusting to being in ketosis mode! Does anyone have any perfume?? I have this weird slightly cabbage-y scent I'm emitting these days!

xo,
Nic

Human Ambassador Associate, The Shake Company
#1 Human Ambassador Associate -- Murray Hill region
Try The Shake Company for yourself!

"Make like Taylor Swift and 'Shake It Off'" —My The Shake Company Group Leader, Lauren S.

♡ 921 likes   I SAID YES!   ♡ 595 likes   He put a ring on it!

To: Ali, Katie, Ashley, Morgan, Gracie, Caitlin, Nicole
From: Jen
Date: February 15 at 6:30 a.m.
Subject: Re: Gal-entine's day annual plan!!

Hi Ladies!

Well, last night was certainly a whirlwind evening!! I cannot believe that happened. I am still freaking out. Did any of you know? Ali, I got the feeling you knew from your last email on this thread :) You are so good at keeping a secret, girl :) YOU GUYS, I AM ENGAGED. HOLY FUCKING SHIT. I AM GOING TO BE A BRIDE! I am literally...like, I can't stop smiling and looking at Pinterest!!! It's seriously amazing. I love my life. I am so glad I knew in my heart that Brad would never do something as idiotic as actually skip out on Valentine's Day for his job!! And now it's official: I am his number-one priority lol. I always knew we had the perfect relationship :) I love him so much it hurts.

Can someone send me all the pics/videos/Snapchats/Instagram stories/tweets/status updates from last night? I want to relive every moment.

Thank you so much, everyone, for coordinating and for keeping a secret. Brad def owes you :) Gracie, I am sorry you missed my big night!!!!!

GOING TO THE CHAPEL AND I'M GONNA GET MARRRRRRRIED!!!!!

Love,
Jen "THE BRIDE!!!!"

To: Ali, Katie, Jen, Ashley, Gracie, Caitlin, Nicole
From: Morgan
Date: February 15 at 9:47 a.m.
Subject: Re: Gal-entine's day annual plan!!

Hey girls!

Yay congrats, Jen!!!!! We're all so excited for you guys. Last night was really fun. And Katie, thanks for organizing and bringing all those dudes! They were realllllly good sports about being a part of a surprise wedding engagement flash mob (is that what they're called these days?). Also, loved seeing Ashley and Layton hit it off (as expected!). It was a great night!! ☺

Jen, we can't wait to start planning with you! I've attached some pics I took on my phone, though my mophie ran out of juice and I don't think I caught anything from the final hour!

Btw, do we still want to do a March book club like we did last year? It would be great to feature someone from the Brooklyn literary scene -- like Jonathan Lethem or Walt Whitman. So excited!!!

Love,
Morgs

To: Ali, Katie, Ashley, Morgan, Gracie, Caitlin, Nicole
From: Jen
Date: February 15 at 9:50 a.m.
Subject: Re: Gal-entine's day annual plan!!

Thanks for sending the pics, Morgy, but I can't use any of these. I look fat.

Does anyone have any *good* pics of me being skinny? Kinda surprised Brad didn't plan a photographer to be secretly snapping shots of us during the proposal! I never knew I could be so happy while at a Dallas BBQ.

Love,
Jen
"The Bride!!!!"

P.S. I can't stop staring at my ring!!!!! It feels so heavy!!! It's *almost* too big!!

"I'm getting married!" —Monica, *Friends*

To: Jen, Ali, Katie, Ashley, Morgan, Caitlin, Nicole
From: Gracie
Date: February 15 at 9:52 a.m.
Subject: Re: Gal-entine's day annual plan!!

Jen! Huge CONGRATULATIONS!!!!! I'm so happy for you!!!!! Can't wait to see all the photos!!! Sorry I had to miss last night, can't wait to hear the story of how it all went down in person!

x, Gracie

To: Jen, Katie, Ashley, Morgan, Gracie, Caitlin, Nicole
From: Ali
Date: February 15 at 9:55 a.m.
Subject: Re: Gal-entine's day annual plan!!

Congratulations!!!!!!!!!!!!!!!!!

Can everyone please upload all their photos from last night to a Dropbox, and I will select which ones we should post for the initial social media announcements!!!!

Planning this wedding is gonna be the most fun ever!!!

Xo,
Ali

P.S. Can everyone please hard delete any photos of me making out last night?? Ben sent the cutest edible arrangement to my office!!!!

march

To: Ali, Katie, Jen, Ashley, Morgan, Gracie, Nicole
From: Caitlin
Date: March 2 at 7:02 p.m.
Subject: Book Club + Saint Patty's???

Hey ladies,

Wanted to follow up using a new thread re: book clubbin' for this month (plus add a little Saint Patty's planning, too).

Here's what I am thinking:

Book club:
- Meet 2-3x a week (I can't do Mondays or Wednesdays or weekends).
- Try to read one book a week (one of my resolutions, and you can read more on my site!).
- All writers have to be women or married to a woman and the book has to have been reviewed by Parul Sehgal at some point. She's so wise. I quote her book reviews all the time. Even for books I haven't read.
- Gluten-free snacks only because I have decided I am celiac.
- Books should not exceed ~275 pages.
- No poetry!

Saint Patty's:
- Morgan mentioned going to an interesting-sounding speaker series on the potato famine, anyone down?
- I will have to stay out of the bar scene (since I am celiac).

Let me know! Also, Nicole, you still owe me $40 for your missed appearance at my CaitlinTalk!

Caitlin
"To live the life you imagined is so bold." —Caitlin, CEO of CaitlinYourLife™

To: Ali, Katie, Jen, Ashley, Morgan, Gracie, Caitlin
From: Nicole
Date: March 3 at 8:15 a.m.
Subject: Re: Book Club + Saint Patty's???

Hey Ladies!

Top of the morning to you! LOL. I love, love, love the idea of reading a book!

I actually know of this really cool up-and-coming young writer who doesn't have commercial appeal yet who is super indie! It might be fun to go with an author that isn't represented or popular in mainstream society yet? The book that she's written is like *Precious* meets *Fifty Shades of Grey*, and it's a really interesting look inside the mindset of a young woman forced to go to extreme measures to financially keep up in modern Manhattan. It will be available as a Kindle Single, and you can actually just PayPal me directly, and I'll make sure the author gets her money! LMK!

For St. Paddy's I'd be down to go out! Can someone research if any pubs are doing anything for St. Patrick's?? Do we know when St. Patrick's is this year??

Love! Nic

To: Ali, Jen, Ashley, Morgan, Gracie, Caitlin, Nicole
From: Katie
Date: March 3 at 8:27 a.m.
Subject: Re: Book Club + Saint Patty's???

Wait, Nicole, who is this mystery author????

As for me, ladies, it should be no surprise that Topher is of the Irish persuasion and has a lot of fun and cute memorable activities planned for us :) So I am out. Would invite you along but I think I want this private time to see where this is going, etc. You know, in the Irish culture, Saint Patrick's day is like, the actual Valentine's Day. That's something Topher told me, and I'll never forget it. Wish I could see you all, too. Good luck with the plans!

As for book club, I really only have time to read the *NYT* Now app and my 10 free *WaPo* articles a month and also watch Tasty videos and Snapchat Stories. LMK what you guys end up picking though, and if it looks good I'll consider.

Katie

To: Ali, Katie, Ashley, Morgan, Gracie, Caitlin, Nicole
From: Jen
Date: March 3 at 9:15 a.m.
Subject: Re: Book Club + Saint Patty's???

Hey ladies,

Count me out for St. Pat's! I am #SweatingForTheWedding and I am not doing carbs/beer/

processed foods/eating after 4 p.m. or before 2 p.m. I know, I know, it's like, I don't really need to lose weight, but I told my trainer I want Michelle Obama arms and my future MiL is already making comments about how wedding dress sizes are like, totally different than street sizes. Haha #killme!!!!

Nicole, I like your book club book idea, but I also don't really understand it, so if you could send a more fleshed-out description of your plan by EOD, that would be great. I am also not sure with all of the wedding planning that I will have time to read, but I am definitely down to circle back on this once I am a Mrs. :) If you gals were interested in poring over the latest issues of bridal magazines with me, that could be a fun magazine club (sort of like a book club, but we read magazines. Keeping print alive, right, Katie?! I know you can get on board with that). Plus, bridal magazines are FOR women, so it still follows all of the rules. That being said, I'll scan some of my favorite pages that explore the art of table cards and email over ASAP. I also want everyone's opinions on what I should do with my hair. As an FYI, I already know I want to wear it down with a bohemian hairpiece so don't say "wear it up." Thanks in advance.

So to recap!!!!!! No St. Pat's for me, probably don't have time to read books, please let me know your thoughts on a) my hair and b) table cards.

Also wait, what is the protocol about bridesmaids that come from Brad's side of the family (aka "Brad'smaids")? He has two sisters and three sisters-in-law and it's like, okay cool, but???? His mom has already basically said things to me in the vein of like, "Oh Debbie, Kara, Janey, and Emily want to know when you'll be picking out dresses for them..." so she definitely is under the impression that this is...happening. Not sure what to do. Caitlin, do you have any CaitlinTalks about #weddiquette? LMK.

Sorry, I digress! No St. Pat's, no books, please save me from my wedding! JK :) I am having the best time.

xoxo,
Jen

PS - Addendum to my book club comments: If you pick a book I have already read, I can participate. LMK if you guys are interested in:

- *Why Men Love Bitches*
- *Gone Girl*
- *Ice Queens Melt Hearts: Why the Silent Treatment Is the True Language of Love*
- *The Secret*
- *Bossypants* by Tina Fey

"There has to be respect in every relationship." —My therapist, Dr. Sol Rosenstein, PhD, LCSW

To: Ali, Katie, Jen, Ashley, Morgan, Gracie, Nicole
From: Caitlin
Date: March 3 at 9:22 a.m.
Subject: Re: Book Club + Saint Patty's???

Hey ladies,

Do you think it's Saint Patty's or St. Patty's or Saint Patty's or St. Paddy's or Saint Patrick's or St. Patrick's? Writing something quick on the blog about how to make a low-gluten, no-sugar green meals (I surprisingly have a big mommy readership, and you wouldn't believe the google search terms about "green food" that lead to my blog -- amazing for ad rev though!), but I can't figure out what the actual spelling(s) of this holiday are. Who here is Irish? Morgan? Google surprisingly yields no definitive result, but I know you girls are smarter than any search engine :)

Also, Jen, I have **a lot of thoughts** about #weddiquette. Give me a few, and I will gather them. Actually I should probably take this opportunity to pitch a story like that to a magazine...Katie, do you have any contacts at *Cosmopolitan* or *McSweeney's*? LMK! All I need is an email, and I can take it from there. I am super good over email.

As far as books go, I am pretty intrigued by *Ice Queens Melt Hearts: Why the Silent Treatment Is the True Language of Love* even though it seems like it could be anti-feminist?? But I like the idea of reading it for counter-intelligence purposes. Sooo I am down for that!!!

Thanks, loves,
Caitlin

CaitlinYourLife.com
"Every step you take is one more step towards another step." —Caitlin
Check out my podcast, *Caitlin in the City*, ranked #405 by Apple's Podcast App!
And review it (only if you plan to leave 5 stars!).

To: Katie, Jen, Ashley, Morgan, Gracie, Caitlin, Nicole
From: Ali
Date: March 3 at 11:40 a.m.
Subject: Re: Book Club + Saint Patty's???

Hey Ladies!

First off, Katie, I am soo excited for you and Toph!!! I think it would behoove us all to do some research on St. Patty's. (I think that's Gaelic for St. Patrick's??) It's important to be lifelong learners! Plus, JFK Jr. was half Irish-American and half Jackie O., and the more I think about it, the more I think I should date men like that!!

Nic: Can you pls do some research and put together an e-book on St. Patty's and Irish history? Keywords: Ireland, Dublin, potato famine, Conor Kennedy, IRA (while we're at it pls also research the best Roth IRAs to invest in!), gluten-free and meat-free corned beef and cabbage options, a summary of the book *Angela's Ashes*, and a brief history of Catholicism (in ~150 words or less). Can you please do this by EOW? I can pay for your time and take $20 off the $250 you owe me for that deposit for Le Bain last month, which reminds me....LADIES, YOU ALL OWE ME $250. While I'm so (SO!) excited V-Day ended up being co-opted by Brad, I'm still out for the deposit.

Speaking of V-Day...totally random thought, but has Kent mentioned me at all to Topher??? I sent him a FB friend request, but he prob doesn't check it that often (a lot of hedge funds block Facebook). Also, I think my phone was on the fritz last weekend 'cause I didn't get any texts on Sunday -- my instinct is Wikileaks or the Russians had something to do with hacking into U.S. phones, so if he tried texting then I prob didn't get it because of cyber-terrorism.

Jen, there is no way you are under ANY obligation to include *any* of Brad's family in your wedding party!!!!! They're lucky they're even invited. (Are you inviting his whole

side? Because I'd like to actually come with a +3, if that's okay. Some college friends are visiting that weekend. That's what you get for planning a NYE wedding, LOL. THANKS IN ADVANCE!!) I have so many strong feelings about this!!!! If they insist on being included, then we can delegate them with throwing a fake party for their side of the family. Like a bro-dal shower. Or more like a Brad-al shower LOL! Can someone write that down??

For St. Patrick's itself -- I vote for a TriBeCa loft party thrown by a son of a wealthy landowner in Ireland. Or a Kennedy descendant (but only from the John, Bobby, or Ted lines). Or a pub on the UES (but west of Lexington, obviously). I'm not opposed to meeting men who are a bit further along in life!! Should I have my intern research this??

xo,
Ali

"People often tell me I could be a great man. I'd rather be a good man." —JFK Jr.

To: Ali, Katie, Jen, Ashley, Morgan, Caitlin, Nicole
From: Gracie
Date: March 3 at 11:52 a.m.
Subject: Re: Book Club + Saint Patty's???

Hi Ladies!

I love this book club idea! I'm already in another one with some ladies at work, and it's so much fun. Does anyone else want to read that book about that woman who overcame female genital mutilation and then went on to establish a nonprofit helping other victims empower themselves through micro-loans? It looks so fascinating -- I just read a synopsis in *The Atlantic* about it. I'm happy to host the first one! We can even do it on St. Patrick's Day, and I can make us some Irish foods :)

Can't wait.
Gracie

To: Ali, Katie, Jen, Ashley, Gracie, Caitlin, Nicole
From: Morgan
Date: March 3 at 1:15 p.m.
Subject: Re: Book Club + Saint Patty's???

Hi Ladies!

Instead of reading a book, which is just so "old media," and since print is dying (sorry Katie :-/), what if we all read *Brooklyn Magazine* and then got together and discussed it? I really think it would help all of you understand me better and get where I'm coming from. Which is literally the L or G train, which you guys seriously still don't even know about.

Maybe you should include Brad's sisters just to start everything off on the right foot? Or you can give them important jobs like guestbook attendant (shout-out to the one *Sex and the City* ep you guys made me watch!).

For St. Patrick's I vote for everyone coming over to my roof and us drinking Guinness and Irish car bombs. (Can we say that?? No offense!) Katie, can you ask Topher if he minds us appropriating his heritage?? Maybe Topher can do a CaitlinTalk for all of us on what it means to be an authentic Irish person celebrating the holiday, and we can use this as a learning experience.

LMK. I'm saving March 17th in the meanwhile.

Attaching a pic to show you guys how lonely my apt is without my girls :(. Isn't the art so cute?!

Morgs

To: Ali, Katie, Jen, Ashley, Morgan, Gracie, Nicole
From: Caitlin
Date: March 3 at 1:25 p.m.
Subject: Re: Book Club + Saint Patty's???

Hey Ladies!

I still vote for *Ice Queens Melt Hearts: Why the Silent Treatment Is the True Language of Love.*

FYI, Morgan (and also any other party included on this email or any other person who reads my words in perpetuity), blahblah legal disclaimer:

CaitlinTalk™ is the intellectual property of Caitlin, who owns the rights to the phrases "Caitlin," "CaitlinTalk," "Talk," "CaitlinMotivation," "CaitlinCommunication," "CaitlinYourself," "CaitlinYourLife," and "Don'tHesitateCaitlinate." If any parties attempt to infringe upon this copyright, FBI warning: Criminal copyright infringement is investigated by the FBI and may constitute a felony with a maximum penalty of up to 5 years in prison and/ or a $250,000,0000 fine. In the criminal justice system, the people are represented by two separate yet equally important groups: the police, who investigate crime, and the district attorneys, who prosecute the offenders.

Love you!
Caitlin

CaitlinYourLife™
Available for speaking engagements!

To: Ali, Katie, Jen, Ashley, Morgan, Gracie, Caitlin
From: Nicole
Date: March 3 at 1:30 p.m.
Subject: Re: Book Club + Saint Patty's???

Ooh, idea!! Does anyone know if there are any libraries in New York that aren't gross, and how to obtain a library card??

I could Yelp it!

~Nic

Mar 3, 1:35 PM

Katie
Print isn't dying!!!!!!!!!!!!!!! I feel like I need to say something

Nicole
Ooo okay! You should!

Katie
Ok back me up if it gets tense??

Nicole
Kk!

To: Ali, Jen, Ashley, Morgan, Gracie, Caitlin, Nicole
From: Katie
Date: March 3 at 1:52 p.m.
Subject: Re: Book Club + Saint Patty's???

Hey ladies,

Morgan, lol, actually, old media isn't *that* old, and no one has said "print is dying/dead" in years. That's a very 2010 outlook on the media landscape, girl :)

Anyway, your comment inspired me to ditch my 10-free-articles-a-month life, and now I have a *New York Times* subscription (digital and print). I am happy to suggest that we swap *Brooklyn Magazine* for a Styles section book club. This will help us stay cultured and informed, as well as contribute to an institution that so many blogs and magazines today owe themselves to. I appreciate *Brooklyn Magazine*, though I have never read it, but I also think since Morgan is the only person who actually lives in Brooklyn, the rest of us may not relate to its content. Thoughts? Happy to start some potential conversation on the topic after I file a post.

I am also down for *Ice Queens Melt Hearts*...but I want to be clear I am reading it ironically!!!!!! And I will want a digital copy so I can read it on my Kindle and no one on the subway will be able to tell what I am reading. (I just told a coworker I was starting *Finnegans Wake* so...).

LMK by EOD if you want to add a Styles section component to the book club. I am happy to share my subscription with up to 2 additional users. Nicole, no offense, but I am still not over the time you hacked into my Hulu, so you're on your own!! :-P JK, love ya (not JK)

PS Oh, also, ladies, in terms of appropriating Topher's Irish heritage, I asked him about it:

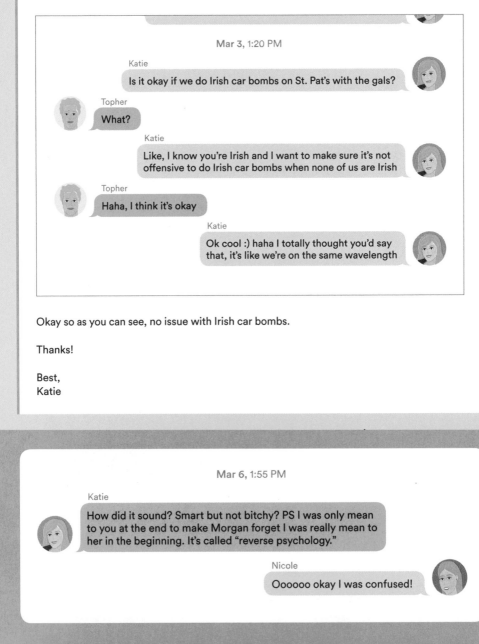

Mar 3, 1:20 PM

Katie
Is it okay if we do Irish car bombs on St. Pat's with the gals?

Topher
What?

Katie
Like, I know you're Irish and I want to make sure it's not offensive to do Irish car bombs when none of us are Irish

Topher
Haha, I think it's okay

Katie
Ok cool :) haha I totally thought you'd say that, it's like we're on the same wavelength

Okay so as you can see, no issue with Irish car bombs.

Thanks!

Best,
Katie

Mar 6, 1:55 PM

Katie
How did it sound? Smart but not bitchy? PS I was only mean to you at the end to make Morgan forget I was really mean to her in the beginning. It's called "reverse psychology."

Nicole
Oooooo okay I was confused!

To: Ali, Katie, Jen, Ashley, Morgan, Gracie, Caitlin
From: Nicole
Date: March 3 at 4:07 p.m.
Subject: Re: Book Club + Saint Patty's???

Hi Ladies!

I'm researching Ireland right now (listening to U2). I'll try to write a book tonight, I'm just a little low-energy right now. All I've eaten today is NicoleVitaminWater (TM). It's like Vitamin Water, but it's just regular water that I chase with a Flintstones gummy vitamin.

I think we should read Steve Harvey's *Act Like a Lady, Think Like a Man*!!! Or we could just get together and watch the movie??

Also, this guy on Tinder wants to go out tonight, but I'm wearing a suit to my temp job today, cause of *Lean In* and #DressForTheJobYouWant, what should I do?????

Love,
Nic

CEO & Founder of NicoleVitaminWater™

To: Ali, Katie, Jen, Ashley, Gracie, Caitlin, Nicole
From: Morgan
Date: March 3 at 4:09 p.m.
Subject: Re: Book Club + Saint Patty's???

Hi ladies,

Wait, Nicole, is this the same guy you've been chatting with on Tinder but haven't met IRL yet? What's his name again, like, Jonah? Or Zach? Something Judd-Apatow-y, right? Didn't he like, stand you up on your first and second dates?

Morgan

PS - Katie, loud and clear on the print is dead thing!

To: Ali, Katie, Jen, Ashley, Morgan, Gracie, Caitlin
From: Nicole
Date: March 3 at 4:12 p.m.
Subject: Re: Book Club + Saint Patty's???

Both times he got pulled into a "fire drill," which is work-speak for an emergency and not an actual fire drill (AS I AWKWARDLY FOUND OUT when I messaged him "are you ok???"). Anyway, we both have busy careers, and it's important that I be with someone really driven!!

That said, I'm ready to lock this down. His name is Seth!!!!!

Should I rent the runway, or just buy a bandage dress at H&M?? Does anyone wanna sneak out of work to get blowouts and mani/pedi/Brazilians???

x,
Nic

To: Ali, Katie, Jen, Ashley, Morgan, Gracie, Nicole
From: Caitlin
Date: March 3 at 4:24 p.m.
Subject: Re: Book Club + Saint Patty's???

Hi Ladies!

Ok, need to jump in here because this is actually like, a major (DJ KHALED VOICE) key that I wrote about on the blog with corresponding outfit of the day pics. (Check it out here!) In case your work computers have blocked my site from your desktop (I totally get it, it's addictive and you want to read it all at once!), I have condensed my best tips for you here, Nic, and for whoever else may benefit from this information**

- **If a guy has stood you up once, he'll probably do it again.** And if he's stood you up twice, honestly, fuck him. Nicole! Your time is valuable. Your job is important. I'm sorry this guy got stuck in an office fire, but is that an excuse to miss a date? And then another date? Know your worth! (This is different from your net worth, which I know is low.)

- **Do not text him for a year so he starts wondering where you've been.** Seriously— change his name in your phone from whatever his name is to DO NOT PICK UP. This totally helps. Don't delete him from your phone because you never know!!! But don't keep that in the back of your head!!!!! I'm serious, Nicole!!!!!

- **Work is not more important than love.** If you want, I can say this into a voice recorder, and you can listen to it as you sleep. This is called an affirmation, and they are available for download on my blog for $.99 each or $5 for 5 (best value!).

- **You cannot be serious with the H&M outfits!** We really need to start building you a wardrobe of investment pieces you can rock all year long. Check out my post about capsule wardrobes here.

I hope this was helpful!! Nicole, you can do better!!!!!!!!!!!!!

Love you love us!!!
Caitlin

"Live your life. Stay strong. Be bold. Be gold." —I don't know the song, but it got me up the last hill in spin class this morning

** CaitlinTalk™ is the intellectual property of Caitlin, who owns the rights to the phrases "Caitlin," "CaitlinTalk," "Talk," "CaitlinMotivation," "CaitlinCommunication," "CaitlinYourself," "CaitlinYourLife," and "Don'tHesitateCaitlinate." If any parties attempt to infringe upon this copyright, FBI warning: Criminal copyright infringement is investigated by the FBI and may constitute a felony with a maximum penalty of up to 5 years in prison and/ or a $250,000,000 fine. In the criminal justice system, the people are represented by two separate yet equally important groups: the police, who investigate crime, and the district attorneys, who prosecute the offenders. **

To: Ali, Katie, Jen, Ashley, Morgan, Gracie, Caitlin
From: Nicole
Date: March 3 at 4:30 p.m.
Subject: Re: Book Club + Saint Patty's???

So should I cancel, or should I sleep with him (literally getting a Brazilian right now, so I'd like to see a return on that investment--look at me!)?? If I sleep with him, should I tell him I'm not looking for anything serious because of reverse psychology??

We really need to read *Ice Queens Melt Hearts*!!! Gotta go, the waxer is asking me to help her hold my butt cheeks apart!!! I love being women!!! Write me back!!

Nic

To: Ali, Katie, Ashley, Morgan, Gracie, Caitlin, Nicole
From: Jen
Date: March 3 at 4:34 p.m.
Subject: Re: Book Club + Saint Patty's???

Hey ladies,

Quick Q, do you think I can pull off a long-sleeved, high-necked wedding dress, or is that too Kate Middleton-esque?? Obviously people will be comparing us, as it is, anyway. Lmk!

Jen

Ultra Trendy BUT Classy Long Sleeve Bridal Dress
Jen
The BIG Day

Gorgeous Engagement Rings for Every Lady
Jen
The BIG Day

I'M THE F*CKIN BRIDE!
Subtle Ways to Tell People You're the Bride
Jen
The BIG Day

Killer Bridesmaids Gifts Under $10
Jen
The BIG Day

THE Perfect Bridal Updo for Elegant Brides

Wedding Dress with Train AND Back Details
Jen
The BIG Day

To: Ali, Jen, Ashley, Morgan, Gracie, Caitlin, Nicole
From: Katie
Date: March 3 at 4:41 p.m.
Subject: Re: Book Club + Saint Patty's???

Hey ladies,

Nicole I've been reading a lot about #Women lately, and my opinion is that you should be getting waxed every three weeks regardless of whether you're having sex or not.

Carole Radziwill of *RHONY* S5-present also says this, and she's literally 50-something dating a guy our age. So I'm just saying, setting yourself up for success is important. It's like having a 401k, which I know you don't have yet, Nicole, but this would be a good step forward.

Anyway, Morgan, do girls in Brooklyn do Brazilians???? Not judging -- just interested in learning about different cultures around the world.

Happy to do *Ice Queens Melt Hearts*, etc. Excited!!!!!!

Katie

To: Katie, Jen, Ashley, Morgan, Gracie, Caitlin, Nicole
From: Ali
Date: March 3 at 5:30 p.m.
Subject: Re: Book Club + Saint Patty's???

Hi Ladies!

I know we can sometimes be a bit indecisive, so I just did a bulk order for *Ice Queens Melt Hearts*!! I'm having it delivered to my office, so just be sure to pick it up from me this week so we all get a chance to read it. Let me know when you're planning on stopping by, so I can have the intern give your name to security. This will be much easier for everyone!!

Please send me $27.99 (I purchased the hardcover instead of the paperback to celebrate our first book club). In addition, everyone STILL owes me for our botched Valentine's Day plans (no offense, Jen! <3 you!). So can everyone PLEASE send me:

$250 (non-refundable Le Bain deposit)

$27.99 (*Ice Queens Melt Hearts* book for book club YAY!!!!)

$20.00 (for everyone EXCEPT Jen, so I can send her and Brad a bottle of '89 Dom -- it's good luck 'cause that was the year I was born and the year the Berlin Wall came down, coincidence?? ;))

TOTAL FOR EVERYONE EXCEPT JEN: $297.99

JEN'S TOTAL: $277.99 (#JointCheckingAccountYesPlease) and yes you can def pull off a long sleeve and a high neck!!

For St. Pattys, I still think we should go to a Kennedy party!!! Does anyone have any contacts at Soho House?? It might be worth the investment for us all to join!

Nic, according to the Amazon summary for *Ice Queens Melt Hearts* you should definitely ignore him while you're on your date tonight! Act like you hate the bar that he picked and pout, but then mention how your ex-boyfriend had great taste. Guys are competitive, and it will drive him crazy, and you'll become a Dreamgirl (see: *Why Men Love Bitches*) instead of a Doormat (see: *Why Men Marry Bitches*). Email us back in front of him -- guys love it when you don't give them your undivided attention!!!!

xo,
Ali

"Men love to be surprised in bed." —Excerpt from an unpublished op-ed I submitted to Cosmo in 2009.

To: Ali, Katie, Jen, Ashley, Morgan, Gracie, Caitlin
From: Nicole
Date: March 4 at 8:01 a.m.
Subject: Re: Book Club + Saint Patty's???

Hey ladies,

Ali, I am going to pay you in installments, and can you do a 0% APR for the first year like banks do? Thank you in advance!!! Also, I think I'll just print out the book from the internet...so I'll deduct $27.99 from what I owe you, and you can just return my copy. Sound good???

Love ya, chicks!
Nic

To: Ali, Katie, Jen, Ashley, Gracie, Caitlin, Nicole
From: Morgan
Date: March 4 at 8:20 a.m.
Subject: Re: Book Club + Saint Patty's???

Hey ladies,

Sounds good, Ali, but in the future maybe it's best to not pay for things first and then ask us for money (just because what happens if someone already figured out a way to get the book, etc., or didn't want to go to Le Bain, etc.). Totally understand you are a woman who likes to #GetShitDone, but don't hold us financially hostage for your aggressive relationship with money and planning!!

I am gonna read this book ironically :) but I also can't wait!

Morgs

To: Ali, Jen, Ashley, Morgan, Gracie, Caitlin, Nicole
From: Katie
Date: March 4 at 8:25 a.m.
Subject: Re: Book Club + Saint Patty's???

Hey ladies,

I'm out of pocket this weekend, because Topher and I are going upstate. Well, we're just going for the day, because he has to pick up something at a Home Depot. But it's probably going to be romantic!! We can look at bathroom and kitchen tiles, and I'll likely drop some hints about our future home!!! He has been using "we" a lot lately (e.g., "I think we should talk"). EEEE!!! SO thrilled and fulfilled.

SO EXCITED for the book club!!!!! Like Morgan, I will also read this book ironically!

Best,
Katie

P.S. I took this photo this morning!!! How adorable do we look!!!

To: Ali, Katie, Jen, Ashley, Morgan, Gracie, Nicole
From: Caitlin
Date: March 4 at 8:35 a.m.
Subject: Re: Book Club + Saint Patty's???

Hey ladies!

SOOOOOOOO EXCITEEDDDDDDD ABOUT THE BOOOOOOOOOK CLUB! Ali, you can return my copy too -- a friend of my agent/publicist/lyricist snagged me a copy from a dollar bin at The Strand. I think there were more copies if you ladies wanna go take a look :)

Again -- soooooo exciteddddddd!!!!!

I can host the first week since travel to Brooklyn might be expensive and booked for the date we choose. Can everyone BYO peanut-free or Soylent-free snacks?

Caitlin

CEO, CaitlinYourLife™

To: Ali, Katie, Jen, Ashley, Gracie, Caitlin, Nicole
From: Morgan
Date: March 4 at 8:39 a.m.
Subject: Re: Book Club + Saint Patty's???

Hi all!

Brooklyn is actually a part of NYC, it's not separate from NYC (there are five boroughs). It costs the same to get to each borough by subway. Cabs are not more or less expensive as distance is a constant. If you guys are down, would love to host a book club night but understand if the subways might confuse!!!!!

Morgs

To: Katie, Jen, Ashley, Morgan, Gracie, Caitlin, Nicole
From: Ali
Date: March 4 at 9:00 a.m.
Subject: Re: Book Club + Saint Patty's???

Hey Ladies!

According to any lifestyle guru and probably also Bethenny Frankel: "You have to spend money to make money." Therefore, I am investing in all of our futures through purchasing the hardcover of *Ice Queens Melt Hearts*. Think about it: don't you think you deserve more than a dollar-bin book or a paperback?? Haven't you guys read Caitlin's blog post on "manifesting your reality"??? Do you really want to manifest someone's old leftover book? I mean, I just think we can do better than secondhand (no offense, Nicole or Nicole The Runway™).

But, I'm hearing your feedback and really taking it in, sooo after you all pay me back (just invoiced you all through Venmo), I will be sure to "check in" before buying in bulk in the future ;)

I would LOVE to go to Brooklyn, Morgan, it just might be sort of hard to organize if we did it on a weekday or weekend. Thoughts??

xo,
Ali

"You are killing it!" —my boss to me this morning (!!!!)

To: Ali, Katie, Jen, Ashley, Morgan, Gracie, Caitlin
From: Nicole
Date: March 4 at 9:06 a.m.
Subject: Re: Book Club + Saint Patty's???

I'll go to Brooklyn!!! Does anyone have Uber codes???

Nicole

Ps. My tinder date was so cute! Sleep with him *then* ignore him, right??

To: Ali, Katie, Jen, Ashley, Morgan, Gracie, Nicole
From: Caitlin
Date: March 4 at 9:09 a.m.
Subject: Re: Book Club + Saint Patty's???

Nicole, why don't you message me off thread, and I'll send you my PowerPoint presentation on this.

Caitlin

To: Ali, Katie, Jen, Ashley, Gracie, Caitlin, Nicole
From: Morgan
Date: March 4 at 9:12 a.m.
Subject: Re: Book Club + Saint Patty's???

Hey ladies,

For *Ice Queens Melt Hearts*, do we have any actionable outcomes we'd like to see after studying this text? What are our intentions?

Morg

To: Ali, Katie, Ashley, Morgan, Gracie, Caitlin, Nicole
From: Jen
Date: March 4 at 9:18 a.m.
Subject: Re: Book Club + Saint Patty's???

Hi all!!

Since I'm the only one engaged to be married, would it make more sense if we skipped the book and I just told you guys over gluten-free biscotti how I was able to make a forever-lasting, loving, and worthwhile relationship work and thrive with the love of my life! Spoiler: it always happens when you stop looking for him! Just trust me. Sure, when I met Brad I was going out every night to meet men, but I think subconsciously I wasn't truly looking for it. Happy to explain more in detail!

Please come to New Jersey? And bring macarons. You just can't find a decent macaron west of the Hudson :(

Lmk, Jen

To: Ali, Katie, Jen, Ashley, Gracie, Caitlin, Nicole
From: Morgan
Date: March 4 at 10:56 a.m.
Subject: Re: Book Club + Saint Patty's???

Hey ladies,

Off-topic, but I'm having a roommate problem, and I need some advice/need to vent. Anyone around?

Morgs

To: Ali, Katie, Jen, Ashley, Morgan, Gracie, Nicole
From: Caitlin
Date: March 4 at 10:58 a.m.
Subject: Re: Book Club + Saint Patty's???

Morgs, I have a PowerPoint on that too. Just got to my site and search: Roomie Probs. Discount code is: Friends20 for $2 off your first PowerPoint.

Love ya, good luck!
Caitlin

To: Ali, Katie, Ashley, Morgan, Gracie, Caitlin, Nicole
From: Jen
Date: March 4 at 10:59 a.m.
Subject: Re: Book Club + Saint Patty's???

Morgan, please vent away!! Is your roommate upset you want to host a CaitlinTalk on the potato famine? Maybe we could rent out an event space for it instead if it's causing problems. (Nic: can you do some research? I am swamped with trying to find photos of animals/nature/seascapes/time periods/colors/textures that speak to what I am trying to say thematically with #HereComesTheBrad or #EverlastingBJ -- still can't decide on a hashtag. HALP!!!)

Do you want me to call my broker and see if he has any apartments available near me in Hoboken?! That would be so fun!!

Ali -- you can send my book back also, since it doesn't really apply to where I am in life anymore. But I'll still attend book club/the potato famine talk if I have time!!

xo,
Jen

To: Ali, Katie, Jen, Ashley, Morgan, Gracie, Caitlin
From: Nicole
Date: March 4 at 3:43 p.m.
Subject: Re: Book Club + Saint Patty's???

Ok! I looked into the potato famine!! They have free WiFi on the subway now at most stations, so I spent a few hours underground and did a bunch of research! It's really sad though! Do you guys wanna Venmo me $16.99 (MP for a book these days!), and I can pass along the info I found out?! I think we should go to a pub and meet Irish guys! Or really any ethnicity!! I'm gonna write "Kiss Me, I'm Irish" on a white tank top that I plan to wear with no bra cause according to the Amazon review for *Ice Queens Melt Hearts*, guys are very visual. So I'd like guys we meet to visualize my nips!!!

Morgs, are you ok??

Love,
Nic

Ghostwriter, Researcher, Sales, Branding Expert & Life Coach

To: Ali, Jen, Ashley, Morgan, Gracie, Caitlin, Nicole
From: Katie
Date: March 4 at 3:50 p.m.
Subject: Re: Book Club + Saint Patty's???

Instead of a book club or a CaitlinTalk, do you ladies just wanna go to a happy hour in Flatiron next Thurs? LMK who is free. I can do between 5:00-5:45, but then I have a dinner with Topher, but seeing you girlies for a drink would be SO FUN!

Katie

To: Katie, Jen, Ashley, Morgan, Gracie, Caitlin, Nicole
From: Ali
Date: March 4 at 4:00 p.m.
Subject: Re: Book Club + Saint Patty's???

Hey Ladies!

So I totally totally get the first days of infatuation where you want to spend all your time together, but as *Why Men Love Bitches* taught us, it's up to women to set the pace of the relationship -- as they say, the Diptyque candle that burns twice as bright burns half as long. (Nicole: Diptyque candles are like Yankee Candles but 10,000% times better -- next time you come over, you should smell one!)

Katie, you should definitely not drop your whole life to see Topher! Not only is it retro and anti-feminist, but according to *The Rules*, men love a challenge! I think it's better to do a combination of seeing him once or twice/week, canceling plans every once in a while to keep him on his toes, and cultivating an Instagram presence to make him completely jealous of who you're with when you're not with him.

Therefore! I think we should still do a St. Patty's party at a bar (I'm down for anything TriBeCa), and you can email us the CaitlinTalk™ beforehand instead! We can meet JFK Jr.-type dudes while respectfully celebrating the rich history of their ancestors! HOT!

Nic: can you put together a PowerPoint on an iPad?

So excited!!!

xo,
Ali

"The supreme art of war is to subdue the enemy without fighting." —Sun Tzu, *The Art of War*

To: Ali, Katie, Jen, Morgan, Gracie, Caitlin, Nicole
From: Ashley
Date: March 4 at 4:10 p.m.
Subject: Re: Book Club + Saint Patty's???

Hey ladies!

Sorry, just getting all of these! No service in CT :(

What if we all went out in Stamford? We could go to my dad's golf club in Greenwich -- they're having a cocktail mixer (I think it's a prix fixe, $200, but $10 of your ticket price goes to teach underprivileged city kids how to play tennis). There will be bagpipers too! Fun, right? It might be a slightly older crowd, but you know, I'm not exactly opposed to being a second wife if it were the right situation ;)

Just a note: this is a very pearls and Vineyard Vines crowd, so maybe we can all wear some fun cocktail dresses or printed dresses? Basically, there's a dress code. Morgan & Nicole -- if you wanna borrow something, I have many options!! Or there's Rent the Runway?

Love,
Ash

To: Ali, Katie, Jen, Ashley, Morgan, Gracie, Caitlin
From: Nicole
Date: March 5 at 12:30 p.m.
Subject: Re: Book Club + Saint Patty's???

Off-topic: After I slept with Tinder Guy I asked if I could borrow a hoodie for the Walk of Shame, and he tried to give me this hoodie that he got for free at work, and I was like, "Oh, your Cornell hoodie looks way warmer, is it ok if I borrow that?" and he completely cares about my well-being because he was like, "Um, ok I guess?" Playing it cool much, dude? ;)

Anyway, we definitely are hanging again because I took his favorite hoodie!! Genius, right? To be honest, I'm really frustrated with him right now because I texted, "The other night was fun ;)" an hour ago and he hasn't written back yet, and then I just texted "???" and he hasn't written back to that either! I hope he's not one of those guys who doesn't really text 'cause he's "busy" working. I'm launching an e-book, a lifestyle-wellness brand, and a passive source of income, Nicole The Runway™, and I STILL find time to text him constantly. Would it be weird if I called his office and hung up when he answered the phone? I just want to hear his voice. SWOON!!!!

x,
Nic

To: Ali, Katie, Ashley, Morgan, Gracie, Caitlin, Nicole
From: Jen
Date: March 5 at 12:45 p.m.
Subject: Re: Book Club + Saint Patty's???

Honestly? Connecticut or even Manhattan seems like a lot of work right now. When you all get engaged, you'll totally understand! We are viewing so many venues next weekend, and I'm already so stressed. Plus, I'm not eating carbs, nightshades, animal proteins, chia seeds, or soy. I'm doing the KaMu diet (all kale + mushrooms) for the wedding, and I'm experiencing a ton of headaches and I feel flu-like symptoms, which I've read is just toxins leaving my body.

Would you all want to come over to my place in New Jersey on March 17th for some self-care and wedding planning??

x,
Jen

To: Ali, Katie, Jen, Ashley, Morgan, Gracie, Caitlin
From: Nicole
Date: March 5 at 1:17 p.m.
Subject: Re: Book Club + Saint Patty's???

Exciting news! I figured out Tinder Guy's work email, and I just sent him an Outlook cal invite for "Weekend in Paris!" for two weeks from now! How romantic am I??

Stay tuned... ;)

x,
Nic

To: Ali, Jen, Ashley, Morgan, Gracie, Caitlin, Nicole
From: Katie
Date: March 5 at 1:27 p.m.
Subject: Re: Book Club + Saint Patty's???

Hey ladies,

I'm out for the happy hour drinks I planned for next Thurs. Topher wants to talk!!! He was like, "I think we need to talk, why don't you stop by next Thursday after work at the Pret a Manger below my office." EEEEE!!! Honestly I didn't think we'd be getting engaged this quickly, but I guess it's true about knowing when you know. (Hopefully he's not proposing in a Pret? Ha!) Anyway, see you ladies soon, I hope!!!!!

Katie

ps. Jen, re: March 17, I can't. I think I am going to surprise Topher with a big Irish celebration to show I care about his heritage.

To: Ali, Katie, Ashley, Morgan, Gracie, Caitlin, Nicole
From: Jen
Date: March 5 at 2:07 p.m.
Subject: Re: Book Club + Saint Patty's???

Hi girls,

Good luck, Katie!! If you do get engaged, let's make sure we schedule our events so that everyone can go to everything. I'll share my wedding cal with you now.

Also please wait until after next January, so we both don't get married in the same calendar year. :) Thanks!

Jen

P.S. I'm off the KaMu diet. I'm starting to question if toxins are a real thing??! Gonna google.

To: Ali, Katie, Jen, Ashley, Morgan, Gracie, Caitlin
From: Nicole
Date: March 5 at 2:10 p.m.
Subject: Re: Book Club + Saint Patty's???

Tinder Guy just declined my "Weekend in Paris" invite.

I need a B12 shot.

Going to die alone.

xoxo,
Nicole

To: Katie, Jen, Ashley, Morgan, Gracie, Caitlin, Nicole
From: Ali
Date: March 17 at 10:30 a.m.
Subject: Re: Book Club + Saint Patty's???

Sorry, I've been MIA for a couple weeks. I've been in a sex cocoon with Ben! (We saw each other 3x last week!) Whatever happened to our St. Paddy's Book Club?! Taking the reins here! No one has mentioned having plans tonight so I'll happily alpha!

Itinerary for St. Patrick's tonight!!!!

7:00 p.m.: Meet at The Half King in Chelsea (I know I mentioned going to TriBeCa, but The Half King should be way more fun! And it's only half a block from my office, so it's more convenient for everyone!)
7:05-7:10: First book club session for *Ice Queens Melt Hearts*!!!
7:10-7:15: Order Guinnesses or perhaps a variety of wine from the Killarney region
7:15-??: Celebrate St. Patrick's Day in a mature, culturally-sensitive-yet-not-appropriating manner

I think we should all wear green!!

xo,
Ali

PS. Everyone please bring cash, and I think it's only fair to buy me drinks to pay down the $ you all owe me for the book and the canceled V-Day reservation!!!

"This feels...cool." —Ben to me this morning *sigh*

To: Ali, Katie, Jen, Ashley, Morgan, Caitlin, Nicole
From: Gracie
Date: March 17 at 10:32 a.m.
Subject: Re: Book Club + Saint Patty's???

Hi all,

I am not going to be able to make book club this round. Have fun!

Thanks,
Gracie

To: Katie, Jen, Ashley, Morgan, Gracie, Caitlin, Nicole
From: Ali
Date: April 1 at 7:01 a.m.
Subject: Bridal ShowShow!!!

Hey Ladies!!

Rabbit rabbit! I was just thinking -- what if we did a bridal shower for Jen super low-key at one of our apartments? We can all do a potluck, play some games, listen to music, and just be super chill. I was just thinking about how the wedding-industrial complex can divert us so much from what is really important -- two people who love each other, and their friends and families gathering to support and nourish that love. Let me know if anyone would like to plan it! Down for whatever. :)

xo, Ali

"True love is the soul's recognition of its counterpoint in another." —Owen Wilson, *Wedding Crashers*

To: Katie, Jen, Ashley, Morgan, Gracie, Caitlin, Nicole
From: Ali
Date: April 1 at 7:02 a.m.
Subject: Re: Bridal ShowShow!!!

JUST KIDDING APRIL FOOL'S BITCHES LOL!!!!!!!!!!!!!

Can everyone please join my #BJShower Slack channel. I'm thinking of a Marie Antoinette/ Louis XVI theme. Powdered wigs, court jesters, harps, etc. I'd like to hold the first planning meeting ASAP. Who is available tonight??

xo, Ali
"A woman only gets eight true loves in a lifetime" —A lesson I learned from the inimitable life of Elizabeth Taylor

To: Ali, Katie, Ashley, Morgan, Gracie, Caitlin, Nicole
From: Jen
Date: April 1 at 8:14 a.m.
Subject: Re: Bridal ShowShow!!!

Ahhhh! OMG! Not gonna lie, ladies, I was just about to reach into my computer screen and strangle Ali!!!! Fuck YOU for that, Ali! Jk! lol! But not really!!!!

Marie Antoinette Bridal Shower

Party Must-Have: Ombre Macaron Tower

 Ali
Wedding Shower of the Year

Fans would be cute as gifts!? No A/C yet :(

 Ali
Wedding Shower of the Year

Dainty Tea Set for Every and Any Party

 Ali
Wedding Shower of the Year

Let Them Eat Cake - Marie Antoinette Tshirt

 Ali
Wedding Shower of the Year

QUEEEEEEEN aka party inspiration!!!

Ali
Wedding Shower of the Year

Champagne Tower for the Perfect Partay

Ali
Wedding Shower of the Year

Okay so basically I'm super excited by all of these ideas, and I think Ali's onto a good start with a theme (we can wear waist trainers and do big curls!). BUT my mom is also really into planning this for me so maybe a few of you can join up with her to help plan????

I gave her all of your emails (work and personal) as well as your phone numbers (work and cell). Can everyone also pass along an emergency contact number in case either of your numbers go to voicemail? We just don't have a ton of time to plan.

Expect to hear from my mom soon!!!!

Xoxo,
#herecomesbradsbride

To: Ali, Katie, Ashley, Morgan, Gracie, Caitlin, Nicole
From: Jen
Date: April 1 at 8:20 a.m.
Subject: Re: Bridal ShowShow!!!

Ladies,

Forgot to add that an emergency number can be your boyfriend, your boss, or your landlord.

Ideally this person is NOT a parent. I don't want to be rude and bother your family :)
I expect there to be a lot of phone calls.

Xo, #AlmostAMrs

To: Ali, Katie, Jen, Ashley, Morgan, Gracie, Nicole
From: Caitlin
Date: April 1 at 11:23 a.m.
Subject: Re: Bridal ShowShow!!!

Hi girls,

Jen, you can give your mom my publicist's number -- 212-555-9788. Ask for Gennie (it's a hard G).

Thanks!
Caitlin

CEO, CaitlinYourLife™

To: Ali, Katie, Jen, Ashley, Morgan, Gracie, Caitlin
From: Nicole
Date: April 2 at 10:53 a.m.
Subject: Re: Bridal ShowShow!!!

Hi ladies!

My emergency contact is my roommate, Kelly S (not sure if her last name is Sanderson or Sandleson). She usually doesn't pick up unknown numbers, so tell your mom to text her!!! 917-555-1248

Thanks!
Nicole

To: Katie, Jen, Ashley, Morgan, Gracie, Caitlin, Nicole
From: Ali
Date: April 2 at 3:07 p.m.
Subject: Re: Bridal ShowShow!!!

My emergency contacts are my interns, the Emmas -- Emma H. and Emma V.

Emma H. is much more responsible, but Emma V. has much better style. They are both available 24/7. Unfortunately they communicate via Instagram private messaging and Snapchat only -- could your mom download one of them?

xo,
Ali

"It is better to be disliked for being who you are than to be loved for who you are not."
—André Gide

To: Ali, Katie, Jen, Morgan, Gracie, Caitlin, Nicole
From: Ashley
Date: April 4 at 8:36 a.m.
Subject: Re: Bridal ShowShow!!!

I don't really have an emergency contact I'm not related to...Sorry, this is really triggering for me. I am going to self-care/look at photos of dogs on Petfinder now...

Love,
Ash

To: Ali, Jen, Ashley, Morgan, Gracie, Caitlin, Nicole
From: Katie
Date: April 4 at 8:40 a.m.
Subject: Re: Bridal ShowShow!!!

Hey ladies,

My emergency contact: You can reach my boss at the *New York Times* story-tagging desk. His name is Adam Havenworth, and he is at 212-555-9345. He knows my name is Katie, I think, but he might not know my last name. If there's any confusion, just say, like, "You know, the girl with a nose for news who tags the stories?"

THANKS!
Katie

To: Ali, Katie, Jen, Ashley, Morgan, Caitlin, Nicole
From: Gracie
Date: April 4 at 3:45 p.m.
Subject: Re: Bridal ShowShow!!!

Hi,

I don't think I need to give an emergency contact (I have a feeling my boss will hate that, haha!), but you all have my email and cell, so if I don't pick up, it just means I am occupied with work or another activity (not that I am dead), and I'll call back when I have time!

Xo, Gracie

To: Katie, Jen, Ashley, Morgan, Gracie, Caitlin, Nicole
CC: HeleneAndRobert.Carrington@gmail.com
From: Ali
Date: April 4 at 4:07 p.m.
Subject: Re: Bridal ShowShow!!!

Hi ladies!

Hmmm...Gracie, humor us and be a team player?? I have cc'ed Jen's mom, Helene Carrington, on this email.

Thanks,
Ali

To: Ali, Katie, Ashley, Morgan, Gracie, Caitlin, Nicole
From: HeleneAndRobert.Carrington@gmail.com
Date: April 7 at 11:00 a.m.
Subject: Jennifer's Bridal Shower

Hi Ladies!

This is Helene Carrington, Jen's mom. You can call me Mrs. Carrington or #mamaofthebride.

Thanks for getting the ball rolling on the bridal shower, Ali! I'm impressed with your email skills. You girls will have to put up with my technological ineptitude haha -- don't be surprised if I butt dial you at all hours of the night! But please pick up when I do.

So I'll keep this as short as possible, as I know you all live busy lives. Since we all know Jen has always loved flowers, I'm thinking we do a garden luncheon bridal shower at our country club in Virginia at the turn of the season. I know Virginia is a trek from New York City and Brooklyn, but I already checked Amtrak train tickets for the last weekend in April, and it looks like it will only be ~$450 per person round trip (a deal!).

Ali, since you're the Maid of Honor I'll let you handle dress code, but please, ladies, be prepared to wear a pastel or muted shade that goes well with your skin tone. If you're not sure, google! Or go to a high-end luxury clothing store and make a consultation appointment with a stylist. As for shoes, just because this will be outside doesn't mean you should sacrifice looking good for being comfortable. I am going to have a photographer on site, so keep that in mind! As for hair and makeup, please call Meegan at Hair Today in VA for consecutive day-of appointments so we can have consistency in looks.

As for gifts, here is a link to Jen and Brad's registry. Keep in mind that in addition to gifts, Jen is asking that everyone make a notable ($250+) donation to a charity of your choice.

Thank you, ladies. Any questions please ask Ali!

All best,
Helene "Mrs." Carrington

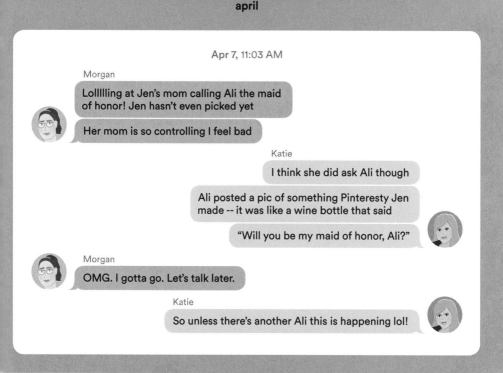

Apr 7, 11:03 AM

Morgan
Lollllling at Jen's mom calling Ali the maid of honor! Jen hasn't even picked yet

Her mom is so controlling I feel bad

Katie
I think she did ask Ali though

Ali posted a pic of something Pinteresty Jen made -- it was like a wine bottle that said

"Will you be my maid of honor, Ali?"

Morgan
OMG. I gotta go. Let's talk later.

Katie
So unless there's another Ali this is happening lol!

To: Helene and Bob Carrington
From: Morgan
Date: April 7 at 1:15 p.m.
Subject: Re: Jennifer's Bridal Shower

Hi Mrs. Carrington!

I didn't reply all to the email thread so this one is just to you.

I wanted to say thanks for planning and let me know if you need me to do anything that you were planning to ask Ali to do as maid of honor. Obviously you've been like another mother to me since first grade :) and I've been excited about this wedding since Jen made me the priest in her fourth-grade recess wedding to William Pelter (haha!).

Anyway! So yeah! Let me know if I can be of any help or anything at all!

Thanks!
Morgan

To: Morgan
From: Helene and Bob Carrington
Date: April 8 at 2:00 p.m.
Subject: Re: Jennifer's Bridal Shower

Hi Morgan,

So nice to hear from you! We are so looking forward to the wedding and having you and your parents there. I'm so thrilled you and Jen have remained friends in New York/Brooklyn.

I wonder if William Pelter will object to his first wife having another wedding! I still chuckle about making cupcakes for her to bring to school so the event could be "catered."

Thank you for the offer to help! Oh, and as a reminder -- Jen mentioned you might stay with your parents while you're in town for the shower, but we would love to have you stay at the hotel with the rest of the group. It's $249 a night plus tax. Mention "Carrington wedding" when you call to book!

See you soon, dear,
Mrs. Carrington

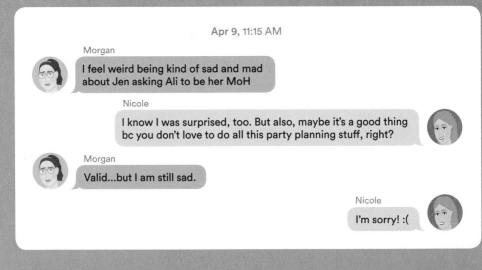

Apr 9, 11:15 AM

Morgan
I feel weird being kind of sad and mad about Jen asking Ali to be her MoH

Nicole
I know I was surprised, too. But also, maybe it's a good thing bc you don't love to do all this party planning stuff, right?

Morgan
Valid...but I am still sad.

Nicole
I'm sorry! :(

To: Katie, Ashley, Morgan, Gracie, Caitlin, Nicole, Helene and Bob Carrington
From: Ali
Date: April 9 at 4:00 p.m.
Subject: Re: Jennifer's Bridal Shower

Hi Ladies,

First off, thanks so much, Helene, for getting the ball rolling! My mom barely knows how to text, so it's amazing how e-savvy you are! Jealous.

I think the Virginia shower idea is very interesting, but I'm wondering if it really makes the most sense from a friends-locale perspective? Since most of Jen's girls are based in New York, I think logistically the shower should happen here. Also, it seems like you have a ton on your plate between your garden and those Daughters of the American Revolution teas and fundraisers for raising awareness about tennis elbow -- I am happy to send my diagrams and color swatches for a shower in the tone of a northern wedding aesthetic (completely different than what you are probably accustomed to!). It will be fun!

Mason jars. Chalk menus. Social media tie-ins. I'm probably speaking another language to you, right!? LOL! So! I am happy to coordinate Jen's bridal shower here in New York for her city friends. Since most of us have big careers, it's hard for us to take off an entire weekend. Some of us work around the clock! (No offense, Nicole.) Maybe you can do a second shower in VA for you and Jen's aunts and cousins that still live nearby? Can't wait to see the photos!!

Sincerely,
Ali

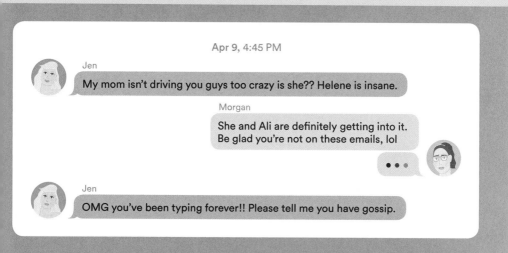

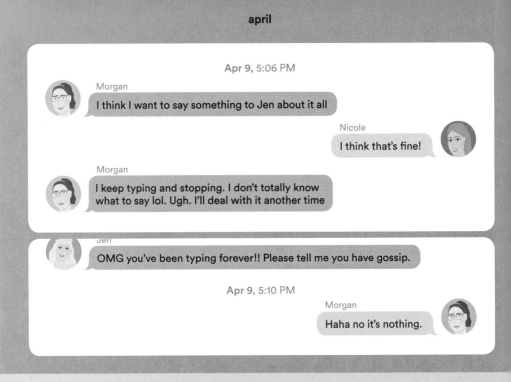

Apr 9, 5:06 PM

Morgan
I think I want to say something to Jen about it all

Nicole
I think that's fine!

Morgan
I keep typing and stopping. I don't totally know what to say lol. Ugh. I'll deal with it another time

Jen
OMG you've been typing forever!! Please tell me you have gossip.

Apr 9, 5:10 PM

Morgan
Haha no it's nothing.

To: Ali, Katie, Ashley, Morgan, Gracie, Caitlin, Nicole
From: Helene and Bob Carrington
Date: April 10 at 6:32 a.m.
Subject: Re: Jennifer's Bridal Shower

Hi Ali and Ladies!

What a fun idea to try to coordinate a separate bridal shower in New York for Jen! I love that she will have a friends-leaning shower and a family-leaning shower, and that everyone is invited and expected to come to both! Thank you for making my Jen feel so special in the time leading up to her wedding.

We look forward to hosting you at our country club in Virginia, and my husband and I will make arrangements for our families to come to New York to celebrate in a…bar? A venue space? Museum? Sorry, dear, it wasn't totally clear where you will be throwing this soiree, but I know it will be fabulous. Count us in!

All best,
Helene

Apr 10, 2:15 PM

Ali
Can you send some communication and management style tips over ASAP?

Jen's mom isn't totally getting it

Caitlin
Yah they are on my blog! Google CAITLINYOURLIFE and then "managing up: how to handle your annoying boss"

Ali
Jen's mom is NOT my boss!!!

To: Ali, Katie, Ashley, Morgan, Gracie, Caitlin, Helene and Bob Carrington
From: Nicole
Date: April 10 at 6:54 p.m.
Subject: Re: Jennifer's Bridal Shower

Hi Helene,

I'm not sure if you know this, but I am an entrepreneur. Like Steve Jobs and Woz (spelling? not sure exactly who he is, I watched the Steve Jobs movie on a plane after taking half an Ambien, lol), but instead of building computers in a garage in Cupertino, I am building something from the ground up, and since my seed funding is just around the corner (fingers crossed!), it's really important I pour all my energy and resources into my company!

Therefore I am asking you all to support me and for the time being I need to embrace self-care and not get further into debt. So unless you can *invest* in me and provide me with free transportation and accommodation, I respectfully decline the Virginia weekend.

Thank you for understanding.

Yours,
Nicole

"Investing in yourself is the best investment you'll ever make." —me (TM)

To: Katie, Ashley, Morgan, Gracie, Caitlin, Nicole, Helene and Bob Carrington
From: Ali
Date: April 10 at 8:30 p.m.
Subject: Re: Jennifer's Bridal Shower

Hi ladies and Mrs. Carrington,

Okay! I totally understand your email. Two parties sound fine, and we'll make sure we show you a real New York soirée.

For your family gathering, just wanted to run some details by you:

Amtrak tickets run around ~$450 for the weekend we're going. Is it correct to say the Carringtons will be providing transportation? Helene, you can just reply all to let us know here. To help keep costs down, I read on Caitlin's blog that there is a social media tie-in that will allow us to enter for one free round-trip ticket! All you have to do is buy Caitlin's e-book, *Caitlin Rules*, and post a photo on Instagram of you reading it with the hashtag #PulitzerPlease and #CaitlinRules, Snapchat story it to all of your friends, and post about it on Facebook and Twitter! SUPER easy! And if you win, Caitlin's publisher's PR team will reimburse you up to $450 for a ticket within 365 days of purchase.

LMACK (that's "Let me and Caitlin know") once you post your pics! Cannot wait!

Until then, please reply all to let Helene know that you are coming so she can purchase the tickets. (Helene, please do a status update on that soon so we can get this garden party started!)

THANKS!

Ali

"May the bodies of your enemies act as your escalator to the top." —Ancient proverb

To: Ali, Katie, Ashley, Morgan, Gracie, Caitlin, Nicole
From: Helene and Bob Carrington
Date: April 11 at 8:30 a.m.
Subject: Re: Jennifer's Bridal Shower

Hi Ladies,

Nicole, are you threatening to not come unless I invest in your company? I believe Mr. Carrington's investments and finances are squared away until EOQ3, but I will check, dear. In any case, we are happy to cover the cost of your Amtrak tickets if it will mean you can all be here for Jen's first bridal party. It has always been a long-term resolution of mine to be more charitable towards the needy, for thine is the kingdom and the power and the glory of God, now and forever, and peace be with you.

Thank you all,
Helene Carrington

"In God all things are possible."

To: Katie, Ashley, Morgan, Gracie, Caitlin, Nicole, Helene and Bob Carrington
From: Ali
Date: April 11 at 8:37 a.m.
Subject: Re: Jennifer's Bridal Shower

Thanks for the e-note, Helene!

Can everyone please save the month of May (entirely) for the New York shower? I am sourcing venues.

Best,
Ali

"God is dead." —Friedrich Nietzsche

To: Ali, Katie, Ashley, Morgan, Gracie, Caitlin, Nicole
From: Helene and Bob Carrington
Date: April 12 at 11:00 a.m.
Subject: Re: Jennifer's Bridal Shower

Hi Ladies,

I did a special bridal shower registry for Jen at Michael C. Fina and Tiffany & Co., so please feel free to buy your gifts now. You can use the money you saved on the train tickets we bought you! Additionally, Ali, the entire "Carrington Clan" is busy in May, so sorry about that. We try to celebrate spring's renewal in our homeland. It might be too crazy to have two showers after all. Maybe we will just stick with the first one. I love Jen, but two showers might be extreme! Glad we worked this out.

Please dress "Southern Shower Chic." (Some brands: Lilly Pulitzer. Or a more affordable option: J.Crew.) Looking forward to seeing everyone!

Warmest,
Helene

CEO of the Carrington family

To: Ali, Katie, Morgan, Gracie, Caitlin, Nicole
From: Ashley
Date: April 12 at 2:45 p.m.
Subject: ???????? but also !!!!!!!!!!

Hi everyone!

So what's the plan? Are we having two parties or one? Sort of confused! I don't get service in Connecticut :(But looking forward to it either way! Can someone just let me know? Ready to do whatever! I'm flexible! So fun! Excited! So just email when there's a for-sure plan! Can't wait!!!!!

Love!!!! Ash

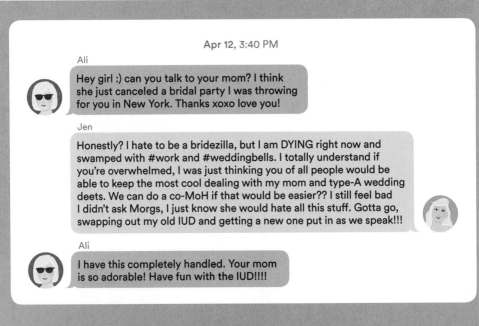

To: Ali, Katie, Ashley, Morgan, Gracie, Caitlin, Nicole
From: Helene and Bob Carrington
Date: April 13 at 10:30 a.m.
Subject: Transportation Details

Hi Ashley and fellow Ladies,

Small twist: Amtrak is out! I was just chatting with my friend Diana, and for her daughter Ambrose's bridal shower, they sent a car to pick everyone up and bring them, so Mr. Carrington and I will do that! We'll send a small bus to pick up all of you girls! It's our pleasure. I don't quite know where most of you live in New York City (my knowledge of New York begins and ends with Bergdorf's -- haha), so I thought it would be easiest for you to meet in front of Jen's apartment in New Jersey at 6:00 a.m. the day of the shower. How fun! Better than the train with all of the other train people, right?

Looking forward to it!

Warmest,
Helene

CEO of the Carrington Family

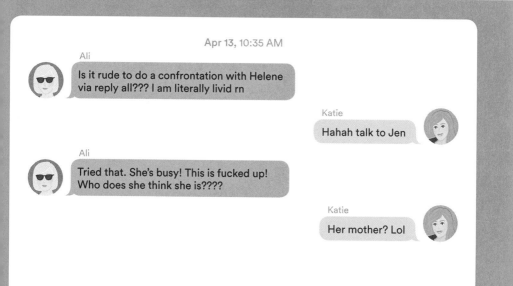

Apr 13, 10:35 AM

Ali
Is it rude to do a confrontation with Helene via reply all??? I am literally livid rn

Katie
Hahah talk to Jen

Ali
Tried that. She's busy! This is fucked up! Who does she think she is????

Katie
Her mother? Lol

To: Katie, Ashley, Morgan, Gracie, Caitlin, Nicole, Helene and Bob Carrington
From: Ali
Date: April 14 at 10:00 a.m.
Subject: Re: Jennifer's Bridal Shower

Hi Ladies and Mrs. Carrington,

Thank you again for handling the details for the family shower! I've done a lot of soul searching and consulting Pinterest, and have decided it would be more fun to have one bridal shower down south. Thank you for hosting! Please let me know if I can help with any of the arrangements. For example, even though the venue may say country club, it might be fun to have on-trend barn details such as party favors of homemade jam, fresh-cut wildflowers, and twinkle lights (lighting is sooo important to our generation). Please let me know if I can send a vision board to help your event planner with details.

~Day-of Logistics~
I've arranged a car and driver to bring everyone to Helene's car in Hoboken. We will meet in front of my apartment no later than 5:00 a.m. I will have a mimosa brunch spread (pre-party!) and will invoice everyone accordingly.

Also, I know it's April, but I am experiencing SAD still! I haven't bought an official SAD light box, but I'm staring at the overhead lighting at work...and it's not changing my mood at all :(. I'm going to ask my therapist (i.e., Kayla at SoulCycle) about coloring-book therapy. I need like a Paris weekend or something to get me out of my doldrums. I miss Ben. I haven't heard back from him in a few weeks, but it's a completely mutual decision for us to consciously uncouple. That said, I'm thinking about texting him something like "Hey stranger" and then pretending like I meant to send it to someone else. Really torn.

xo,
Ali

Apr 14, 11:06 AM

Morgan
Wait which guy is Ben?? Re: Ali's email lol

Ashley
I can't remember. Honestly everyone in this part of CT is named Benjamin so...No idea.

To: Helene and Bob Carrington
From: Ali
Date: April 15 at 8:03 a.m.
Subject: KILL ME!

Okay, so the New York party is officially dead in the water, so let's all go to Helene's fucking 1980s shower!!! I will play the long game. It's gonna be so boring that everyone will be excited to have me plan everything going forward. This is literally the worst thing to happen to me since I had to ride third row at SoulCycle and it threw off my chakras for WEEKS.

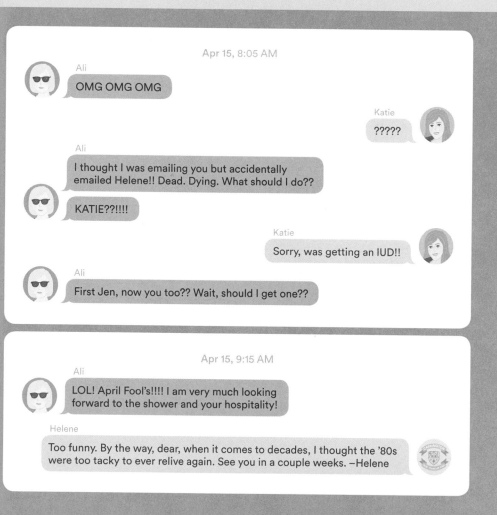

Apr 15, 8:05 AM

Ali
OMG OMG OMG

Katie
?????

Ali
I thought I was emailing you but accidentally emailed Helene!! Dead. Dying. What should I do??

KATIE??!!!!

Katie
Sorry, was getting an IUD!!

Ali
First Jen, now you too?? Wait, should I get one??

Apr 15, 9:15 AM

Ali
LOL! April Fool's!!!! I am very much looking forward to the shower and your hospitality!

Helene
Too funny. By the way, dear, when it comes to decades, I thought the '80s were too tacky to ever relive again. See you in a couple weeks. –Helene

To: Ali, Katie, Ashley, Morgan, Gracie, Caitlin, Helene and Bob Carrington
From: Nicole
Date: April 17 at 1:24 p.m.
Subject: Re: Jennifer's Bridal Shower

Hi Helene and Ladies,

Thank you again for providing transportation to Virginia! Can't wait!!

Ali -- no need to include me on the Uber/champagne brunch. Once again, I am in start-up mode over here. I'll just go on a Tinder date the night before with a guy in Hoboken and sleep over at his place.

xx,
Nicole

Use the code "JENSHOWER" for 5% off at Nicole The Runway!

To: Ali, Ashley, Morgan, Gracie, Caitlin, Nicole, Helene and Bob Carrington
From: Katie
Date: April 19 at 1:59 p.m.
Subject: Re: Jennifer's Bridal Shower

Hey Ladies!

I'll probably be staying over at Topher's the night before. Helene -- to catch you up: Topher is my boyfriend. He went to Villanova (Go Wildcats, lol!), MBA at Wharton, does something in finance -- he's told me, but it's so boring so I just focused on his jawline (swoon) and nodded.

Anyway, gotta run! Have a conf call now! We're updating the tag categories at the *New York Times*. All the news that's fit to tag! Ha!

xo,
Katie

To: Ali, Katie, Ashley, Morgan, Gracie, Nicole, Helene and Bob Carrington
From: Caitlin
Date: April 21 at 2:02 a.m.
Subject: Healthy and Mindful Shower!

Hi ladies!

I'm so looking forward to the shower! I can't wait to get some air and embrace nature on the grounds at your country club.

Not sure if you received my rider that Gennie sent over -- she said you haven't confirmed for some reason? Did you not receive it? Should she send you a hardcopy? We can FedEx overnight.

Anyway, I've embraced a clean-eating lifestyle change. Here are the foods that jibe with the CaitlinLifestyleYouAreWhatGoesInYourMouth™ plan:

Acceptable foods:
- Kale
- Dandelion root
- Locally sourced millet
- Farm-raised (preferably where the animal is raised on an organic diet as well) duck
- Truffles
- Kombucha (made within hours of consuming it)
- Arame (a sea vegetable collected off the coast of Japan -- should be easy to find at your local market)
- Hemp milk

List of UNACCEPTABLE/POISONOUS FOODS!!!! ☠
- Anything WHITE
- Olive oil
- Iodized salt (causes inflammation!)
- Nightshades
- Dairy
- ANY kind of non-duck meat (btw -- if I made a documentary on why eating meat is bad, would that be helpful? It seems no one's done that before!)
- 99% of vegetables that are in a Western diet
- Fruit (sugar ughhhhhh)

Hope this isn't a pain! Can't wait!!

Caitlin

CEO & Founder of CaitlinYourLife™
"I am emboldened to live with courage." —Caitlin, CEO & Founder of CaitlinYourLife™

To: Ali, Katie, Ashley, Morgan, Gracie, Caitlin, Helene and Bob Carrington
From: Nicole
Date: April 21 at 11:15 a.m.
Subject: Re: Healthy and Mindful Shower!

Caitlin and I eat the same diet pretty much, so that goes ditto for me!

xo,
Nicole

Use the code "JENSHOWER" for 6% off at Nicole The Runway!

To: Ali, Katie, Ashley, Morgan, Gracie, Caitlin, Nicole
From: Helene and Bob Carrington
Date: April 22 at 2:30 p.m.
Subject: Re: Healthy and Mindful Shower!

The menu has been decided, ladies. Please choose salmon, chicken, or a garden salad.

Warmest,
Helene

CEO of the Carrington Family

Apr 22, 2:35 PM

Ali

Did no one see that I'm suffering from seasonal depression????

Katie

Can I interview you for a piece?? Would you go on the record saying you're totally depressed and feel like you're spiraling? Your story can help a lot of people!

To: Ali, Katie, Ashley, Morgan, Gracie, Nicole, Helene and Bob Carrington
From: Caitlin
Date: April 23 at 9:07 a.m.
Subject: Re: Healthy and Mindful Shower!

Hi Helene and fellow women in my tribe,

No need to change the menu. I'll be bringing my own juice with me anyway. I'm strongly considering a Juicetarian lifestyle.

Best,
Caitlin

Founder & CEO, CaitlinYourLife™
Ask me about my line of CaitlinVitamins!

To: Caitlin, Katie, Ashley, Morgan, Gracie, Nicole, Helene and Bob Carrington
From: Ali
Date: April 29 at 9:00 a.m.
Subject: Re: Healthy and Mindful Shower!

Hi Helene and Ladies!

I wanted to personally thank Helene for throwing such a lovely bridal shower. I thought the garden salad and hard dinner rolls were a fun throwback to American foods before the culinary arts began to embrace locally sourced artisanal foods, and it really made me grateful to return to the food capital of the world! I thought your speech was lovely, and since you said that there "wasn't enough time" for me to do my prepared speech, I'll be modifying a version of it for my wedding speech. Get ready to laugh and cry—it's going to be beautiful! I hired a grad student who studies with Zadie Smith to ghostwrite it for me.

Thank you again for sending transportation to pick us up. On the return trip home, I had the driver drop us all off in Manhattan after he dropped Jen in Hoboken since it isn't safe to travel on transportation from New Jersey after 7 p.m. Thank you again for your hospitality.

Just to confirm, any and all details regarding Jen's wedding should go through me first. This is a peaceful transfer of power. I'm running point on this now.

xo,
Ali

"Money can buy a lot of things, but it can't buy good taste." —Me, Ali, April 29th, 8:59 a.m.

may

To: Ali, Katie, Jen, Ashley, Gracie, Caitlin, Nicole
From: Morgan
Date: May 6 at 2:00 p.m.
Subject: Vacation, all I ever wanted

Hey bitches :)

Read this amazing piece in *Wired* the other day about off-the-grid living and it gave me an idea: what if we did a long weekend "unplugged" this summer? We could rent a cute Airbnb in Rockaway Beach and do face masks, listen to music, and not look at our phones! We could also make sage bundles!

I know this sounds very "Brooklyn" to you, but who's down? Can try to put together a basic plan with a Doodle for available weekends.

Let me know!
Morgan

To: Ali, Katie, Jen, Ashley, Gracie, Caitlin, Nicole
From: Morgan
Date: May 6 at 7:08 p.m.
Subject: Re: Vacation, all I ever wanted

Hi ladies,

No one has responded to this yet, so bumping it to the top of your inboxes!

xMorgan

To: Ali, Katie, Jen, Ashley, Gracie, Caitlin, Nicole
From: Morgan
Date: May 8 at 10:00 a.m.
Subject: Re: Vacation, all I ever wanted

Hi ladies!

Just wondering if you're all getting this email about the Rockaways and unplugging and face masks?

LMK!
Morgan

May 11, 8:01 AM

Morgan
Hey are you getting my emails about the Rockaways?

Jen
OMG yes so sorry I will respond now!

May 11, 8:02 AM

Morgan
Hey did you get my email about doing a weekend in rockaway beach this summer?

Katie
hmmmm no!! I don't think so! Can you resend?

May 11, 8:05 AM

Katie
Ugh morgan just texted me about Rockaways I was hoping she'd forget about it lolol ahh I am so mean

Ali
No worries. I will handle.

To: Ali, Katie, Ashley, Morgan, Gracie, Caitlin, Nicole
From: Jen
Date: May 11 at 8:52 a.m.
Subject: Re: Vacation, all I ever wanted

Hey ladies!

Sorry, I've been so busy #wedding #planning, and I've been lost in a sea of food charts and arm toning tricks. You guys have to feel my bicep next time we hang (but tell me if I look too bulky!).

This sounds fun, Morgs, but how would we get to the Rockaways?? What about hurricanes? Is there Zika in Queens? Would hate to be stranded in the middle of a #Sandy-like storm :(Maybe we should do something a little safer, like Paris?

Bisous, Jen

"It sounds like a logistical nightmare, and for that reason I'm out." —What Mark Cuban would say to you on *Shark Tank*, Morgan

---

To: Katie, Jen, Ashley, Morgan, Gracie, Caitlin, Nicole
From: Ali
Date: May 11 at 10:11 a.m.
Subject: Re: Vacation, all I ever wanted

Hey Ladies!

Great news! Since this is the last summer all of us are still single (we are so *Sex and the City* before Charlotte marries Trey!), I think we should all do a summer share house somewhere fun! I googled Rockaway Beach, and it looks super cute, but really difficult to get to, and also it's technically part of New York City, and I think it would be much more fun and relaxing to get out of dodge and go to the country and be somewhere remote so we can truly unwind.

Is everyone in for doing a share house this summer in the Hamptons!?!?!?! #CrushingItIn The631ThisSummer!!!! Daytime parties, aka darties. Lounging by the pool. Hanging with Gwyneth and Jessica (that's *Seinfeld*, Morgs!). Meeting dateable guys. I'm so excited!!!!

I vote for Amagansett, but I'd be willing to do Montauk for more of a bohemian/Surf Lodge vibe. If everyone's in, I'll lock down a place!!! Since Jen's wedding will be so pricey (happy to spend the $!!!!), I vote for sharing rooms! LMK by EOD!!!!

xo, Ali

"The summer in the Hamptons has rejuvenated our bodies and souls. This was the greatest summer of our lives." —all of us, next fall!!!! ;)

To: Ali, Katie, Jen, Ashley, Gracie, Caitlin, Nicole
From: Morgan
Date: May 11 at 11:22 a.m.
Subject: Re: Vacation, all I ever wanted

Hey Ladies!

Oh thanks, Ali! That sounds fun! But was anyone down for Rockaways and sage bundles if

I did a Zipcar? I have a $100 credit on my account and wouldn't mind using it to transport us all down to the beach and back. As much as I love the Surf Lodge, prices tend to be kind of nuts. I mean, I could def afford it but I am just thinking of Nicole.

Morgan

To: Ali, Katie, Jen, Ashley, Morgan, Gracie, Caitlin
From: Nicole
Date: May 11 at 11:40 a.m.
Subject: Re: Vacation, all I ever wanted

HI LADIES,

GOOD NEWS. NICOLE THE RUNWAY HAS ITS FIRST OFFICIAL INVESTMENT!!! MY UNCLE JOSEPH GAVE ME $850 IN SEED MONEY SO I AM DEFINITELY DOWN TO GO TO MONTAUK THIS SUMMER. FIRST ROUND'S ON ME! I AM SO EXCITED. I CAN'T ACTUALLY FIGURE OUT HOW TO TURN OFF THE CAPS ON THIS PHONE BUT IF I COULD, I WOULDN'T, BECAUSE THAT'S HOW EXCITED I AM! IF I HAVE ONE MORE INVESTOR BEFORE THE TIME WE HAVE TO BOOK I WOULD ALSO BE DOWN TO UBER FROM THE UES TO MONTAUK INSTEAD OF TAKING THE JITNEY. LET ME KNOW!!!

NICOLE

CEO OF NICOLE THE RUNWAY

May 11, 5:15 PM

Caitlin

 Honestly I am happy for Nic but she doesn't know the first thing about biz. Do you think it's rude to tell her she needs to NOT spend her investment dollars on Montauk???

Ashley

I am not sure but I just had to drive out three miles from the Choate campus to get service so PLEASE FaceTime me like, now, and give me an update? I am missing EVERYTHING!

To: Katie, Jen, Ashley, Morgan, Gracie, Caitlin, Nicole
From: Ali
Date: May 12 at 9:09 a.m.
Subject: Re: Vacation, all I ever wanted

Great news, Nicole!!! Congrats!!!! <3 Really quick, was just crunching numbers and you still owe me for Gal-entine's Day and also some various other times I spotted you money, which actually comes out to around $900. It's kismet!!! You can just Venmo me.

Also -- really quick: EVERYONE still owes me for Gal-entine's Day. If you Venmo me today, I'd be happy to put down the deposit for our place in Montauk (with everyone paying me back no later than Monday). YAY!!!

Love! Ali

"I love the Hamptons!" —All celebrities

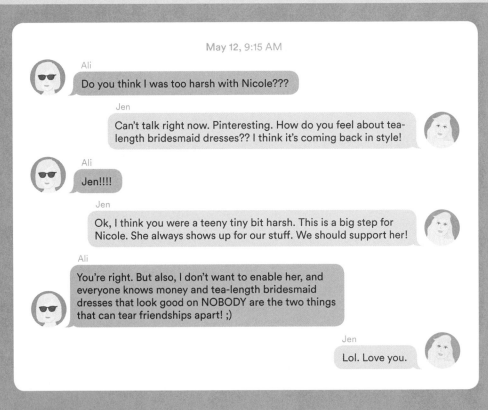

May 12, 9:15 AM

Ali
Do you think I was too harsh with Nicole???

Jen
Can't talk right now. Pinteresting. How do you feel about tea-length bridesmaid dresses?? I think it's coming back in style!

Ali
Jen!!!!

Jen
Ok, I think you were a teeny tiny bit harsh. This is a big step for Nicole. She always shows up for our stuff. We should support her!

Ali
You're right. But also, I don't want to enable her, and everyone knows money and tea-length bridesmaid dresses that look good on NOBODY are the two things that can tear friendships apart! ;)

Jen
Lol. Love you.

May 12, 9:50 AM

Ali

Huge congrats, Nicole!!!! Can't wait to see all the amazing things Nicole The Runway does! Pretty soon I'm going to be borrowing money from you!!!!

Nicole

Lol. Just Venmo'd you $20. Will send the rest after series A! YAY!!!

To: Ali, Jen, Ashley, Morgan, Gracie, Caitlin, Nicole
From: Katie
Date: May 12 at 10:34 a.m.
Subject: Re: Vacation, all I ever wanted

Hi gals,

I'm down for a Montauk trip, but I'm gonna try to pitch it as a story to Styles first. Thinking for heds (that's journo-speak) something along the lines of:

For New Yorkers, a New Way to Cool Down

Or

Andy Cohen Was Right, the Hamptons Are for Your Mom's Friends (something he said on Bravo once that really stuck with me)

I doubt anyone has written about this yet, so I think I could get $$$$ for my unique perspective. Would all of you be willing to be photographed and interviewed on the record for this? Just watched *Spotlight* and feeling super inspired.

Morgan, do you know anyone actually going to Rockaways? Would love to do a one-on-one to show contrast of locale.

Ali, I figure if I give you a big role in this story it's like free press, and then I won't owe you for V-Day. Lmk!

Xo, Katie

"Journalism is the greatest job. I loved it." —Nora Ephron

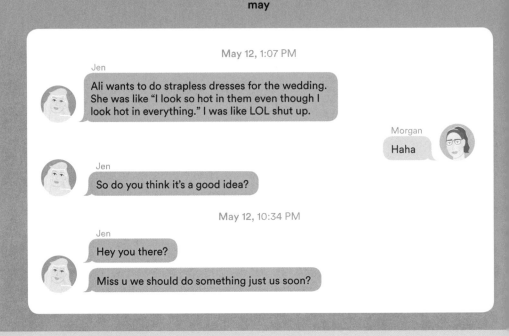

Jen

Ali wants to do strapless dresses for the wedding. She was like "I look so hot in them even though I look hot in everything." I was like LOL shut up.

Morgan

Haha

Jen

So do you think it's a good idea?

May 12, 10:34 PM

Jen

Hey you there?

Miss u we should do something just us soon?

To: Ali, Katie, Jen, Ashley, Morgan, Gracie, Caitlin
From: Nicole
Date: May 13 at 3:00 p.m.
Subject: Re: Vacation, all I ever wanted

Hey girlies,

After careful consideration I think Nicole The Runway should not attend any summer weekend getaways.

BECAUSE I WILL BE TOO BUSY APPLYING TO HOST MY FIRST EVER ENTREPRENURE (SP?) CONVENTION!!

The plan is amazing! Nicole The Runway-Fest will host 100 of the world's newest and most innovative businesses. It's $200 for the business to apply (cha-ching for me!) and if accepted, $1000 to set up a booth at Javits (RIP Hillary 2016 :(still so sad honestly). But I am ready to #MakeJavitsGreatAgain by infusing it with new talent and the future of business! Plus, folding tables only cost $50 for a one-day rental and everyone has to BYO everything for their own booth, so I end up MAKING $950 on each table! Again, cha-ching!! Why don't more people do this??

XO, NICEOLE

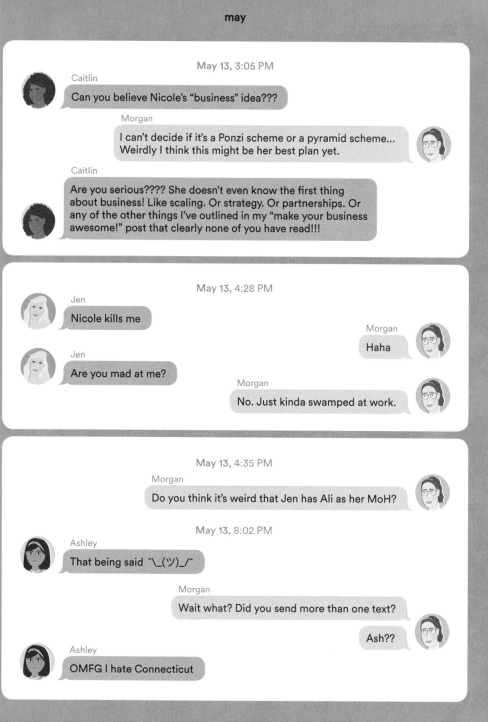

May 13, 3:05 PM

Caitlin
Can you believe Nicole's "business" idea???

Morgan
I can't decide if it's a Ponzi scheme or a pyramid scheme...
Weirdly I think this might be her best plan yet.

Caitlin
Are you serious???? She doesn't even know the first thing
about business! Like scaling. Or strategy. Or partnerships. Or
any of the other things I've outlined in my "make your business
awesome!" post that clearly none of you have read!!!

May 13, 4:28 PM

Jen
Nicole kills me

Morgan
Haha

Jen
Are you mad at me?

Morgan
No. Just kinda swamped at work.

May 13, 4:35 PM

Morgan
Do you think it's weird that Jen has Ali as her MoH?

May 13, 8:02 PM

Ashley
That being said ¯_(ツ)_/¯

Morgan
Wait what? Did you send more than one text?

Ash??

Ashley
OMFG I hate Connecticut

To: Katie, Jen, Ashley, Morgan, Gracie, Caitlin, Nicole
From: Ali
Date: May 13 at 8:45 p.m.
Subject: Re: Vacation, all I ever wanted

Hey Ladies,

I think that's a great idea, Nicole!!! I would love to invest in it! Let's take $50 off what you owe me, and I will get 25% net proceeds of Nicole The Runway-Fest. I've been looking to get into a secondary source of income for a while -- you never know how life will turn out, and if I become a stay-at-home mom or end up divorced with an ironclad prenup, it would be great to have some extra money coming in that I don't need to work for! I feel like I'm rising from the ashes of my seasonal depression, and am excited for facing the future and treating my life as a business, and investing in Ali.

First goal: Summer share in Montauk! This will be so much fun, and since it's a huge undertaking, I think it's best if we (I) divide and conquer. I say we go out one weekend a month. We'll prob meet guys with houses around Memorial Day and will mostly stay at their places anyway!

Nicole: I strongly urge you to reconsider. Do you know where all your potential investors will be this summer? In the city? Nope. In Montauk, or Southampton (if they're old!). As John Lennon said, "If I'd lived in Roman times, I'd have lived in Rome. Where else? Today America is the Roman Empire and New York is Rome itself." You have to go where the action is, and this summer that is the Hamptons, but the fashionable part. Also, if you don't come we're left with an odd number of people, and that really doesn't work for the share houses I'm looking at! Just focus on getting the $ together. Can you ask your dad??

Katie: I think the article is a great idea! I know you hate when I say article, but is something really considered a "piece" if it's just a blog? Love you. Just being honest. If we have a party, could you put it on your corporate card and write it off as a business expense? Is Topher going to be out there? What about Kent? I so don't care either way, just curious.

Morgan: Montauk has a very bohemian by way of Goop vibe, and I would love it if you could bring that certain down-to-earth artsy Brooklyn vibe to our group. Can you make us flower crowns and cut-offs?? Should we all send our jeans to you? Lemme know!

Jen: I know you are crazy busy with the wedding planning, and all the fittings and registering for KitchenAid mixers and whatnot, but I really think this could be your last chance for a fun summer of girly freedom before you know, you're summering with Brad's family and dealing with his mom's moods (/alcoholism)! Come onnnnnn. You know you want to!!! What happens in Montauk stays in Montauk! WHICH REMINDS ME, everyone make sure they're up to date on the HPV vaccine!!!!

Caitlin: Since you're super into the tech/Instagram/lifestyle scene, can you please get us on the lists for all the best parties?? If this summer ends and one of us hasn't blown either or both of the Winklevoss twins, YOU HAVE FAILED US ;)

Ashley: Please buy some hot non-teacher clothes! You can still wear your pearls!!

Gracie: Are you coming? If you can't make it, no prob!!

SO EXCITED!!!!!!

xo,
Ali

"But oh—those summer nights!" —*Grease*

 SURF LODGE Fun spot to meet guys named Tyler or Trevor!

 DITCH PLAINS BEACH Surfing classes which teach you how to "be in the moment!"

 SLOPPY TUNA Authentic beach bar for a more authentic Long Island experience! Caveat: A lot of young Billy Joel types :-/

 SOUTHAMPTON Old-people Hamptons!

 OUR HOUSE Pro: Right on the beach!!! Con: A Wall Street trader allegedly killed his wife in the master bedroom :(

 THE ENDZ SALON Hair salon to get beachy Gisele waves!

 LIGHTHOUSE Historical Instagram spot!

WAY DOWN THERE!

MONTAUK

To: Gracie
From: Morgan
Date: May 14 at 8:00 a.m.
Subject: hey :)

Hey Gracie,

So...well, let me first say that I am sorry I haven't reached out earlier to hang out, just the two of us. My life has been super busy lately -- no excuse, I know -- but it would be great to just chill with you over a drink or coffee or something. I also started going to a great yoga place in Bushwick. It's just a juice bar but they have a really big supply closet where they host Bikram. It's $6 a class, plus the membership to the juice bar ($115 a month). Let me know if you ever want to join. It's worth it bc all of the juice is organic and free trade.

BUT...

My main reason for emailing (and you might have guessed this already if you've been keeping up with the crazy chains for the last few months) is that I have sort of an issue with Ali and Jen right now and I don't know how to handle without making it All About Me.

So......you know how Jen asked Ali to be her MoH? I was pretty shocked. I know Jen and I are very different people but we GREW UP together. I've known her since first grade. And we're still friends! Great friends! And I was surprised not to be asked. I almost kind of... expected it? So my feelings are like, half mad, half hurt, half embarrassed that I was under the impression that I'd be MoH no question, and then we get the email from Jen's mom (who I know, like, well!!!!) and it's as if I am a stranger to her. Ali has already taken over in so many respects and as much as I appreciate her type A personality (esp. bc I am very type B), it's just not FUN. So much of it's all about spending money and taking Instagrams and making sure everyone knows we're having a great time that it's actually just no longer about Jen at all. It's about Ali asserting herself as the leader of the pack, which I think we can all agree she has already done, over and over again, for a really, really long time.

Anyway it's made me kind of distance myself from Jen. Ever since March, she keeps texting me complaining about Ali over-planning certain wedding events (which, honestly? what the fuck?), and I don't have it in me to be like, you know what, this is what you wanted. So stop complaining. It's like she doesn't realize how much she hurt my feelings. Maybe she doesn't. IDK. She's obsessed with this wedding.

If you have any advice for me, I'd love to hear it. You've always been a great friend and are really good at facing problems head-on...which is something I'm working on.

I don't really plan on saying anything to Ali or Jen right away, but I would love to hear what you think I should say. LMK.

Morgs

From: Katie
BCC: Everyone Katie has ever met
Date: May 14 at 8:30 a.m.
Subject: Help for a story!!!!!!!

Can everyone send me a good quote about why it's fun to go away for the summer? It's for a story I am writing.

Thanks!
Katie

To: Morgan
From: Gracie
Date: May 14 at 3:00 p.m.
Subject: Re: hey :)

Hey Morgs,

I'm so sorry you're going through this right now. I tend to just skim most of the long emails that go around (haha -- this should come as no surprise!) but I have to be honest, I was really surprised Jen didn't choose you to be maid of honor. Just to see it from her perspective for a second, I could see her choosing Ali because she knows Ali is obsessed with details and loves all of this stuff, and maybe she didn't want to bog you down with all the boring parts? I know if I personally had to send out a million emails about things like what time we should start pre-partying for a bachelorette party months from now, I would kill myself. So maybe she wanted to spare you that?

That said, my therapist always talks about the importance of directness and Speaking Your Truth. Michelle Obama is a huge hero of mine, and I always think about this interview she did with Oprah (nobody knows this but I secretly LOVE Oprah and I read O every month. It's my guilty pleasure along with $20 yoga classes :/) and she talked about how it's really important to not play games and to just Stand in Your Truth and Find Your Way. So I think you should be direct with Jen. Ask her to get together one-on-one. Tell her your feelings were hurt and where you're at now in your friendship, while allowing her to have her own experience and reasons for doing things. Take in each other's perspectives. All of my close friends and family drive me at least 70% crazy, but in the end it's completely worth it. I think you owe it to your long friendship to be real and honest with her, then let the chips fall where they may. I believe in you. :)

Btw, I gotta say -- as much as I can't stand Hamptons types, a Montauk summer sounds sooo nice right now! I'll do it if you do it. Let me know how it goes!!

Love, Gracie

To: Gracie
From: Morgan
Date: May 14 at 4:55 p.m.
Subject: Re: hey :)

Gracieeeeee,

You should be a therapist! Honestly! Let me know what I can Venmo you for this.

I love your advice, and I would like to think you are right -- maybe she was sparing me? But then why didn't she just ask me first and be like, maybe this isn't for you but like, I love you and we're friends? The thing about getting together with her and being direct is that I read this article a while ago that said women use too many "I feel" statements when they are talking, and I am conflicted because I FEEL like shit, and I want Jen to know that I FEEL like she hates me.

Would you mind (bc you are so so so so so so so so so so so so good at this) mocking up a script where I have lines about what to say to Jen and then we imagine what Jen might say back but we avoid things like me saying "I feel"? And then you can come to my place or to my office at your lunch break and practice with me? The L is down but you can Lyft?

That would honestly be so helpful.

Thank you, G <3
Morgs

To: Morgan
From: Gracie
Date: May 14 at 6:07 p.m.
Subject: Re: hey :)

Hey Morgs,

Not sure if I am able to do that (work is busy), but I am sure if you google it there are lots of tips for constructive criticism with friends. When I have a sec I'll google something for you that I am remembering reading about directness. Also, have you ever thought about going to therapy? SoulCycle doesn't count! ;) Gotta run! Chin up, girl.

xo,
Gracie

To: Ali, Katie, Ashley, Morgan, Gracie, Caitlin, Nicole
From: Jen
Date: May 15 at 8:00 a.m.
Subject: OKAY

Hey ladies,

I truly need one last summer with my girls. I am going to make this easy for you.

Montauk Weekend Share House
A weekend in June = $476 pp
A weekend in July = $575 pp
A weekend in August = $702 pp

Thinking we do one weekend per month, starting on June 11-13.
Leaving after work at 4:45p.m. on June 11.
Jitney pickup on 5th and 59th.
Returning by train June 13 at 11:30p.m.

Anyone who wants to UberCopter can. I'm gonna rough it this time around (will likely 'copter out for August).

I know what you're thinking -- it's so much money and you're already paying so much to do wedding stuff and I know and I am so grateful, but let me just say I would do it for you in a heartbeat. And I will, when/if you guys get married!!!

If anyone can't make it, let me know ASAP!!!!

xo, Jen

To: Katie, Jen, Ashley, Morgan, Gracie, Caitlin, Nicole
From: Ali
Date: May 15 at 9:43 a.m.
Subject: Re: OKAY

Way to take charge! Love you, Jen, let's do it!!!!!!

<3 Ali

P.s. Is everyone seeing my Venmo requests from Gal-entine's Day??

"Meet me in Montauk!" —*Eternal Sunshine of the Spotless Mind*, my fav movie with Jim Carrey since *Liar Liar*

june

To: Ali, Katie, Jen, Ashley, Morgan, Gracie, Caitlin, Nicole, Sherri Gold
From: Helene and Bob Carrington
Date: June 1 at 6:17 a.m.
Subject: Here come the Bridesmaids!

Hello Ladies,

I hope you had a wonderful Memorial Day weekend. Jen's father and I got some badly needed R & R in the Vineyard with our old friends Helen, Ira, Mary, and Ted. I'd love to share some photos -- would any of you girls be able to walk me through uploading some of them from my camera on to my computer?

But now it's time to get back to work! My friend Helen called in some favors and her good friend Helmut, who is apparently the head designer at Oscar de la Renta, said he might be able to create some custom-made dresses!!!! Jen and I will both work closely with him on our dresses, but I was thinking he could take a pass at the bridesmaid dresses as well. This is such an amazing opportunity -- how often does one get a customized *haute couture* dress!!!! I am just so excited! Plus, you'll be able to wear the dresses again -- which reminds me: let me know if any of you ladies would be interested in serving on the Young Patrons Society for the Gala of the Royal Horses. While it's based here in Virginia, the cause is just so important -- I fear that by the time you young women are my age, thoroughbred horses might be a distant memory. :(

But onto happier news! Please send me your measurements immediately. Be honest -- dresses tend to run smaller with European sizes and all. It's much easier to have them taken in than let out! I've been Pinteresting photos into a scrapbook from the society pages since Jen was a baby. I'm thinking that we model the dresses in the vein of Princess Diana's bridesmaid dresses!!! How elegant. You ladies will be responsible for the cost of your own dress -- but I spoke with my doctor, and I'd love to provide you ladies with Botox and fillers the morning of the wedding. You are such a spirited group of young ladies, but with that comes laugh lines and wrinkles! I will schedule all of you for a quick session with my doctor the morning of the wedding, unless I hear otherwise.

Please send me your measurements ASAP as possible.

Warmest regards,
Helene Carrington

P.S. I had my accountant crunch some numbers and hired an infographic designer to illustrate the all-in cost of the dress (see attached). Don't worry, we're getting a great deal.

The Oscar dress is SOOO cheap!

$200
full-body spandex

$300
alterations

$150
dyed shoes

Plus hair + make-up + teeth whitening + spray tans + waxing/lasering 😬

To: Ali, Katie, Jen, Ashley, Morgan, Gracie, Caitlin, Nicole, Helene and Bob Carrington
From: Sherri Gold
Date: June 1 at 7:50 a.m.
Subject: Re: Here come the Bridesmaids!

Hi Helene,

While I would simply adore joining the Young Patrons Society, I believe for me it would be best to focus Nicole's efforts, both personal and professional, into a more streamlined plan.

Would it be possible for you to set up a lunch with Helen, the head designer, Nicole, myself, and any others you may feel would be a good fit for Nicole The Runway investors? This will help us ensure we are prepared to handle the production of Jen's bridesmaid dresses. Thank you so much for asking Nicole to do this. It is a great marketing opportunity for Nicole The Runway, and don't worry -- free of charge for you!

Some background: Oscar has always been a huge inspiration to Nicole, especially after she watched the first *Sex and the City* movie where Carrie tries on one of his dresses for the "you're 40 and that's old" bridal shoot. Amazing and brave. Nicole applauds your efforts to create a grand aesthetic for Jen's wedding and would love to be a part of it.

Here's what Nicole is thinking: Sequins. Halter tops. A throwback to Jen's college years with eleganza. Purple. Scrunched hair. A bold lip. A bold shoe.

Show Helmut my notes and let me know your thoughts. Our team lawyer will draft an NDA for you shortly (just provisional!).

XO,
Sherri Gold
CFO, Nicole The Runway

"Be the leading lady of your own life." —Nicole quoting Kate Winslet, *The Holiday*

Jun 1, 7:55 AM

Caitlin
Nicole got Sherri Gold?!?!?!?!?! I'm DEAD.

Ashley
Who's that??

Caitlin
Are you kidding??! She was one of Goop's original advisors. Everyone in the lifestyle business tells the story about how Gwyneth was originally planning on calling it POOP, and then Sherri was like, actually instead of starting it with the P for Paltrow, let's start it with the G for Gwyneth, and the rest is history!! She is a genius!!!!! How the fuck did Nicole get her?!!?!

To: Sherri Gold
CC: Ali, Katie, Jen, Ashley, Morgan, Gracie, Nicole, Helene and Bob Carrington
From: Caitlin
Date: June 1 at 3:09 p.m.
Subject: Re: Here come the Bridesmaids!

Hi Sherri and Ladies,

It's so wonderful to finally "meet" you! I've been studying your work for years, and I can't believe I'm emailing with the person who was on the team in the early aught-teens that invented the hashtag! #LifeDreamAccomplished

If you have a moment, I would love to bring by my deck on CaitlinYourLife™ -- it's part lifestyle, part wellness, part gratitude, part metaphysical, part miracle coaching. As everyone on here can attest, the CaitlinYourLife™ system not only works, but it changes your soul.

My next few weeks are pretty busy, but I can squeeze in a meeting with you anytime.

All the best,
Caitlin

Founder & CEO, CaitlinYourLife™

"I was stuck in a rut! Then I did CaitlinYourLife, and realized I was allergic to negative thoughts and gluten, and now I'm truly living my best life! Thanks, Caitlin!" —Charlotte Zork

"CaitlinYourLife has changed mine! I can't wait to recommend this to everyone I know! It's the best investment I ever made!" —Miranda Jobs

---

To: Ali, Katie, Jen, Ashley, Morgan, Gracie, Caitlin, Nicole, Helene and Bob Carrington
From: Sherri Gold
Date: June 1 at 10:45 p.m.
Subject: Re: Here come the Bridesmaids!

Oh sorry, ladies!

I meant for that email to go only to Helene Carrington (even though I addressed it to the ladies as well). So sorry! Not good with "e-communications" clearly! Mercury must be in retrograde!

Thank you!
Sherri Gold

To: Ali, Jen, Ashley, Morgan, Gracie, Caitlin, Nicole, Helene and Bob Carrington, Sherri Gold
From: Katie
Date: June 2 at 10:50 a.m.
Subject: Re: Here come the Bridesmaids!

Hey ladies,

Happy to do whatever on the bridesmaid dresses, just LMK. Also, does anyone know if all of Europe truly does not have WiFi? Isn't that so weird? Topher told me this before he left on his 6-week business conference to Paris and London. I can't believe they have no internet there -- or phones!!!!

God bless the USA, honestly.
Katie

To: Katie, Jen, Ashley, Morgan, Gracie, Caitlin, Nicole, Helene and Bob Carrington, Sherri Gold
From: Ali
Date: June 2 at 12:19 p.m.
Subject: Re: Here come the Bridesmaids!

Hi Ladies,

Thanks so much for this email -- the Oscar de la Renta idea is so cute, and I can't wait to see your Mother of the Bride creation! Have you thought about wearing a Mother of the Bride skirt suit? I think you would look gorgeous in it! Not everyone can pull off a boxy look, but you have that sporty, androgynous figure that I am so jealous of!

As for our dresses, I've been keeping it under wraps, but I've actually selected several possible bridesmaid-dress looks. My plan was to surprise Jen with it and let her choose, but the cat's out of the bag now! They are all beautiful and tasteful, while still being very current and not like, you know, something your mother would pick out for you.

I'll be wearing a different dress since I'm the Maid of Honor. I wish I got to wear the dresses you girls will wear though! All these options are so cute!! Honestly? I'm jealous! I love the Royal Wedding idea, Helene! My dress will actually be designed by the same person who designed Pippa Middleton's dress. Don't envy me though, I've been doing squats (and kegels -- hello, Jen's cousin Harrison!!) since Jen told me I'd be the MoH.

Photos of the dresses are attached. Please let me know by end of day.

xo,
Ali

Say yes to the bridesmaid's dress!

To: Ali, Katie, Jen, Ashley, Morgan, Caitlin, Nicole, Helene and Bob Carrington, Sherri Gold
From: Gracie
Date: June 2 at 4:20 p.m.
Subject: Re: Here come the Bridesmaids!

Hey Ladies,

Just catching up on this thread...and wasn't sure if I was added here by accident. I'm not a bridesmaid, am I?

Gracie

To: Ali, Katie, Ashley, Morgan, Gracie, Caitlin, Nicole, Helene and Bob Carrington, Sherri Gold
From: Jen
Date: June 2 at 4:22 p.m.
Subject: Re: Here come the Bridesmaids!

Of course you are!!!! I musta been so frazzled with #WeddingPlanning that I forgot to send you a "Will U B My Bridesmaid" singing telegram at work! Sorry about that!!! I'll make it up to you with a different singing telegram at work, I promise! This is gonna be so fun! So excited!!

<3
The soon to be Mrs.!!!!

To: Ali, Jen, Ashley, Morgan, Gracie, Caitlin, Nicole, Helene and Bob Carrington, Sherri Gold
From: Katie
Date: June 3 at 2:43 a.m.
Subject: Re: Here come the Bridesmaids!

Hey ladies,

Europe DOES have Wifi...do you think Topher got confused? Does anyone know how to spell "hotel" in Euro? I am having a stressful time!!

Okay, let me run you through a play-by-play. Mrs. Carrington, if you have any advice feel free to chime in. I know dating looks different since you were our age, but so many tenets of finding and keeping a man are the same, so while I may not totally take all of your advice, I'd really like you to take the time to give me some :) Thank you!!!

1. Topher and I meet at Diner because he found my cell phone.
2. We order eggs EXACTLY THE SAME WAY (scrambled) and talk about what we do for work as we eat.
3. We TAKE A WALK (to the subway), because we are really enjoying each other.
4. He tells me he has to MEET HIS FAM for a New Year's Day walk in the park, and we depart, but we exchange numbers.
5. I don't text him for 3 days and load him into my phone as NO DO NOT TEXT HIM, YOU CLINGY PSYCHO.
6. It works.
7. He texts me on day 4 and asks if I want to meet up at a bar in Gramercy.
8. I do.
9. We have sex after we go to the bar.
10. We start hanging out 3 days a week, including one weekend night/sleepover.
11. He says I AM PRETTY a lot.
12. He introduces me to his second cousin when we see him on the 6 train.
13. I MAKE SURE to not ask where this is going or how he is feeling as all books say acting like you are a human with emotional needs is a real NO-NO.
14. All of a sudden it's March, and you all remember Saint Patrick's Day.
15. He is SUPER BUSY so I make sure he knows I am 100000% available on his schedule.
16. But then when we make a plan I cancel last minute, so he knows if he doesn't hold tight to me I WILL LEAVE.
17. 2 weeks go by and we don't hang out AT ALL.
18. I also do not call or text!!!!
19. He texts me to come over late at night in April.
20. We fall back into our routine bc we're just like that, you know?
21. I'm finally like, so where is this going, etc. And also I say I love you.
22. And he seems SHOCKED.
23. Like...it's been 4 months, dude. It's normal!!!!!!!!!!
24. And then he says he loves me too but he said it really softly. It sounded like something else but I could just tell.

And now he's been "on business" for weeks...without wifi????????????????

And I googled it and Europe does have the internet. It's not a third-world continent. I'm not an idiot.

I am really mad and sad and all I want to do is write him a huge email detailing everything I feel and just send it to him and be like I AM DONE WITH THIS. WHAT DO I DO??

Also I am down for anything bridesmaid-dress related. LMK!

Katie

"Sometimes you just gotta take out the trash." —My roommate to me last night (I think she meant it literally, but honestly it changed my life)

To: Katie, Jen, Ashley, Morgan, Gracie, Caitlin, Nicole, Helene and Bob Carrington, Sherri Gold
From: Ali
Date: June 3 at 11:01 a.m.
Subject: Re: Here come the Bridesmaids!

Hey Ladies,

I'm so sorry you're going through this, Katie :(Honestly? I always thought Topher was totally cute and fun, but thought you were the real prize in the relationship. As my favorite yoga booty ballet barre teacher always says, "This terrible thing will be the best thing that ever happened to you! Take all of your feelings and heartbreak and put it into this squat!"

You're awesome. You have a big-time career in journalism a la Diane Sawyer or like a younger, cooler, more internety Katie Couric, who has my fantasy work/life/New York scene /Hamptons scene balance down. And what does Topher have? A sick apartment. Probably a trust fund. Looks good in a pair of Bonobos. Dimples for days. That's it. Honestly, I'm not even sure how you were with him for so long. I don't even know how you slept with him. I always secretly thought having sex with him must be like having sex with a pair of corduroy pants.

But!!! He must realize what he's lost! Here are some ideas!

1) Instagram offensive -- we need to take tons of pics in Montauk this weekend with a BUNCH of hot guys in ambiguous positions with you and post them.

2) I'm just gonna say what we're all thinking: what if you hooked up with Topher's boss? I just did a quick search and he looks cute! (You don't mind a dad bod and a Paul Giamatti face, do you?)

3) Text him "Let's just say you are soooo much bigger than my ex. P.S. You have to stop sending me flowers at work!! Fine, I'll go to Necker Island with you this weekend!" Then a minute later text him: "Sorry. Wrong person."

4) Go on a revenge diet a la Khloe Kardashian. You are GORGEOUS as you are, but nothing helps one's self-esteem like losing 10 lbs. Then when you get back with him, you'll prob put on 5 lbs, but on the plus side, your boobs will get bigger, so win-win!

5) We could all show up to that benefit thing he's on the board of. Something involving microloans or lacrosse? Helene, would you wanna buy a table for us? Tax write off!!!

6) Go absolutely NO CONTACT (a la *Ice Queens Melt Hearts*), except for texts.

7) Write a long letter getting all of your feelings out, then put it in the ocean, but near his fam's house in Nantucket, so he might find it one day!

8) Spend time with your friends!!! I'm totally there for you. Do you wanna get a blowout later? Or SoulCycle? Or go out to the Meatpacking District and meet guys who look like Topher and who you can work out your feelings on?? I'm down for whatever!

9) Being single at this time in your life is the absolute best! 90% of marriages end in divorce or resentment or something like that -- so it's better to be free and find the perfect person for you and not just settle!!!

BTW, I found the perfect MoH dress, are you getting my calls, Jen??

xo,
Ali

"Revenge is a dish best served locally sourced." —Me

To: Sherri Gold
CC: Ali, Katie, Jen, Ashley, Morgan, Gracie, Nicole, Helene and Bob Carrington
From: Caitlin
Date: June 3 at 3:32 p.m.
Subject: Re: Here come the Bridesmaids!

Hey ladies & Sherri :)

Katie, I'm so sorry you're going through this! But! Nothing in the Universe Is a Mistake (TM pending). I highly recommend you explore the CaitlinYourLife™ approach to retransformation during this critical time.

CaitlinYourLife Guide to Breakups and Breakthroughs!

1) My e-book *Nothing in the Universe Is a Mistake* (20 pages) is available for $19.99

2) One-on-one coaching sessions available via text, 24/7 availability (24 days over 7 months, during business hours) -- a $5,000 value, discounted at 5%

3) Reclaiming the Caitlin-Goddess Within™ -- All of the above, plus I would give you your own personalized mantra, eating plan, and Instagram photography session -- a $15,000 value, available for just two payments of $7,400 if you sign up by end of day!

We will get through this together!!!

For bridesmaid dresses, I would be happy to barter one personal coaching session in exchange for the cost of the Oscar bridesmaid dress.

Sherri & Nicole, did you get my prospectus??

xo,
Caitlin

CEO of CaitlinYourLife™
"The Universe is my bitch." —Caitlin, CEO of CaitlinYourLife™

To: Ali, Jen, Ashley, Morgan, Gracie, Caitlin, Nicole, Helene and Bob Carrington, Sherri Gold
From: Katie
Date: June 3 at 4:15 p.m.
Subject: Re: Here come the Bridesmaids!

CAN YOU ALL PLEASE GOOGLE "MADISON HARRISON"???? SHE JUST LIKED FOUR OF HIS INSTAGRAMS AND 19 OF HIS FACEBOOK PICS, AND I CAN'T BREATHE!!!!!!!!

Katie

To: Katie, Jen, Ashley, Morgan, Gracie, Caitlin, Nicole, Helene and Bob Carrington, Sherri Gold
From: Ali
Date: June 3 at 4:19 p.m.
Subject: Re: Here come the Bridesmaids!

OMG!!!! Ok, she has a private Instagram, so the most logical thing to do here would be to create a burner Instagram account of a really hot guy and catfish her into accepting the request, right? I'm gonna make a profile, buy thousands of fake followers to make it look legitimate, then request her. Fingers crossed!!!

xo,
Ali

"I ain't sorry." —Beyoncé

To: Ali, Katie, Jen, Ashley, Morgan, Gracie, Caitlin, Nicole, Sherri Gold
From: Helene and Bob Carrington
Date: June 3 at 5:02 p.m.
Subject: Re: Here come the Bridesmaids!

Dear girls,

Can you please remove me from this thread? It's clogging up my electronic-mail.

Warmest wishes,
Helene

Jun 3, 6:30 PM

Gracie

Hey Jen, hope you're doing well! I wanna thank you so much for including me as a bridesmaid, but I was just looking over my budget and with saving up for grad school, I'm not sure I can afford the Oscar dress. I'd still love to help out in any way for your big day (guestbook attendant? Lol). Hope this is ok :) I wanted to bring it up before Montauk this weekend and let you know ASAP.

Jen

Ok. Wow. Um. No prob. See you this weekend!

To: Ali, Katie, Jen, Ashley, Morgan, Gracie, Nicole, Helene and Bob Carrington, Sherri Gold
From: Caitlin
Date: June 5 at 7:02 a.m.
Subject: Re: Here come the Bridesmaids!

Hey girls,

Did a deep dive on Madison Harrison. Was able to use my cousin's LexisNexis account to research. Here's what we know, Katie:

- Graduated Vanderbilt 2011 with a BA in comm
- Skis every winter in the Berkshires
- Was an intern at Bloomberg after college and now works there full-time on their PR team
- Blonde hair is not fake (TBTs show it's natural)
- Oldest of 3, only girl, two younger brothers are named Jacob and Max
- Summers in Nantucket -- seems to have family there
- Salary is $97,000 + bonus
- 5'7" and 131 lbs
- Blue eyes
- Former lacrosse superstar
- Volunteers at senior citizen home

Katie, which pics did she like?????

Caitlin

Madison Harrison
vivre. rire. amour. 😊💙   **948** posts   **1.7k** followers   **629** following

💙 537 likes   Good morning!!

💙 542 likes   "I have always preferred the reflection of the life to life itself." - François Truffaut

To: Ali, Katie, Jen, Ashley, Morgan, Gracie, Caitlin, Nicole, Sherri Gold
From: Helene and Bob Carrington
Date: June 5 at 8:04 a.m.
Subject: Re: Here come the Bridesmaids!

Hello Ladies,

Can everyone please send me their measurements by this afternoon? Note: Oscar goes off European sizes, so I highly recommend you round up. Again, it's much easier to have something taken in than let out. Alterations will be necessary of course -- the house of Oscar requires that you work with one of his designated ateliers in New York. This is so exciting!

I checked with Bob about purchasing a table for the tennis-elbow charity -- and while it's a cause close to my heart, or rather, elbow (haha!), we are maxed out for our charitable write-offs this year. If any of you are looking to attend a gala, Bob and I will be attending the Black and White Ball this fall in DC. Our friends Camilla and Edward Blackandwhite (his ancestors actually invented the cookie) host it every year, and it is such fun! Our table is booked up, but I believe they have tickets available and 5% of it is a tax write off!

Gotta run! Send me those measurements! If I don't receive them by end of day, I'll just eyeball your Facebook photos and round up!

Warmest,
Helene

CEO of the Carrington Family

P.S. Nicole, just to clarify, you're not involved in this process at all. Thanks for your interest!

To: Ali, Jen, Ashley, Morgan, Gracie, Caitlin, Nicole, Sherri Gold, Helene and Bob Carrington
From: Katie
Date: June 5 at 8:19 a.m.
Subject: Re: Here come the Bridesmaids!

Ughhhh, fuck Madison Harrison!!!!!!!! She just liked 2 more of his pics. Where does she live? Is she in NYC? If not, should we Zipcar and do a drive by?

Mrs. Carrington, I am a 6 but please round down to a 2. I don't eat when I'm heartbroken.

Katie

To: Ali, Katie, Jen, Ashley, Morgan, Gracie, Caitlin, Sherri Gold, Helene and Bob Carrington
From: Nicole
Date: June 7 at 1:15 p.m.
Subject: Re: Here come the Bridesmaids!

Hey ladies,

Do you think I could just copy the Oscar pattern for Nicole The Runway? I am trying to pour all that I have into my business and it would be a fun project for me to try to recreate the gown.

LMK, Nicole

CEO, Nicole The Runway

To: Ali, Katie, Jen, Ashley, Morgan, Gracie, Caitlin, Nicole, Sherri Gold
From: Helene and Bob Carrington
Date: June 7 at 9:02 p.m.
Subject: Re: Here come the Bridesmaids!

Hi Nicole + others,

I don't think that's appropriate. Plagiarism of fashion is a real underground issue right now, and I don't want to add fuel to that fire.

Best,
Mrs. Carrington

To: Ali, Jen, Ashley, Morgan, Gracie, Caitlin, Nicole, Sherri Gold, Helene and Bob Carrington
From: Katie
Date: June 8 at 11:04 a.m.
Subject: Re: Here come the Bridesmaids!

Hi all,

Topher just posted an Instagram, and Madison was the first like.

I am going for a 45-minute emergency SoulCycle because I really need to clear my head, get in a positive place, align my body with my mind, and focus on making this bitch's life a fucking nightmare.

Katie

To: Ali, Sherri Gold, Nicole, Katie, Gracie, Ashley, Morgan, Jen, Caitlin
From: Helene and Bob Carrington
Date: June 8 at 11:36 a.m.
Subject: Re: Here come the Bridesmaids!

Hi Ladies,

Please just excuse me from these emails, and I will send you another one when it's time to talk dresses again.

Best,
Mrs. Carrington

CEO of the Carrington Family

To: Katie, Jen, Ashley, Morgan, Gracie, Caitlin, Nicole, Sherri Gold, Helene and Bob Carrington
From: Ali
Date: June 8 at 2:46 p.m.
Subject: Re: Here come the Bridesmaids!

Hey Ladies,

Okay, I just did a deep dive on Madison Harrison.

Facts:

- You are WAY prettier than her. I went deep on her Facebook and found a bunch of pics she had removed from her timeline that she was still tagged in. (Evil laugh!) I'm not trying to be petty, but her eyes are really small for her head. Seriously. I'm surprised she can even see out of them. Her face is kinda manly too. Her jawline is very intense. As you know, I'm a girl's girl and would never hate on another woman out of pettiness, but I am just telling the truth here.

- She loves corgis. Wow, that's *original*. No one in the entire history of the world has ever claimed to love corgis before. Gross.

- She volunteers with this charity helping blind people. Okay, well, that's actually kinda nice, but you don't have to Instagram it all the time. So showy.

- She was in Paris last month. She took a photo with a macaron and captioned it "délicieux! #LeMarais." So...it looks like Topher met her during his business trip to Paris. This is so season 2 of *Sex and the City* I can't even take it. He is the worst! While you were here pining away over him and totally depressed and staying completely loyal to him by doing Everything But, he was hanging out with some basic girl that eats macarons, which is just so 2008. Everyone knows the It Food in Paris right now is the FoieGrasEsCarSant (foie gras infused croissant stuffed with escargot).

- She lives in the West Village -- should we hang out outside her apartment and see if Topher shows up? Should one of us wait outside Topher's apartment to confront him?

- Should we do that thing Jared Kushner's dad did where he set up a prostitute to have sex with his brother-in-law then had photos taken of it? We could see if we can TaskRabbit a hot dude to hit on Madison then take photos and send it to Topher from a burner phone. We should probably check on the legality of this. I slept with a lawyer last year -- would it be weird if I texted him out of the blue about this??

- We could hire someone in another country to hack into Topher's cloud and read his texts. Again, Morgs, you were thinking about taking the LSAT -- is this legal??

Also, is everyone packed for Montauk this weekend??!!! SO EXCITED!!!!!!!

xo,
Ali

"Keep Calm and Hack the Cloud" —Poster I'm having made

To: Ali, Jen, Ashley, Morgan, Gracie, Caitlin, Nicole, Sherri Gold, Helene and Bob Carrington
From: Katie
Date: June 8 at 3:02 p.m.
Subject: Re: Here come the Bridesmaids!

Hi ladies,

All good ideas here. I think my best bet is a) confronting Topher and letting him know how fucking little I care, and b) finding out Madison's phone number and placing lots of "cash orders" for TaskRabbits to bring Monistat to her office at Bloomberg, as well as c) sitting outside her apartment just to see what she looks like IRL. It's hot out so if anyone wants to join me, I'll spring for soft serve with toppings for anyone willing to play the Clyde to my Bonnie. LMK.

I packed for Montauk already and am Amazon Prime-ing some essentials to hit the rental house on Saturday afternoon. No time to go to Duane Reade -- I am having a crisis!!!!!!

See you gals this weekend! And BTW I am so hooking up with the first dude I see at Sloppy Tuna.

Everything is totally normal and calm!! Bye!!!

Katie

To: Ali, Katie, Jen, Ashley, Morgan, Gracie, Caitlin, Nicole, Sherri Gold
From: Helene and Bob Carrington
Date: June 8 at 3:45 p.m.
Subject: Re: Here come the Bridesmaids!

Hey Ladies!

Is there a way I can "mute" this conversation unless it pertains to dresses? My phone is pinging constantly, and I'm not sure how to get it to stop.

Warmest,
Helene

CEO of the Carrington Family
Sent from an iPhone

To: Ali, Katie, Jen, Ashley, Morgan, Gracie, Caitlin, Sherri Gold, Helene and Bob Carrington
From: Nicole
Date: June 9 at 8:07 p.m.
Subject: Re: Here come the Bridesmaids!

What is everyone planning to bring to Montauk?? I need to pack, and I'm so stressed!!!! It's so ironic since I'm literally the CEO of a top fashion start-up! It's like what they say about the cobbler's children! I think they say they don't have shoes? So sad.

LMK what to pack!!!

Xo,
Nic

CEO of Nicole The Runway

To: Ali, Katie, Jen, Ashley, Morgan, Gracie, Nicole, Sherri Gold, Helene and Bob Carrington
From: Caitlin
Date: June 10 at 1:14 a.m.
Subject: Re: Here come the Bridesmaids!

Hi Ladies,

Below is a packing list I think you will find helpful. And remember, a white t-shirt is your best friend! For the upcoming 36 hours:

- Jean shorts
- White pants
- Totes for the beach
- Bikini (are we swimming?)
- Flowy tops (???)
- Beach towels
- Sheets?
- Does the rental come with pillows?
- Hair ties
- Converse
- Sandals
- Wedges
- Leggings
- Sports bra
- Nikes
- Heels
- No-show socks
- Tank tops
- Dress (3)
- Maxi skirt
- Satchel bag
- Off-the-shoulder tops
- Sunscreen
- Makeup
- Hair products
- Baseball cap
- Small purse
- Tees
- Sweatshirts
- Sweater
- Jacket in case it's cold
- Boots in case it rains
- Flip-flops

Everyone who is doing the Jitney, meet at 59th and Lex at 10:00 a.m. on Friday morning. There is a Starbucks nearby for those who can't survive without their java!

UberCopter-ing gals, see you there!

Make sure everyone is beach-ready by 1:00 p.m.

FRIDAY PLANS:
1:00 p.m.: Beach
2:00 p.m.: Swimming???
2:30 p.m.: Tanning
3:00 p.m.: Lunch at the rental (light bites only)
4:00 p.m.: Power napping
5:00 p.m.: Shower schedule begins (alphabetical order)
7:00 p.m.: Reservation at Surf Lodge
10:00 p.m.: SLOPPY TUNA!!
1:00 a.m.: Uber it home

Read my blog if you need more packing tips. I like to roll my jeans to save space!!

Caitlin

CEO of CaitlinYourLife™

To: Ali, Katie, Jen, Ashley, Morgan, Gracie, Caitlin, Sherri Gold, Helene and Bob Carrington
From: Nicole
Date: June 10 at 3:14 p.m.
Subject: Re: Here come the Bridesmaids!

Hey Ladies!

I just thought of some more things we should pack!

* going-out tops
* push-up bras
* tampons
* condoms
* IUDs -- I don't have one, but I'm thinking of getting one for the weekend
* cute sandals

For the schedule, I think I might skip out on the 3:00 p.m. lunch. I need to eat every two hours. Would anyone wanna grab lunch earlier with me around noon? Are there any cute restaurants in Montauk? I could do something farm-to-table. Lemme know! Also, how's everyone getting out to Montauk? Should we all Uber it?

xx,
Nicole

NiCEOle <3

To: Katie, Jen, Ashley, Morgan, Gracie, Caitlin, Nicole, Sherri Gold, Helene and Bob Carrington
From: Ali
Date: June 10 at 7:02 p.m.
Subject: Re: Here come the Bridesmaids!

Hey Ladies!

We're taking the jitney at 10:00 a.m. on Friday! Read above :)

Getting my mani/pedi/waxing right now!

Can someone pick up Starbucks for me for the jitney on Friday?? I'll take a grande iced with cashew milk!

xo,
Ali

"Next stop, Hamptons!" —The Jitney driver on Friday!

To: Ali, Katie, Ashley, Morgan, Gracie, Caitlin, Nicole, Sherri Gold, Helene and Bob Carrington
From: Jen
Date: June 11 at 10:05 a.m.
Subject: Re: Here come the Bridesmaids!

Hey Ladies!

I'm on the jitney, and I'm wearing a bandage dress I took out of storage!! I left my ring at home in the safe to make sure it doesn't get stolen! Hurry!!!! Just told the driver to wait for everyone!!!

~Jen

To: Ali, Katie, Jen, Ashley, Morgan, Caitlin, Nicole, Sherri Gold, Helene and Bob Carrington
From: Gracie
Date: June 14 at 9:02 a.m.
Subject: Re: Here come the Bridesmaids!

Hey Ladies,

I just wanted to say this weekend in Montauk was so much fun. I just uploaded some photos to Facebook. Feel free to tag yourselves :)

A relaxing weekend at the beach was exactly what I needed -- did everyone make it back to the city okay? Jen, Morgan, and I were a bit worried when no one came back to the house on Saturday night. When we left for the city at 2:00 p.m. on Sunday no one had come back yet, but we're assuming everyone had lots of fun and met people! We checked your Instagrams to make sure you were all still alive :)

Can't wait to hit up the beach again next week!! Next time you all should get in the water -- it felt so good!

Dreaming of Montauk,
Gracie

p.s. You don't need to include me in any reservations next time -- I'll prob just bring food again :)

To: Ali, Katie, Ashley, Morgan, Gracie, Caitlin, Nicole, Sherri Gold, Helene and Bob Carrington
From: Jen
Date: July 6 at 11:17 a.m.
Subject: PROBLEM 911 ASAP HELP SOS

LADIES,

MY MOM'S BFF AND HER HUSBAND WERE ARRESTED FOR CONSPIRACY TO COMMIT INSIDER TRADING. THEY ARE CURRENTLY BEING HELD WITHOUT BAIL AT SOME JAIL SOMEWHERE, I DON'T KNOW, IT'S EXTREMELY LIFETIME MOVIE MEETS MADOFF HEADLINES.

BUT THAT'S NOT THE ISSUE, THE ISSUE IS THAT MY MOM'S BFF IS/WAS OUR CONNECTION TO OSCAR AND SINCE THE ARREST, ALL OF THE FASHION DESIGNERS ARE DENOUNCING THEIR RELATIONSHIPS WITH HER TO DISTANCE THEMSELVES FROM THE DRAMA (THIS IS PR 101)!!!

SO NOW WE WILL NOT GET OUR DRESSES AND THE WEDDING IS 25 WEEKS OUT!!!!!!!!!

I HAVE NO IDEA WHAT TO DO! WE NEED BACKUP. DOES ANYONE KNOW ANYONE ANYWHERE THAT CAN GET US HIGH-QUALITY RUNWAY-TYPE DRESSES FOR ROUGHLY THE SAME COST AS WE WERE GETTING THE OSCAR GOWNS FOR?

FUCK! FUCK FUCK FUCK FUCK!!!!!!!!!!!!!!!

I AM GONNA START CALLING YOUR EMERGENCY CONTACTS.

BYE,
JEN

To: Katie, Jen, Ashley, Morgan, Gracie, Caitlin, Nicole, Sherri Gold, Helene and Bob Carrington
From: Ali
Date: July 6 at 11:25 a.m.
Subject: Re: PROBLEM 911 ASAP HELP SOS

Hey Ladies!

Omg, Jen, this is so exciting and terrible!!! I'm not sure how to ask this delicately, but was Helene involved at all? If so, should we distance ourselves from your mom right now?? Do you guys remember Evan? Or Devin? I gave him (Kevin??) an over-the-pants HJ in the bathroom of Surf Lodge last month, and I think he mentioned he's a lawyer -- should I get in touch with him for legal advice?? I'll track down his work email.

For dresses, should I just go to Barney's and try to eyeball some dresses and get what I think would look good on everyone?? Off-the-rack is our last option, but at least we can have fallback dresses then. Don't freak out, Jen!!!! Can everyone PLEASE source some dresses and send me options??!

This counts as a family emergency right?? I'm gonna leave work -- I can't even focus right now!!! Can everyone meet me at Saks??

I'm so sorry your mom might go to jail :(

xo, Ali

"In the midst of chaos, there is also opportunity." —Sun Tzu, *The Art of War*

To: Ali, Katie, Jen, Ashley, Morgan, Gracie, Caitlin, Nicole, Sherri Gold
From: Helene and Bob Carrington
Date: July 6 at 11:45 a.m.
Subject: Re: PROBLEM 911 ASAP HELP SOS

Hey Ladies,

For the extremely successful, white-collar crime is simply a part of the cost of doing business. One comfort in my life is knowing that I raised Jennifer to become a woman who doesn't take pleasure in the misfortune of others. As our friend George from Kennebunkport always says, "When you point your finger at someone, there's still other fingers on your hand that are pointing back at yourself." Wise words, indeed. I'll be in touch shortly regarding alternative dress options.

Helene

"Everything in life is elusive." —Gloria Vanderbilt

To: Ali, Katie, Ashley, Morgan, Gracie, Caitlin, Nicole, Sherri Gold, Helene and Bob Carrington
From: Jen
Date: July 6 at 11:52 a.m.
Subject: Re: PROBLEM 911 ASAP HELP SOS

Ladies!!

Seriously?! It's not my mom going to jail, it's her BFF (and more importantly, her connection to the guy at Oscar de la Renta).

I don't know what to do. I can meet at Saks in 20. Will you be there? Can everyone meet? Everyone has personal days saved up, right??

Jen

To: Ali, Katie, Jen, Ashley, Gracie, Caitlin, Nicole, Sherri Gold, Helene and Bob Carrington
From: Morgan
Date: July 6 at 11:55 a.m.
Subject: Re: PROBLEM 911 ASAP HELP SOS

Hey Ladies,

This is so terrible!! Helene must be so upset! I don't know how to really put this but...will we be getting our money back for the Oscar dresses? This is so embarrassing, but I really don't have an extra $1,100 on me now, between the share house and the wedding expenses and my new juice bar membership -- I go so often, it's so worth it though! I've amortized it so each cold-pressed juice is only like $9.

I'm just going to put it out there: I really need to get my money back for the Oscar dress before I can buy a new dress. If I can't for some reason, then um, I guess I can just sit out being a bridesmaid.

Sorry to do this. Just trying to be truthful here.

Love,
Morgs

To: Morgan
From: Gracie
Date: July 6 at 11:59 a.m.
Subject: Re: PROBLEM 911 ASAP HELP SOS

Morgan,

Good email!!!

Gracie

To: Ali, Katie, Ashley, Morgan, Gracie, Caitlin, Nicole, Sherri Gold, Helene and Bob Carrington
From: Jen
Date: July 6 at 12:09 p.m.
Subject: Re: PROBLEM 911 ASAP HELP SOS

Ladies, I totally get this is an inconvenience of the highest proportions and it fucking sucks. I am trying so hard to keep it together but it feels like a bad omen. I mean, COME ON...this only happens in movies!

I am in Saks, please meet me!!! We can figure this all out later, money-wise.

Jen

To: Ali, Katie, Jen, Ashley, Morgan, Gracie, Caitlin, Sherri Gold, Helene and Bob Carrington
From: Nicole
Date: July 6 at 12:22 p.m.
Subject: Re: PROBLEM 911 ASAP HELP SOS

Hi gals,

I'm at Saks right now. I can't find the up escalator to the ball gown department but I am sure I will find it soon. Paused in perfumes to write this. I would hate it if Morgan had to drop out.

You are right, Jen, this really does only happen in movies. Luckily, in movies, there's always something or someone that saves the day.

Drum roll pleeeeeease.

Nicole The Runway is happy to step in and save us all from spending too much on the replacement gowns. Sherri Gold, as you remember from the emails, is helping to set me up with a small seamstress company here in the city to make custom clothing and accessories in addition to renting out my quality closet of vintage Forever 21. I used the investment I got from my uncle to pay for the services and also threw in 15% of my company if we can keep manufacturing rentable wears. Sherri says this is "blue sky" (???) for now, but she also encouraged me to reach out to my network to offer this once-in-a-lifetime opportunity to my best friends.

I would really love nothing more than to book my first gig as a designer and clothesier (that's French and I just made it up) for you, Jen. With Jen's blessing and her mother's, please visit my showroom on 37th and 7th to get measured and fitted. I am sending along some sketches of designs I think could work, but keep in mind they're just artist renderings.

I found the escalator! Be up soon!

Nicole

CEO, Nicole The Runway
"We make all of your dreams come true."

To: Ali, Katie, Jen, Ashley, Morgan, Gracie, Caitlin, Sherri Gold, Helene and Bob Carrington
From: Nicole
Date: July 6 at 12:26 p.m.
Subject: Re: PROBLEM 911 ASAP HELP SOS

Wait, I am in Bloomingdale's. Hold on.

Nicole

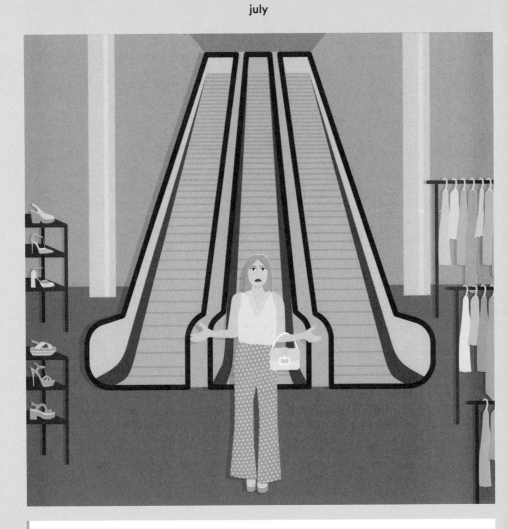

To: Ali, Katie, Jen, Ashley, Gracie, Caitlin, Nicole, Sherri Gold, Helene and Bob Carrington
From: Morgan
Date: July 6 at 12:52 p.m.
Subject: Re: PROBLEM 911 ASAP HELP SOS

I'm in a Lyft Line carpool thing, and they keep picking up more people!!! We keep going deeper into Brooklyn. I'm not exactly sure where we are right now, but I think I see the ocean!!! :(How long are you guys going to be there for??

Morgs

To: Ali, Katie, Ashley, Morgan, Gracie, Caitlin, Nicole, Sherri Gold, Helene and Bob Carrington
From: Jen
Date: July 6 at 1:47 p.m.
Subject: Re: PROBLEM 911 ASAP HELP SOS

Hi Ladies!

Okay, none of you are here, so I'm taking matters into my own hands! I've tried on a bunch of bridesmaid dresses at Saks, and I HATE EVERYTHING!!!! Why is this happening to me??!!!!! I am a good person -- I don't understand this!!!!!

I am SO stressed out. I have been keeping this on the DL -- but every once in a while, at some point every day I search online for every guy I've ever so much as gone to second base with and look up everything about him, and secretly fantasize about meeting him somewhere and having sex with him. Like the really dirty kind. Where there's no face touching. Or having to hang out with each other's mothers. Or having to pretend to care about his job or feelings. And sometimes I look at Brad while he sleeps, and while I love him SO much it hurts, I just stare at his face and can't believe that I'm going to have to spend the rest of my life with this person. And what if I'm settling?? I have so many dreams, and maybe he's holding me back! I think about taking a year off and getting to travel to places like St. Bart's or the Seychelles and really finding myself. And sometimes I dream about Brad dying in a tragic way but something quick and painless, like his plane goes down on his way to Las Vegas for his bachelor party, and then I get all Jackie Kennedy and wear the black veil and I'm this super strong widow that has to start over. And it's so sad and I spend my life devoted to Brad's memory and start a foundation in his name. Then to escape the pain I go to Tuscany for a year, like *Under the Tuscan Sun*-style, or maybe Jamaica and have a fling with a Taye Diggs lookalike or maybe I *Eat Pray Love* it but without the India part. And then I reinvent myself as a career woman, and I invent an app maybe or I move back to the city and become a relationship columnist for the *New York Star* or maybe I work with orphans in Kansas or somewhere like that. And then I meet someone who I'm super attracted to and he's more fun and smarter than Brad, and when I watch the new guy sleep I think about how grateful I am that Brad was in my life and that he loved me enough to tragically die so that I could go on and live this way better life that I was meant to live.

Do you think these feelings are normal?? Are you guys close by?? I'm in the ladies room at Saks outside the dress department. I'm sitting on the floor of stall 4. See you soon.

xo,
Jen

To: Ali, Katie, Jen, Ashley, Gracie, Caitlin, Nicole, Sherri Gold, Helene and Bob Carrington
From: Morgan
Date: July 6 at 1:52 p.m.
Subject: Re: PROBLEM 911 ASAP HELP SOS

HELP IS ON THE WAY, DEAR!!! I just got off the FDR at 61st and I am cruising through the park. I'll be there so soon. Nicole, did you find her?

Morgan

To: Ali, Katie, Jen, Ashley, Morgan, Gracie, Caitlin, Sherri Gold, Helene and Bob Carrington
From: Nicole
Date: July 6 at 3:09 p.m.
Subject: Re: PROBLEM 911 ASAP HELP SOS

You guys,

I made it out of Bloomingdale's and into Saks and found our girl huddled by some faux fur capes from Zac Posen's winter line. She is OKAY (thank g-d for waterproof mascara) but a little shaken up. She keeps repeating the words "one dick forever?" and sobbing into a Ralph Lauren tennis skirt left behind by another shopper (we had to purchase this, as it was ruined by her bronzer).

Morgan got here a little while later and we managed to get to Cafe SFA on the 8th floor for some beef sliders. Mrs. Carrington, we charged this to your house account, which I hope you don't mind. Morgan and I have been talking her off a ledge for about an hour, and once she ate she seemed to have higher spirits, plus we saw Andy Cohen and a Housewife. Plus, Brad texted just to say I love you, so now she's back to her usual self of telling us how much better our lives would be if we could just find love. ALL IS WELL.

We also all decided that yes, it would be best for Nicole The Runway to take over the bridesmaids' dresses. More details on that soon. Mrs. Carrington, perhaps we should do a call with you and me and Sherri Gold, from the emails?

Can everyone do 37th and 7th in an hour?

Best and regards,
Nicole the CEO, and the FIXER

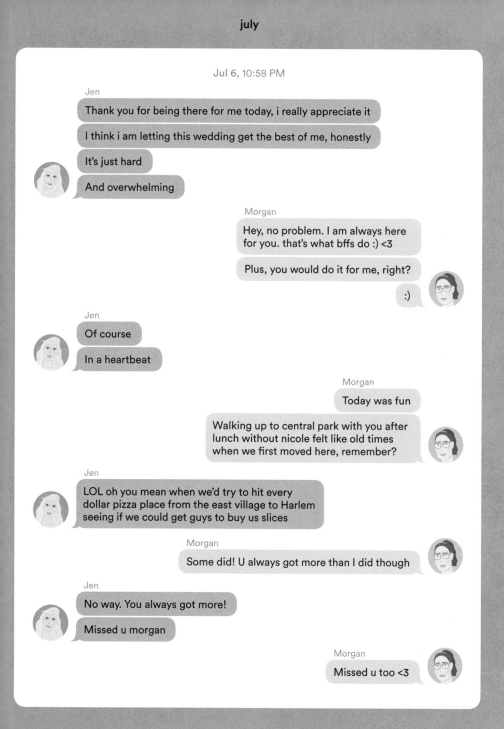

Jul 6, 10:58 PM

Jen

Thank you for being there for me today, i really appreciate it

I think i am letting this wedding get the best of me, honestly

It's just hard

And overwhelming

Morgan

Hey, no problem. I am always here for you. that's what bffs do :) <3

Plus, you would do it for me, right?

:)

Jen

Of course

In a heartbeat

Morgan

Today was fun

Walking up to central park with you after lunch without nicole felt like old times when we first moved here, remember?

Jen

LOL oh you mean when we'd try to hit every dollar pizza place from the east village to Harlem seeing if we could get guys to buy us slices

Morgan

Some did! U always got more than I did though

Jen

No way. You always got more!

Missed u morgan

Morgan

Missed u too <3

To: Katie, Jen, Ashley, Morgan, Gracie, Caitlin, Nicole, Sherri Gold, Helene and Bob Carrington
From: Ali
Date: July 6 at 11:30 p.m.
Subject: Re: PROBLEM 911 ASAP HELP SOS

Hey Ladies!

Thanks so much, Nicole, for taking the lead on this. I was in a meeting and had basically no cell reception. It was crazy. I had nothing to do but just think thoughts and listen. That must have been what it was like to be a #WorkingWoman in the nineties. Except back then there weren't cell phones, so when you'd go out, you'd give guys your office number to call you at. God, can you imagine how exciting that must have been?? You're stuck at work, typing on a typewriter or something, and at any point you could get a phone call -- and it's either your boss or some dude you met and since there was no caller ID, you had to answer the phone in your sexy voice all the time! I'm glad that we've made strides in women's rights, but things must have been so much more exciting in the nineties.

I regress! Anyhoo, I love the idea of us supporting Nicole The Runway soooo much, but since this is your first major event, I think we should go with an actual dress designer that has things like "experience." I will find everyone's bridesmaid dress and a separate maid of honor dress for myself -- it should stand out a bit more, that's just tradition. I am still working with Pippa Middleton's designer on some drawings for my dress, but for the bridesmaid dresses, I think we should get some from David's Bridal!! They have some really cute options! I found this long skirt-suit dress -- it's technically in the mother of the bride section, but I think you girls have the gravitas to pull it off! Nicole -- maybe we could Nicole The Runway it for the farewell brunch the next day! What do we think?? I'm happy to go by David's Bridal and take some photos.

Let me know! I'm ready to pull the trigger!

xo, Ali

"If you pay attention, all will be revealed." —Fortune Cookie I opened (but didn't eat)

To: Ali, Katie, Ashley, Morgan, Gracie, Caitlin, Nicole, Sherri Gold, Helene and Bob Carrington
From: Jen
Date: July 7 at 9:07 p.m.
Subject: Re: PROBLEM 911 ASAP HELP SOS

Hi ladies,

Ali, I appreciate this so much but I am pretty sure my mom is already really into the Nicole The Runway idea. I don't hate it either, honestly! When Morgan, Nicole, and I went to SFA we talked a lot about how cute we might look in NTR wear. I am sort of married (hahahahahahaha) to the idea now.

Jen

To: Ali, Katie, Jen, Ashley, Morgan, Gracie, Caitlin, Nicole, Sherri Gold
From: Helene and Bob Carrington
Date: July 8 at 2:02 p.m.
Subject: Re: PROBLEM 911 ASAP HELP SOS

Hello Ladies,

I've decided: Nicole The Runway will provide the bridesmaid dresses. Sherri and I just had a wonderful conference call -- I think you girls will be thrilled with the final product! :)

FYI: If you would like to be reimbursed for the "Oscar" dresses, Bob says to contact your family's attorney about getting in touch for damages. Oscar has rebranded and will now be known as Oscar!, but due to legal ramifications they aren't able to be affiliated with any previous "Oscar" commitments. As we said at Swiss boarding school, *tant pis*.

Ali -- Sherri and I discussed it, and I've decided you will be wearing the Nicole The Runway bridesmaid dress as well to adhere to a uniform look. I've ordered one in your size.

I am signing off this thread for now and turning off my cell phone and all e-communications while I spend a badly needed two weeks at a spa/body transformation retreat in Sedona.

Warmest,
Helene

CEO of the Carrington family

To: Katie, Jen, Ashley, Morgan, Gracie, Caitlin, Nicole, Sherri Gold, Helene and Bob Carrington
From: Ali
Date: July 8 at 2:14 p.m.
Subject: Re: PROBLEM 911 ASAP HELP SOS

Okay we can just come back to this and discuss at a later time!!! Enjoy Sedona, Helene.

xo,
Ali

To: Ali, Jen, Ashley, Morgan, Gracie, Caitlin, Nicole, Sherri Gold, Helene and Bob Carrington
From: Katie
Date: July 17 at 2:14 p.m.
Subject: Re: PROBLEM 911 ASAP HELP SOS

Hi ladies,

Unfortunately I am going to have to bail on this weekend's Montauk excursion. I am still feeling the effects of last weekend's house-rager with those volunteer firemen. Who knew tequila was no longer my friend? Okay, yes, I knew. But I trusted that bitch anyway.

So I am out this weekend. Gonna lay low, watch some *SVU*, hard boil some eggs, do a face mask, etc.

Oh btw did I mention Topher has been texting me nonstop? He's literally obsessed. I knew playing hard to get was going to work.

xo, have fun, Katie

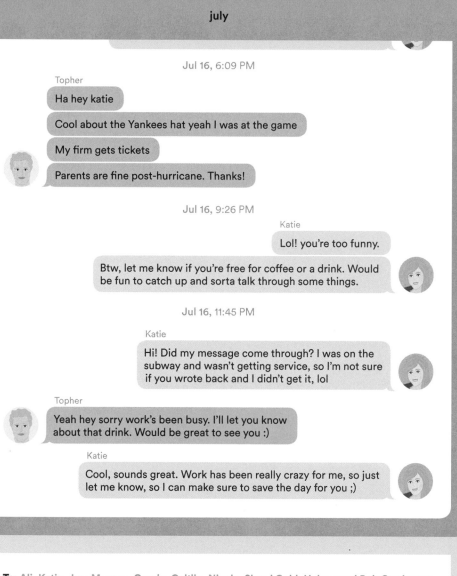

Jul 16, 6:09 PM

Topher

Ha hey katie

Cool about the Yankees hat yeah I was at the game

My firm gets tickets

Parents are fine post-hurricane. Thanks!

Jul 16, 9:26 PM

Katie

Lol! you're too funny.

Btw, let me know if you're free for coffee or a drink. Would be fun to catch up and sorta talk through some things.

Jul 16, 11:45 PM

Katie

Hi! Did my message come through? I was on the subway and wasn't getting service, so I'm not sure if you wrote back and I didn't get it, lol

Topher

Yeah hey sorry work's been busy. I'll let you know about that drink. Would be great to see you :)

Katie

Cool, sounds great. Work has been really crazy for me, so just let me know, so I can make sure to save the day for you ;)

To: Ali, Katie, Jen, Morgan, Gracie, Caitlin, Nicole, Sherri Gold, Helene and Bob Carrington
From: Ashley
Date: July 17 at 3:15 p.m.
Subject: Re: PROBLEM 911 ASAP HELP SOS

OMG show us the texts?? Dying to see. I knew he'd come back to you :)

Ash

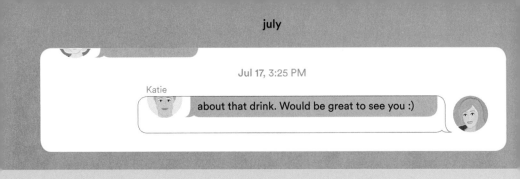

Jul 17, 3:25 PM

Katie

about that drink. Would be great to see you :)

To: Ali, Katie, Ashley, Morgan, Gracie, Caitlin, Nicole, Sherri Gold, Helene and Bob Carrington
From: Jen
Date: July 17 at 4:08 p.m.
Subject: Re: PROBLEM 911 ASAP HELP SOS

haha, just got your text. that is AMAZING. get him, girl! will miss you this weekend.
Jen

To: Ali, Katie, Ashley, Morgan, Gracie, Caitlin, Nicole, Sherri Gold, Helene and Bob Carrington
From: Jen
Date: July 22 at 10:13 a.m.
Subject: Re: PROBLEM 911 ASAP HELP SOS

Hi ladies!

Such a fun weekend! Some notes moving forward: The security deposit only comes back on this rental if we leave everything in the same condition as it was when we arrived, so WHOEVER threw up on the chaise lounge, please deal with it.

Phew, now that that's out of the way (don't want any drama with my gals), I'll just say the best thing to happen this weekend was ME LEAVING MY ENGAGEMENT RING AT HOME...at first it was freaking me out to not have my rock, but then it was like I was single and the guys at the bar had no idea. I was getting so many free drinks. I think that guy Paul really was into me! Do you guys think I should find him on Twitter and DM him? Just to be friends. He works in food and I love food so it's a good networking opp!

Anyway that's all to report here, nothing weird or bad to say! Looking forward to this weekend. Can't believe it's already the end of July!

HERE COMES THE BRIDE!

xo,
Jen

To: Katie, Jen, Ashley, Morgan, Gracie, Caitlin, Nicole, Sherri Gold, Helene and Bob Carrington
From: Ali
Date: July 22 at 11:05 a.m.
Subject: Re: PROBLEM 911 ASAP HELP SOS

Hey Katie & Ladies,

Hope you're feeling better. :)

So Katie...If someone knew something that could potentially destroy someone else's relationship with someone, should someone tell her friend even though it might hurt her feelings in the short term but actually help in the long term through knowing the truth? What would you do?

PLEASE WRITE ME BACK ASAP.

xo,
Ali

"You have to be honest with your friend. I'd want to know." —RandySixtyNine, Reddit/r/relationships

"People always kill the messenger, dude." —GaryMRA, Reddit/r/relationships

To: Ali, Jen, Ashley, Morgan, Gracie, Caitlin, Nicole, Sherri Gold, Helene and Bob Carrington
From: Katie
Date: July 22 at 6:47 p.m.
Subject: Re: PROBLEM 911 ASAP HELP SOS

Ali, what???

Lol no idea what you're talking about, but I'm OMW to drinks with Topher (wish me luck, I got a glamsquad blowout and makeup and manicure). I'm wearing push-up bra, spanx suit, and an LBD. I am 8 lbs down this week. First drink after juice cleansing. I'm so excited. I have a spray tan. I can't stop shaking.

If you were to see me, you might think, omg it's Karlie Kloss!...but guys, it's me!

...And I am taking back my life.

Katie

To: Katie, Jen, Ashley, Morgan, Gracie, Caitlin, Nicole, Sherri Gold, Helene and Bob Carrington
From: Ali
Date: July 22 at 6:59 p.m.
Subject: Re: PROBLEM 911 ASAP HELP SOS

Katie,

Before you meet Topher tonight, there's something you need to know.

I wish I didn't have this information, and I wish I never walked into Sloppy Tuna on Saturday night -- if we had gone to The Crow's Nest like I wanted, we wouldn't be in this position!!! But that's neither here nor there, CAITLIN...

I scheduled an emergency therapy session, have been reading Reddit and Yahoo Answers non stop since it happened, and have tried to find clarity in SoulCycle...and I realize I would want to know if I were in your position: we saw Topher making out with a girl on Saturday night. It wasn't Madison. It was someone else. He was kissing her and had his hand on her butt, and we all followed him out and they left together. We tried to get an Uber to follow them, but Morgan didn't wanna pay the 3.5 surge pricing (sorry!). I've attached a photo. I'm so sorry to be the one delivering this news.

Do you want us to come over tonight??

Love you lots,
Ali

"If you can't handle me at my worst, then you don't deserve me at my best." —my new Tinder bio

To: Ali, Jen, Ashley, Morgan, Gracie, Caitlin, Nicole, Sherri Gold, Helene and Bob Carrington
From: Katie
Date: July 23 at 9:02 a.m.
Subject: Re: PROBLEM 911 ASAP HELP SOS

Hey Ladies!

Wow, last night was insane! My therapist has encouraged me to explore different forms of writing, so I wrote what I am calling a shay (short play -- so cute!) reenacting what happened with Topher. Does anyone have any contacts at the Sundance Institute or connections to Lin-Manuel Miranda?

THE BALLAD OF TOPHER AND KATIE - A SHAY by Katie

KATIE AND **TOPHER** MEET UP AT **THE BAR. KATIE** HAS JUST READ THIS EMAIL FROM **ALI.** SHE REFUSES TO CRY BECAUSE SHE FINALLY GOT A SMOKY CAT EYE TO WORK AND SHE CANNOT SQUANDER THIS MOMENT.

[ENTER TOPHER]
TOPHER
HEY KATIE, NICE TO SEE YOU AGAIN.

KATIE
OH HI, YEAH! IT'S BEEN SO LONG. I'VE BEEN REALLY BUSY WHICH IS GOOD, I'VE BEEN WRITING A LOT LATELY.

TOPHER
THAT'S GREAT!

KATIE
YEAH IT IS.

TOPHER
SO WHAT DID YOU WANT TO TALK ABOUT? YOU LOOK GREAT BY THE WAY.

KATIE
I DO? OH, I MEAN, THANK YOU. YEAH. I STARTED SEEING A TRAINER AGAIN AND MY ROOMMATE HAS ME DOING THIS VINEGAR CLEANSE, SO YOU'RE PROBABLY NOTICING THE BENEFITS OF THAT.

TOPHER
[SMILES] SO...WHAT'S UP? WHAT DID YOU WANT TO TALK ABOUT?

KATIE
I JUST FEEL LIKE YOU HATE ME!

TOPHER
HATE YOU? KATIE—

KATIE

NO, IT'S TRUE, TOPHER. DON'T INTERRUPT ME. EVERYTHING FELT LIKE IT WAS
GOING REALLY WELL. WE WERE TALKING ALL OF THE TIME, HANGING OUT,
YOU EVEN KNEW WHEN MY PERIOD WAS. THAT'S NOT SOMETHING I SHARE
WITH EVERYONE, TOPHER. THEN ALL OF A SUDDEN IT'S LIKE, OH YOU HAVE TO
WORK SO MUCH, AND OH, EUROPE DOESN'T HAVE WIFI. I GOOGLED IT,
TOPHER. THERE *IS* INTERNET IN EUROPE.

TOPHER

[SILENT, LOOKING AT DRINK, THINKING ABOUT HOW DEEP AND MYSTERIOUS
GIRLS REALLY ARE THE BEST IN BED]

KATIE

I THOUGHT WE HAD SOMETHING SPECIAL, BUT IT TURNS OUT I WAS JUST ASS
TO YOU. I WAS JUST SOME GIRL YOU FUCK AND THEN GO TO WORK AND
BRAG ABOUT TO YOUR FINANCE BUDDIES. YOU ARE A COLD, HEARTLESS,
LIFELESS SOCIOPATH, AND YOU NEVER DESERVED ME.

STAGE LEFT: THE **BARTENDERS** AND **OTHER PATRONS** ARE ALL STARTING
TO STARE IN **KATIE** AND **TOPHER**'S DIRECTION. **KATIE** NOTICES THIS AND STARTS
TO TURN RED IN THE FACE.

KATIE

OH, THAT'S ALL YOU HAVE? SILENCE? COOL, TOPHER. REALLY AWESOME.
YOU KNOW, I THOUGHT YOU WERE DIFFERENT.

PATRON ONE, A HOT GIRL, STARTS TO LAUGH WITH HER FRIEND AT THE BAR.
TOPHER STARTS TO FEEL LIKE AN IDIOT. I MEAN, ALL OF THESE PEOPLE ARE GOING
TO THINK HE'S A FUCKING ASSHOLE! HE'S SEEN THIS IN MOVIES BEFORE.

TOPHER

YOU HAVE ME ALL WRONG, KATIE. COME ON, CALM DOWN.

KATIE

OH, I HAVE YOU ALL WRONG? EXPLAIN HOW I HAVE YOU ALL WRONG?
I AM PRETTY SURE YOU AREN'T THAT COMPLICATED, NO OFFENSE.

TOPHER

LOOK. THIS IS HARD FOR ME TO SAY. I DO LIKE YOU. I'M JUST...UM. UM...I'VE HAD MY...
HEART BROKEN BEFORE SO...IT'S HARD FOR ME TO, UM...BE VULNERABLE.

KATIE

[PERKING UP] WAIT, YOU DO LIKE ME? WHAT DO YOU MEAN?
TELL ME. TALK TO ME. I AM HERE FOR YOU.

TOPHER

I AM SO AFRAID OF GETTING HURT.

THE END

So this is the craziest part about the night w/me and Topher: So I walked into the bar and he was already sitting there and I was all like, "hey" all cool and stuff and he was like, "Wow." LOL he literally was like, "WOW, you look amazing." We can thank my 7-day no-calories cleanse!!!!!! (Thanks, Caitlin!!!!) Of course I was just like, "Thanks."

Then I just went to town on him. I was like, "You know what CHRISTopher? Fuck YOU. Fuck. You. Fuck you for leading me on. Fuck you for letting me let my guard down for you, which I never do by the way!!! And fuck you for letting me believe you were worth believing in."

He couldn't say anything he was honestly silent, and it was like he was obsessed with not making eye contact with me. I think I scared him!! I almost felt bad but I held it together. I barely said a word after that. I was just like, "You lost this."

You know how when you throw down the gauntlet with a dude you don't expect things to actually like go the way you want them to? Well. That did not happen this time. He basically told me he was too afraid of getting hurt and that he has always been in love with me and that he thinks I'm the one, but I have to put up with him learning how to really love. So I told him I'd think about it (lol) but of course on the INSIDE I was like, "I do!!" And imagining our wedding. We're going to be so happy together.

Oh and when I asked him about the girl in the pic, he just said it was his cousin visiting. Which makes total sense!

Xoxo,
Katie

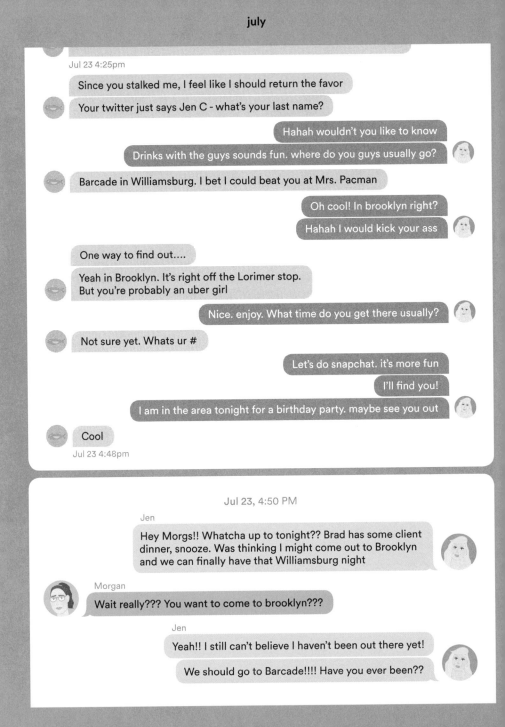

Jul 23 4:25pm

Since you stalked me, I feel like I should return the favor

Your twitter just says Jen C - what's your last name?

Hahah wouldn't you like to know

Drinks with the guys sounds fun. where do you guys usually go?

Barcade in Williamsburg. I bet I could beat you at Mrs. Pacman

Oh cool! In brooklyn right?

Hahah I would kick your ass

One way to find out….

Yeah in Brooklyn. It's right off the Lorimer stop.
But you're probably an uber girl

Nice. enjoy. What time do you get there usually?

Not sure yet. Whats ur #

Let's do snapchat. it's more fun

I'll find you!

I am in the area tonight for a birthday party. maybe see you out

Cool

Jul 23 4:48pm

Jul 23, 4:50 PM

Jen

Hey Morgs!! Whatcha up to tonight?? Brad has some client
dinner, snooze. Was thinking I might come out to Brooklyn
and we can finally have that Williamsburg night

Morgan

Wait really??? You want to come to brooklyn???

Jen

Yeah!! I still can't believe I haven't been out there yet!

We should go to Barcade!!!! Have you ever been??

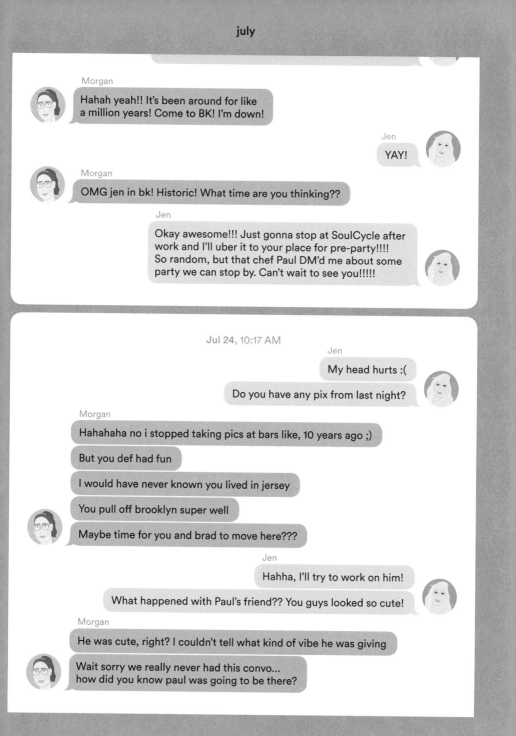

Jen

So cute!! You should def go out with him! Do people in williamsburg go on dates? Or just hangs?

Ohh! He randomly found me on twitter and dm'd me about that party in Williamsburg, and i was DYING to see your place, so thought two birds one stone. Cause we're talking about potentially collaborating with his food business and my PR business. So I can prob write the whole night off!

Morgan

Oh fun! So it was like, for work?

Jen

Totes. Brad's getting up so I'm gonna ask him to make me a smoothie. Talk later!

To: Ali, Katie, Jen, Ashley, Morgan, Gracie, Caitlin, Sherri Gold, Helene and Bob Carrington
From: Nicole
Date: July 24 at 12:54 p.m.
Subject: Re: PROBLEM 911 ASAP HELP SOS

Hi ladies + Mrs. Carrington + Sherri Gold,

Working on the dresses now. I still need fits from Ali and Gracie. They look stunning.

Mrs. C, I totally took your advice with the notching up of the color palette and you are so right -- blush pink IS the new black. Your taste is impeccable. Thanks for taking me out to dinner last week to discuss. Your design tips are really helping NTR take these gowns to the next level. We are so grateful!

Ali, please let me know your availability. Can also do a deskside fitting and send my intern.

God the summer is really flying by!!

XO,
Nicole

CEO of Nicole The Runway!!!!

august

To: Katie, Jen, Ashley, Morgan, Gracie, Caitlin, Nicole
From: Ali
Date: August 1 at 9:00 a.m.
Subject: Keep Calm and Get Your Bachelorette On!

Hey Ladies!

I'm SO excited for Jen's bachelorette weekend!!!!! We're gonna get so lit, lol!!!!

This summer has gone by so fast! We need to plan this ASAP.

Logistics: Let's do this over Labor Day weekend!!! We can Airbnb out the Montauk place!

Options!!
- Las Vegas -- kinda cliché, but Katy Perry did her bachelorette there
- Paris
- Southern Portugal -- Goop did a guide to SoPu, so that would basically be our itinerary
- Seychelles -- Jen mentioned during her Brad-dying fantasy she's always wanted to go, so this might be fun

Activities!!
- Classes: Pole dancing, how to give blow jobs, and Thai cooking class
- Dancing: Let's get bottle service so we don't have to worry about getting in!
- Spa day: Spa treatments so we can relax and de-stress from the long flight. Let's look into packages for two-hour massages, mani/pedis, facials, and seaweed wraps
- Outfits: I'm going to get us matching going-out tops that say "From Miss to Mrs." (Jen) "Bride Squad" (the bridesmaids) and "Backup Bride" (me)
- Dinners: Let's go out for fancy dinners every night! There's a concierge service I saw on Gilt that for a fee can get you into the most exclusive restaurants around the world. I think it's worth the investment!

Let me know where everyone wants to go! I think SoPu would be the most fun! If I don't hear from everyone in the next hour, I'm gonna start making some executive decisions, lol!

Btw, I just friended Justin from Sloppy Tuna on Facebook! Should I message him or wait??

So excited!!

xo,
Ali

"The only time you should text a man first is never." —*Ice Queens Melt Hearts*
"Don't offer to pay until you have a joint checking account." —*Ice Queens Melt Hearts*
"Never accept a Monday-night date." —*Ice Queens Melt Hearts*

To: Ali, Katie, Jen, Ashley, Morgan, Caitlin, Nicole
From: Gracie
Date: August 2 at 6:18 a.m.
Subject: Re: Keep Calm and Get Your Bachelorette On!

Hey Ladies!

I thought we did the Montauk share house *for* Jen's bachelorette? It's really pricey. If you want to have an official night out for Jen's bachelorette, then let's just do it in Montauk, and I'll rally and go to whatever Sloppy Surf Lodge Talkhouse type place you girls want!

Love,
Gracie

To: Ali, Katie, Jen, Ashley, Gracie, Caitlin, Nicole
From: Morgan
Date: August 2 at 10:59 a.m.
Subject: Re: Keep Calm and Get Your Bachelorette On!

Hi ladies,

Going to echo Gracie here -- was the Montauk summer not the bachelorette?

Best,
Morg

To: Ali, Katie, Jen, Ashley, Morgan, Gracie, Caitlin
From: Nicole
Date: August 2 at 1:02 p.m.
Subject: Re: Keep Calm and Get Your Bachelorette On!

Hey ladiesssss,

With the success of Nicole The Runway I am excited to announce I can totally afford SoPu or the Seychelles! It feels amazing to be able to say yes to the plans! That being said, let's go wild. Paris? Russia? Are we allowed to go to Russia? You know, as like, Americans. TBD.

I am so excited to celebrate Jen's last fling that I'll even spring for the bottle service myself. I think I can write it off in my taxes. I am now an LLC. It's all thanks to Sherri Gold. You guys, she is unreal.

Morgan and Gracie, I am happy to help finance your trips :)

xo, Nicole

CEO of Nicole The Runway
"Dream On" —The bedazzled words on my sleeping mask

To: Ali, Jen, Ashley, Morgan, Gracie, Caitlin, Nicole
From: Katie
Date: August 4 at 5:02 p.m.
Subject: Re: Keep Calm and Get Your Bachelorette On!

Hi girls,

I am down for Jen's bach, but I am approaching a busy month, personally. Things with Topher are just so fraught right now; he has so many insecurities about himself and his ability to both accept and give love, and I just feel like I need to stand by my man right now in this pivotal moment for us.

Can we put this off for just 4-6 weeks?

Katie

To: Ali, Katie, Jen, Ashley, Morgan, Gracie, Nicole
From: Caitlin
Date: August 4 at 9:28 p.m.
Subject: Re: Keep Calm and Get Your Bachelorette On!

Hey Ladies!

Labor Day weekend works best for me since I already reserved it! Should we do a combination bachelor/bachelorette party? It might be more fun! We can invite Brad's friends to Montauk! I'll make a pitcher of kombucha-tinis!

Nicole -- did you and Sherri get my cal invite? I'd love to grab 30 mins with the two of you!

Best,
Caitlin

CaitlinYourLife™
Reclaim the Soul Goddess Within Retreat! (Only a few spots left!)

To: Ali, Katie, Jen, Morgan, Gracie, Caitlin, Nicole
From: Ashley
Date: August 5 at 11:00 a.m.
Subject: Re: Keep Calm and Get Your Bachelorette On!

Hi gals,

Labor Day weekend sounds AH-MAZING! Did I tell you Choate is going 100% DRY CAMPUS this year? Something about 14-year-olds having keg parties or something. Anyway, that kind of sucks, no? I will be drinking for 2 at Jen's bach (me and other me, the one who has to be sober through this job).

I can fly out of Bradley or meet you all at JFK or LGA. What does everyone prefer? I say let's do SoPu.

Ashley

To: Katie, Jen, Ashley, Morgan, Gracie, Caitlin, Nicole
From: Ali
Date: August 6 at 4:45 p.m.
Subject: Re: Keep Calm and Get Your Bachelorette On!

Hey ladies,

There are soooooo many people's schedules to accommodate, lol! It looks like August 30th - September 3rd works for everyone!!!!

South Portugal, aka SoPu, is IN. It should be SO cheap when we're there because tapas are tiny.

I've done some organizing: Plane tickets - Expedia.com...and hotels - http://www.hotels.com -- I heard they have some good deals!

YAY THIS IS GONNA BE SO FUNNNNNNN!!!!!!!!

~Ali

ps -- We better brush up on our Spanish!

"This was the greatest trip of our lives!" —us, after SoPu!

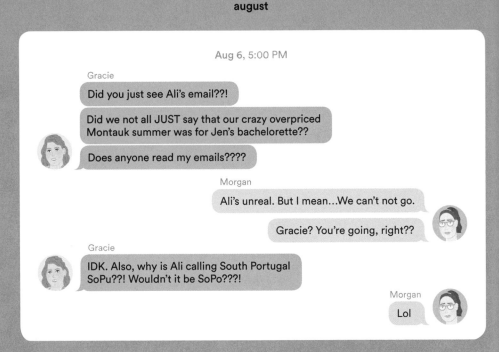

Aug 6, 5:00 PM

Gracie
Did you just see Ali's email??!

Did we not all JUST say that our crazy overpriced Montauk summer was for Jen's bachelorette??

Does anyone read my emails????

Morgan
Ali's unreal. But I mean...We can't not go.

Gracie? You're going, right??

Gracie
IDK. Also, why is Ali calling South Portugal SoPu??! Wouldn't it be SoPo???!

Morgan
Lol

To: Ali, Katie, Jen, Ashley, Morgan, Gracie, Caitlin
From: Nicole
Date: August 7 at 3:09 a.m.
Subject: Re: Keep Calm and Get Your Bachelorette On!

Amazing! Does anyone know how to get to the airport?

xo, Nicole

To: Katie, Jen, Ashley, Morgan, Gracie, Caitlin, Nicole
From: Ali
Date: August 8 at 11:24 p.m.
Subject: Re: Keep Calm and Get Your Bachelorette On!

Hey Ladies!

Change of plans!! Surf Lodge Boy and I have been texting, and I think things are going great! He does something in finance or tech or perhaps fintech (fun! I love hybrids.

They're like the cronuts of jobs). He mentioned he and his ex-gf just broke up in June, so I'm thinking he's prob going through a player phase from mid-June to mid-August, but by late August he will be depressed from that and ready to lock it down by Labor Day. What guy wants to spend his fall alone just watching football instead of apple picking? I think it's really important we spend Labor Day weekend together so we can solidify everything -- SO I think we should go to SoPu the last weekend of August!!! Also, Surf Lodge Boy has a wedding that weekend, and I already know the hashtag for it so we can view it/analyze it from afar during Jen's bach weekend. Fun!

Flights: I found a deal! Can everyone take off a day or two from work? I'm thinking we leave Wednesday and come back the following Tuesday? After travel days, we'll basically just be there for a long weekend, which is enough time to have fun and completely embrace the Portuguese culture! Should we hire a translator? I'm SOOOOOO excited!!!!!

I'll plan a detailed itinerary based on Goop's guide to SoPu. This will totally work for the wedding diet too, because tapas are so cute and tiny and I think we only have to tip like 5% or something!

When is Brad's bachelor party in Vegas again??

THIS WILL BE SO FUN AHHHHHHH!!!!

Love you, ladies!

xo,
Ali

"Only kiss on the first date if you're absolutely sure you're going to marry him."
—Ice Queens Melt Hearts

To: Ali, Katie, Jen, Morgan, Gracie, Caitlin, Nicole
From: Ashley
Date: August 10 at 12:15 a.m.
Subject: Re: Keep Calm and Get Your Bachelorette On!

Hi ladies,

I guess this schedule sounds amazing (!!!!), but I do have to do a quick check with my boss to see if I can get the days off.

I *also* did a quick check on the hotel site and it looks like there's one hotel that comes flush with all of the sheets and bedding we need, but there's also Zika and Ebola to think about, so if everyone wants, we can each pack a separate suitcase with all of that stuff. Don't wanna take chances! It is an extra $75 per suitcase on the flight but I think it will be worth it. Since there are 8 of us, I think we should be safe with 3 hairdryers. Please reply all to let me know who is bringing. I can coordinate from CT!

Love,
Ash

To: Ali, Katie, Jen, Ashley, Gracie, Caitlin, Nicole
From: Morgan
Date: August 10 at 2:28 p.m.
Subject: Re: Keep Calm and Get Your Bachelorette On!

Hey ladies!

Since we all bought those Oscar dresses -- and are hemorrhaging money this summer in Montauk -- I SERIOUSLY hope we get that deposit back (I need to watch a YouTube video on how to get nail polish remover out of a 19th-century farm table)....I was thinking, SoPu sounds really expensive! Is everyone sure they wanna do that? I'm taking a bunch of unpaid days off for the wedding as it is. I don't know. If everyone really wants to do this, I guess I can try to figure out a way to make it work? Maybe we can all stay in one hotel room together, lol?

What does everyone think? I'll be at yoga, but I'll have my phone on me.

Morgs

To: Katie, Jen, Ashley, Morgan, Gracie, Caitlin, Nicole, Helene and Bob Carrington
From: Ali
Date: August 12 at 3:05 p.m.
Subject: Re: Keep Calm and Get Your Bachelorette On!

Hey Ladies + adding Helene,

Helene -- do you or Bob have any friends in South Portugal that have a villa or castle we can stay at for Jen's hen party? Please let me know ASAP!

Also I think they do those weird plugs in Europe, so can someone eBay Portuguese hairdryers, and we can all Venmo you back for it? I just sent everyone a spreadsheet on Slack of presents I think everyone should get for Jen! (Sorry, Jen -- it's a surprise!)

I'm about to buy my plane ticket!!! Everyone's in, right??

xo,
Ali

"Be confident, but don't be yourself." —*Ice Queens Melt Hearts*

To: Ali, Katie, Jen, Ashley, Morgan, Gracie, Caitlin, Nicole
From: Helene and Bob Carrington
Date: August 14 at 12:00 p.m.
Subject: Re: Keep Calm and Get Your Bachelorette On!

Hi Ladies,

I hope that everyone has been having a wonderful summer so far. I tried to look up some of your Montauk photos on Facebook, but Facebook must have been down because it kept denying me access to the albums. I should give my friend Karen Kempner Zuckerberg a call this week about it...

Unfortunately Bob and I only have contacts in the northern Portugal/western Spain area, so I'm afraid that's not much help. I had a fun idea though! My friend Diane was telling me about this show called *The Biggest Loser* where everyone has a contest to work out a lot and get in shape (from what I hear it's not about weight loss, but simply about getting healthy and focusing on your muscle tone -- which your generation seems very into!). Have you ladies heard of it? I thought it might be fun if I got you all a gym membership as a "thank you" from the Carrington family for being such good friends to our Jennifer. Since I don't know New York/Brooklyn that well, I saw that Equinox has locations everywhere. How about I purchase you all memberships that expire at the end of the year? It will expire on December 31st, the day of Jennifer and Bradley's wedding, but I spoke with a membership coordinator, and you would be able to continue your membership at some nominal cost. Perhaps whoever attends the gym the most wins a prize? My Equinox contact told me they can send me weekly updates as to how many people have attended the gym and for how long that week. How fun!

Warmest,
Helene

CEO of the Carrington Family
Daughters of the American Revolution Fall Fling at Monticello: Buy a Table Here (1% tax deductible)

To: Ali, Jen, Ashley, Morgan, Gracie, Caitlin, Nicole, Helene and Bob Carrington
From: Katie
Date: August 14 at 7:19 p.m.
Subject: Re: Keep Calm and Get Your Bachelorette On!

Hi everyone!

While I was at first a little hesitant on SoPu since I don't want to go all exotic on Topher at this crucial turning point in our relationship (seriously, you guys, once I get him over this emotionally devoid hump, it's wedding bells), I am now totally down to go. Can I invite Topher, though?

Here's the thing: He won't stay with us, he'll just stay *near* us. And I'll do day hangs with him and then maybe also sleep over there (so there's more space for all of you in the SoPu-house!), and that way he and I won't go rogue on our routine and there can still be a chance we will make it as a couple. And you guys want this for me right? I have put everything on hold: my career job searching, writing articles for blogs, etc. So please please please be flexible about this :) Ahhh! I just want love, too, you guys! Trying to force Topher into an emotional state has made ME emotional.

Anyway I feel like the free gym memberships are an amazing idea. I also want to work on my (hopefully not needed!) revenge body.

Helene, I am...the biggest loser!

Katie

"Life is fleeting, love out loud." —A GIF I saw on Tumblr

To: Ali, Katie, Jen, Ashley, Morgan, Caitlin, Nicole, Helene and Bob Carrington
From: Gracie
Date: August 14 at 9:00 p.m.
Subject: Re: Keep Calm and Get Your Bachelorette On!

Hi all,

Wow! So many emails :) Mrs. Carrington, such a generous offer, but I already pay a chunk of change for my yoga membership, so I'll just stick with that.

Unfortunately, with regards to SoPu, I am unable to make it work financially. But I hope it is the best best best time for Jen! Let the countdown to the wedding begin!

Gracie

To: Ali, Katie, Jen, Morgan, Gracie, Caitlin, Nicole, Helene and Bob Carrington
From: Ashley
Date: August 15 at 1:23 p.m.
Subject: Re: Keep Calm and Get Your Bachelorette On!

Hi Mrs. C,

As I am in CT I will likely not be able to join a gym in NYC! But there's a great equestrian club here I'd be interested in joining if you were able to pay for that? I'll send you a brochure with pricing options.

Thx,
Ash

To: Ali, Katie, Jen, Ashley, Morgan, Gracie, Nicole, Helene and Bob Carrington
From: Caitlin
Date: August 16 at 10:00 a.m.
Subject: Re: Keep Calm and Get Your Bachelorette On!

Hi ladies,

I just put up a new blog post interviewing the woman who wrote *Want Him? Ignore Him!* and I have to say, Katie, you would really benefit from reading it at this time.

Nuggets I learned:
- Never go out of your way
- Never change your schedule
- Never let him know you care
- Don't ever start the conversation
- Definitely don't let him know you have already told your friends about him
- "Forget" his job and ask him every time you see him what he does, this helps to make him feel insecure and thus more vulnerable around you
- Always have three options for dates so the men can sense your short attention span

Katie, are you following any of these?

I worry!

Also -- just got two ad buys for fall so I am SO in for SO-Pu!

Caitlin

Know someone who would love my blog? Follow me on Twitter, Facebook, or LinkedIn!

To: Katie, Jen, Ashley, Morgan, Gracie, Caitlin, Nicole, Helene and Bob Carrington
From: Ali
Date: August 16 at 3:43 p.m.
Subject: Re: Keep Calm and Get Your Bachelorette On!

Hey Ladies!

1) Topher DEFINITELY can't come. (Helene, avert your eyes here) HOES BEFORE BROS!!!! This is a huge moment for us to show female solidarity and support the sisterhood of our traveling pants! Also, if you bring Toph then Surf Lodge Boy will probably also want to cancel his wedding plans and join us, and that might be too much too soon, you know?

2) The gym memberships sound great, Helene! Sign us up!!! Quick question: can you get me the all-access Equinox membership. I'm in the West Village, but according to my internet stalking, Surf Lodge Boy just bought a condo in TriBeCa, so I imagine I'll be hitting up the gym near his apartment most mornings! You're the best!

3) I just bought my SoPu ticket, ahhh it's really happening!!!!!

4) Just bought Jen's ticket too -- can everyone Venmo me their share ($298.43) for it today? Plus the $$$ you still owe me from the Valentine's fiasco/most exciting day of Jen's life -- if everyone can just Venmo me a quick $500, I'll call it even and you can all just pay for my meals and drinks and spa treatments in SoPu!

5) Should I text Surf Lodge Boy our travel dates to keep him in the loop and let him know I have a full and exciting life with or without him? Should I invite him to the wedding, or is it too soon? I want him to WANT to be my plus one!

xoxoxo,
Ali

"How's your day?" —Surf Lodge Boy to me just now!!!!!!!!!!!!!!

To: Ali, Katie, Ashley, Morgan, Gracie, Caitlin, Nicole, Helene and Bob Carrington
From: Jen
Date: August 16 at 5:03 p.m.
Subject: Re: Keep Calm and Get Your Bachelorette On!

Hey Ladies!

I can't believe we're going to SoPu so soon!!!! I'm so excited!!!! Brad just got on the plane for his bachelor party Vegas weekend. According to him, it will be lots of golf and touring the Hoover Dam...right. :)

Is anyone going out tonight? Williamsburg might be fun!

Also -- do we need to get vaccinated for Portugal??

LMK about tonight!

Jen

To: Ali, Katie, Jen, Ashley, Gracie, Caitlin, Nicole, Helene and Bob Carrington
From: Morgan
Date: August 16 at 5:10 p.m.
Subject: Re: Keep Calm and Get Your Bachelorette On!

Another Williamsburg night??? Jen are you having a crisis??

I am very down, obviously, to host you in my "home borough" if you are interested in coming over the bridge. Last time Jen came out (last month I think?) we went to Barcade. (That was the place I did my 24th birthday. I think most of you were busy that night or some of you got lost on your way over??) It was extremely fun and we ended up meeting up with Paul from Montauk, you know, that chef. For a work thing for Jen. So who knows, ladies, BK might be good for your careers!

If you wanna head down tonight we can go out for a quick dinner and then hit up a bar??

PLEASE COME BC NOW I AM SO EXCITED!!
Morgan

To: Ali, Katie, Jen, Ashley, Morgan, Gracie, Nicole, Helene and Bob Carrington
From: Caitlin
Date: August 16 at 5:40 p.m.
Subject: Re: Keep Calm and Get Your Bachelorette On!

Okay we're all in the Uber for Girls' Brooklyn Night Out! Nicole is driving because she's doing Uber on the side and handing out Nicole The Runway promo cards to people we're picking up in UberPool. Be there in ~30.

Caitlin

Sent from a tiny keyboard on an iPhone X

To: Ali, Katie, Jen, Morgan, Gracie, Caitlin, Nicole, Helene and Bob Carrington
From: Ashley
Date: August 16 at 5:47 p.m.
Subject: Re: Keep Calm and Get Your Bachelorette On!

Hi ladies!

I am so sad I have to miss this. Currently chaperoning a back-to-campus dance at Choate. I swear to god, all of these boys have boners and you can see them in their khakis.

EW! I MISS NEW YORK.
Ash

To: Katie, Jen, Ashley, Morgan, Gracie, Caitlin, Nicole, Helene and Bob Carrington
From: Ali
Date: August 16 at 6:56 p.m.
Subject: Re: Keep Calm and Get Your Bachelorette On!

Hi ladies,

Did you know there's a 129 Franklin Road in a totally different part of Brooklyn? It's different than 129 Franklin Avenue. Whoops! We'll be a bit late, Morgs, sorry. In Manhattan (if you don't know) there's just numbers and avenues. It's like a grid? I'll show you a pic when we meet up tonight.

Jen should be there on time because she Uber'ed from Jersey.

Some notes on what I wanna do in SoPu, while I have the time:
* I want to try "Pu" food
* Maybe do henna tattoos? Is that a thing there?
* Get a really good Insta story
* Is there brunch in Portugal???
* Buy "local souvenirs" for friends back home
* Get incredibly drunk
* Find a local man to show me the sights and maybe sneak back to the USA with me?
* Have a great time with my girls

Seriously, Morgan, where is Brooklyn??? Why is this taking so long?

Ali
[Scene from the *Sex and the City* movie]
CARRIE: "*New York* magazine says Brooklyn is the new Manhattan."
MIRANDA: "Whoever wrote that lives in Brooklyn."

To: Katie, Jen, Ashley, Morgan, Gracie, Caitlin, Nicole, Helene and Bob Carrington
From: Ali
Date: August 16 at 7:06 p.m.
Subject: Re: Keep Calm and Get Your Bachelorette On!

Update: Uber is taking so long, and I think they put on Surge, so we're just gonna call it a night and head back to Manhattan. Love you, Morgs!! Hope you didn't wait for us! Can we PLEASE do brunch sometime soon??

Ali

"Don't waste the pretty!" —*He's Just Not That Into You*
"Release your past and say, 'Today's the day I start with me!'" —Patti Stanger, *Become Your Own Matchmaker*

To: Ali, Katie, Morgan, Ashley, Gracie, Caitlin, Nicole
From: Jen
Date: August 25 at 9:26 a.m.
Subject: Gate 5B

See you guys at the airport! SoPu here we come! I'M SO EXCITED!!

september

To: Ali, Jen, Ashley, Morgan, Gracie, Caitlin, Nicole
From: Katie
Date: September 1 at 4:42 p.m.
Subject: #aboutlastnight

Hey ladies,

I understand that you all probably won't want to read this email with an open mind (or as we say in journalism, objectively). But please hear me out.

I know that Ali was the one to say it, but I realize now none of you were totally fine with me inviting Topher along for the bachelorette party. I didn't realize that I would spend so much time with him while we were there, and I also didn't realize the place he was staying was a two-hour boat ride from the place we were staying. I also didn't realize he would get so drunk on the first night in SoPu and break into our hotel room and throw up all over Nicole. I wanted so badly for this to work that I was blinded to my bad #dicksbeforechicks behavior.

But the thing is, Topher and I are definitely going to end up together. We're meant to be. I feel it. It sounds crazy and I know (now) that he's dating that girl Madison and loves her, but that's temporary. And if you guys can't see that then what kind of friends are YOU? Anyway. Hope you accept my apology.

Katie

To: Katie, Jen, Ashley, Morgan, Gracie, Caitlin, Nicole
From: Ali
Date: September 1 at 5:32 p.m.
Subject: Re: #aboutlastnight

Hey sen-whore-as!!

First off, I just want to say that SoPu was so sick!!! It was not only one of the best weekends of my life, but I feel like it changed all of us a little bit!! I feel like we might have done our part to change SoPu a bit too -- I love how wherever we went, people called us "Meninas Rasas Americanas!!" Did we ever find out what it actually means? Probably something like "super fun and culturally sensitive squad of American girls!" I still can't believe they don't speak Spanish there! I'm surprised more people don't speak it just to interact with tourists... At least we learned "please," "thanks," and "does that have gluten in it?" SO FUN!!!

Just wanted to say, sorry if I drank too much! I feel like my limits might be different over international waters! Jen, I hope Brad totally laughed it off when I stole your phone when you were sleeping and requested dick pics then wrote back "Lol! Is it cold in NJ? Btw, I'm currently fucking a hot Portuguese guy right now whose dick is way bigger and I've never loved you, and I think we should call off the wedding. Lol!!!" He seemed kinda uptight about it, but it might be because it was 2 a.m. his time before his "big meeting" the next day! Btw, how did it go? Tell him I hope it went ok, and sorrryyyyyy again :/

I've noticed everyone's been posting pictures all weekend, and I LOVE your enthusiasm, but I think it would be better if you all uploaded all your photos to my Dropbox, and I'll do a final selection for what we should put online. I'll pick only the ones that make all of us look skinny and hot! Also, Nicole/Morgs/Katie, are you getting my texts?? Can you please take down ANY and ALL photos taken from my left side?? This is seriously ruining my life right now.

Katie -- I believe I said everything I have to say about Topher tagging along when we had that fight when he threw up all over Nicole. And then when he used our bathroom Saturday night for hours and then all of us had to go down and get ready for our big night out at the SoPu McDonald's where we kept having to buy and eat all that questionable non-organic McDonald's food because we were getting yelled at for using all their sinks and outlets --

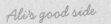
Ali's good side

Ali's bad side

FARO AIRPORT Just a quick 20-hour flight from NYC, including a tight layover in Moscow!

LISBON Starbucks: European coffee! Close to SoPu!

ALBUFEIRA McDonald's -- Excellent bathrooms!

ALGARVE Portuguese Hamptons!

CANIÇO Really fun dancing on the top of a cliff! *Some of us* couldn't get ready in time, but we'll def go here next time we're in SoPu!

SPAIN The birthplace of tapas!!!!

OCEAN The Atlantic! Same ocean as in the Hamptons!

so much so that all of us got a bad case of umm, what's the Portuguese word for diarrhea again?? But at least we all got to end our fun night out early by hitting up a pharmacy where we got to mime our bathroom troubles to the pharmacist who then gave us UTI medicine, which I expect will seriously mess up our pH levels for months to come. But what happens in SoPu stays in SoPu!

Re: Topher -- I'd suggest therapy (SoulCycling and also psychological), a revenge diet, reading the book *Women Who Love Too Much*, and watching the *Sex and the City* ep where Big tells Carrie he's moving to Paris, and then she's like, "You know what? No. I deserve real love!"

Real quick -- since I had to put down my credit card for that tapas dinner we didn't get to go to and also my card was charged for damages to the room -- I thought I told everyone that they use different plugs there and you can't just jam your blow dryer in?? -- can everyone please send me their share of $379 USD. (Plus the $ you all still owe me from the V-Day catastrophe/Jen's engagement. No rush! But please pay me by EOD.)

Really quick -- does anyone know if Portugal has its own Facebook? I looked up João on Facebook, and the only profile that came up was a guy with a girl in his main pic and said he was born like in 2000, lol. That can't be him, right?? Also, can someone Tinder a lawyer and ask about international laws of consent?

Love you girls!!!

Once again please use ONLY the designated hashtags!!
#JensBacheloretteSquad
#JensLastFlingBeforeTheRing

xo,
Ali

"Apenas a ponta??" —João to me!! I think it means "beautiful eyes"! SWOON!!!

To: Ali, Katie, Jen, Ashley, Morgan, Gracie, Caitlin
From: Nicole
Date: September 6 at 2:07 a.m.
Subject: Re: #aboutlastnight

Hey Ladies!

I had such a great time!! Really quick -- does anyone know if you only got one out of the three HPV vaccines, if it's still valid? Everything all cool on my end, I think I'm just experiencing some jetlag in my SoNi, if you catch my drift. (South Nicole -- lol!)

Ali -- I'm seeing all your texts, but I can't respond since somehow my Verizon bill was over $3k from SoPu -- apparently I was on roaming the entire time! Sherri is on the phone with Verizon as we speak, and we might even get a sponsorship deal from them out of this mishap -- so exciting! She is seriously amazing. I'll try to take some of the photos down, but can you just untag yourself?

xx,
Nic

CEO of Nicole The Runway
Aspiring *Forbes* magazine 30 Under 30 winner

To: Ali, Katie, Jen, Ashley, Gracie, Caitlin, Nicole
From: Morgan
Date: September 8 at 11:43 a.m.
Subject: Re: #aboutlastnight

Hey Ladies!

SoPu was so fun! I seriously wish we were all back at the McDonald's right now!!

Is anyone hitting up the Equinox tonight? I'm still pretty jetlagged and not up to a workout yet but was gonna stop by and load up on free razors, if anyone needs anything!

Instead of apple picking, I think we should go to Dia:Beacon! Everyone keeps Instagramming photos from it, and I am dying of FOMO!!!

Love you pretty girls!
Morgs

To: Ali, Katie, Ashley, Morgan, Gracie, Caitlin, Nicole
From: Helene and Bob Carrington
Date: September 12 at 8:01 a.m.
Subject: Intervention

Hi Ladies,

Helene here. Happy to see you gals had such a good time in SoPu. I couldn't help but notice how thin all of your arms looked in the Facebook photos I saw! Did you all contract a parasite or worm of some kind? Good for you!

This may sound serious, and I am praying to my rosary it isn't, but I am wondering what you girls know about the following products and items (photos are attached):
- Waist trainer (?)
- SugarBearHair Gummies
- Fit Tea
- NoFat Wraps
- Maple Syrup + Agave Syrup + Acorn from an Overfed Squirrel Bottled Nectar
- PharmaFreak Ripped Freak Hybrid Fat Cleanse

As I was doing Jennifer's laundry in her childhood bedroom (I often wash the sheets 3x a week despite no one actually sleeping there -- a housekeeping tip from me to you, for free!), I found a decoupaged shoebox of the items listed above. At first I was confused because the shoebox was covered in Mod Podge photos of Nick Carter and various Backsync Boys and outfits from Delia's catalogs. I assumed the box was old and full of old stuff. But the expiration dates on most of the products read 2020, so it makes more sense that she was just hiding this stuff in the old box, right? I know, I sound like I'm off my wagon, so I'll be honest: I did take a Ritalin pill from the box (I know what Ritalin is) so my mind is racing a little bit, but I am also multitasking and baking a three-layer fudge soufflé as I write this, so, you know.

Anyway, I am worried about Jennifer. I knew about the Ritalin and that she had been getting pills from Jacob Masterson, the 8th grader who lives next door to us. I was fine with that because I know Jacob was helping his mom save money to finally divorce Jacob's father, and so I felt like it was a charitable gift with a kickback (like buying a sensible cotton t-shirt where all the proceeds go towards charity!). I was not prepared to see the rest of these items. A waist trainer? Fit Tea? I saw Fit Tea on Teresa Giudice's Instagram after she got out of jail (she always was such a bad representation of New Jersey, but she and I do share a lawyer). Does it work? Should I buy it?

Wondering if we should hold an intervention. I really only think Jennifer needs to lose 5 lbs., 20 lbs. tops. Let me know if you would like to attend/speak. I will have it catered.

All best,
Helene

CEO of the Carrington Family

To: Ali, Ashley, Morgan, Gracie, Caitlin, Nicole, Helene and Bob Carrington
From: Katie
Date: September 12 at 10:23 a.m.
Subject: Re: Intervention

Hi everyone,

Wow. Helene, I don't know what to say. This problem sounds serious. And because I am working overtime to prove that I am a good friend, and that I believe in chicks before bros, especially after what took place in SoPu (please ask me off thread for details as I do not want to bring up the past), I am totally willing to plan the intervention.

To take a page from Ali's book, I am thinking: a theme. Those who have succumbed to their illnesses. Anna Nicole Smith. The Craigslist Killer. These people all had dreams, and their dreams died with them. Is your life worth looking thin in your wedding dress? I know many here would say yes, but I'll direct you to a specific trend piece I saw in *Teen Vogue* (they honestly do amazing work, by the way) about men who want to get thin -- anyway, I'm off topic.

If we're going to get it catered, I think we need to surround Jen with things that make her feel comfortable. No processed sugar, no carbs, no starchy root vegetables, no stevia or Splenda. I suggest 0% Fage (4 WW points for a cup) and celery (0 WW points and burns more calories than they're worth).

If everyone can chime in and just validate me for being an amazing friend during this time and say that they forgive me for what happened in SoPu along with their RSVP for the intervention, that would be great. You can also leave me a voicemail.

Katie

To: Katie, Ashley, Morgan, Gracie, Caitlin, Helene and Bob Carrington
From: Nicole
Date: September 12 at 3:14 p.m.
Subject: Re: Intervention

Hi ladies!

Thanks for organizing, Katie. I will definitely be attending the intervention and this will give me the opportunity to bring my dry cleaning and wash-and-fold receipts to you so you can pay me back. Did you know 90% alcohol-based vomit is extremely hard to get out of polyblend? Something about it being mixed with stomach acid making it a strong substance that locks into fibers?? I don't know the science, but the bill is $1,349.85. Thank you in advance!!

I will bring celery (3-4 stalks). As for location, there is an event room at Equinox, and I think they do this kind of thing all the time. I will ask them when I go tomorrow (that's right, Helene, I am currently clocking in a 7-day workout with no skip days! Am I your fav or what?).

Your business partner (this is for Helene) and friend (everyone else and Helene),

Nic

CEO, Nicole The Runway

To: Katie, Ashley, Morgan, Gracie, Caitlin, Nicole, Helene and Bob Carrington
From: Ali
Date: September 12 at 5:02 p.m.
Subject: Re: Intervention

Hi ladies,

One of my former interns, Emma S. (current interns are Emma H. and Emma G.), is actually an interventplanner. Like an event planner but an intervention planner. Seriously, she does this kind of thing all of the time.

Helene, what's the budget? Do we want to do floral arrangements? What's the current headcount for guest attendance? Will there be a registry? I'll admit it's kind of tacky to hold an intervention within one calendar year of a wedding + bridal shower, etc., but Jen is so beloved, so I am sure friends and family won't mind!

LMK, Ali

"Wow, thank you for planning such a thoughtful intervention." —Jen, after her intervention

---

To: Ali, Katie, Morgan, Gracie, Caitlin, Nicole, Helene and Bob Carrington
From: Ashley
Date: September 14 at 9:05 a.m.
Subject: Re: Intervention

Hi gals,

I won't be able to make the intervention, but I agree it sounds super fun! I don't think any of those items you found in Jen's childhood bedroom sound TOO crazy, but also several family members of mine *have* passed away from OD'ing on ephedrine so *shrug!*. I will be bummed to miss out. Being in Connecticut is like being on another planet. Also can anyone let me know if they took home 2 of the tank tops we got silkscreened in SoPu? I am missing mine and really wanted to wear it for the homecoming game here (for the colors, I assume most of the parents here won't know what "Jen's Sluts" means in the SoPu language (Spanish??)).

Best of luck and all my love to Jen and those affected.
Ash

To: Ali, Katie, Ashley, Gracie, Caitlin, Nicole, Helene and Bob Carrington
From: Morgan
Date: September 16 at 9:34 p.m.
Subject: Re: Intervention

Hi ladies,

I just got the Paperless Post invite to Jen's intervention (#Jentervention). I love the gold confetti look, even for a fall intervention. I'll be there :)

Does anyone want to meet up prior at Veselka for eats? Been dying for their pancakes and ever since my office moved to Bushwick I feel like I almost never venture into Manhattan. LMK. I figure we'd want to eat beforehand, not sure if 4 stalks of celery will sustain us. Also does anyone wanna get tix to Tegan and Sara for next month?

Morgs

To: Ali, Katie, Ashley, Morgan, Gracie, Nicole, Helene and Bob Carrington
From: Caitlin
Date: September 17 at 11:53 a.m.
Subject: Re: Intervention

Hey ladies,

I have some great weight loss solutions up on the blog today. I'm talking about the difference between matcha and green tea as well as the benefits of 0% fat Greek yogurt as a replacement for sour cream. Join me for my Twitter chat! #CaitlinChats at 4pm EST.

Caitlin

CaitlinYourLife™
Find me on Twitter! #CaitlinChats

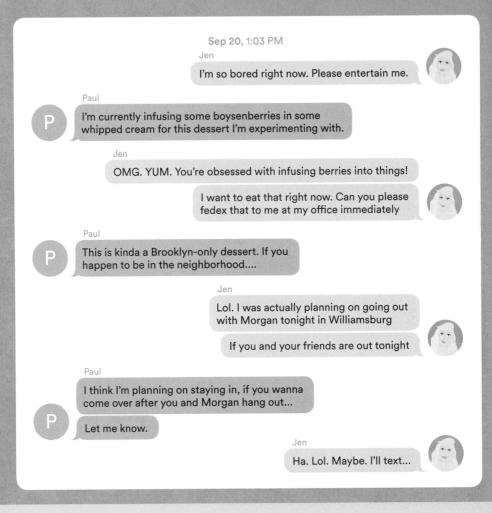

Sep 20, 1:03 PM

Jen
I'm so bored right now. Please entertain me.

Paul
I'm currently infusing some boysenberries in some whipped cream for this dessert I'm experimenting with.

Jen
OMG. YUM. You're obsessed with infusing berries into things!

I want to eat that right now. Can you please fedex that to me at my office immediately

Paul
This is kinda a Brooklyn-only dessert. If you happen to be in the neighborhood....

Jen
Lol. I was actually planning on going out with Morgan tonight in Williamsburg

If you and your friends are out tonight

Paul
I think I'm planning on staying in, if you wanna come over after you and Morgan hang out...

Let me know.

Jen
Ha. Lol. Maybe. I'll text...

To: Ali, Katie, Ashley, Morgan, Gracie, Caitlin, Nicole
From: Jen
Date: September 20 at 1:34 p.m.
Subject: Tonight!

Hey Ladies!

I know we're all planning on meeting at Equinox tonight in the Village but just wanted to see if you'd want to meet at the one in Brooklyn Heights instead? Brad has to work late (again), so I was thinking maybe we could grab some Skinnygirl margs in Williamsburg after? Is everyone in??

I am going to wear an autumnal flower crown!!!! Tell me if you like it for the wedding???

Love!
Jen

To: Katie, Jen, Ashley, Morgan, Gracie, Caitlin, Nicole
From: Ali
Date: September 20 at 1:41 p.m.
Subject: Re: Tonight!

Hi Jen + Ladies,

Let's keep our Equinox date at the one we planned on in the city tonight, okay? We can hit up Williamsburg after! I just think the equipment and workout will probably be better in the city since Manhattanites are so intense compared to the 'burbs of Brooklyn. Please be there at 6:30 p.m. SHARP, EVERYONE.

xo,
Ali

"Addiction is a decision. An individual wants something, whatever that something is, and makes a decision to get it." —James Frey, *A Million Little Pieces*, former Oprah's Book Club selection

---

To: Katie, Ashley, Morgan, Gracie, Caitlin, Nicole, Helene and Bob Carrington
From: Ali
Date: September 20 at 1:52 p.m.
Subject: #JENTERVENTION!!!!!!!

Ladies! This is go time!!! Why is Jen obsessed with Brooklyn all of a sudden?! Was there a trends piece I don't know about??

SCHEDULE

5:30 p.m.: All of us will be waiting in the back room of Equinox where we will surprise Jen with her intervention. DO NOT BE LATE, PEOPLE!!!!
6:00 p.m.: Morgan will "surprise" Jen at work and bring her to Equinox
6:30 p.m.: Morgan and Jen will arrive

6:45 p.m.: We will share stories of how Jen's waist trainer and stevia addictions have affected all of us
7:30 p.m.: The drug counselor I hired (rated #1 in Intervention Specialists on the Upper East Side, and has personally gotten THREE Real Housechildren weaned off of sugar) will incept Jen and help her face her addictions.
8:00 p.m.: Jen will realize we are right!!!!!!!!
8:05 p.m.: We all hug Jen and have a group cry.
8:15 p.m.: We do a "gentle yoga" class to release the toxins and chains of our past

So excited!!!!! Helene, I told the interventionist to bill you directly, if that works?

xo, Ali

JESSIE: "I'm so excited! I'm so excited! I'm so...scared!"
ZACK: "Hey, don't be scared! Listen, we'll get through this." —*Saved by the Bell*

To: Ali, Katie, Ashley, Morgan, Gracie, Caitlin, Nicole
From: Helene and Bob Carrington
Date: September 20 at 4:19 p.m.
Subject: Re: #JENTERVENTION!!!!!!!

Hey Ladies!

Sorry, Bob and I can't make the intervention -- we got last minute tickets to a regatta gala on the Potomac. Please let me know how it goes and give Jen our love! Send photos!

p.s. How are the Equinox memberships going?? Who do you think has lost the most weight?

Warmest,
Helene

CEO of the Carrington Family

To: Ali, Katie, Ashley, Gracie, Caitlin, Nicole, Helene and Bob Carrington
From: Morgan
Date: September 20 at 5:19 p.m.
Subject: Re: #JENTERVENTION!!!!!!!

Hi ladies,

Helene are you sure you're unable to attend tonight? I know part of the reason we're doing this is because you seemed concerned about Jen's addiction to addicting things. If you're not invested in coming, do you think we're overreacting?

Let me know in the next 5 bc I'm on my way to pick up Jen...

Morgs

To: Ali, Katie, Ashley, Gracie, Caitlin, Nicole, Helene and Bob Carrington
From: Morgan
Date: September 20 at 6:27 p.m.
Subject: Re: #JENTERVENTION!!!!!!!

Okay we're here, walking in, is everything set?

Morgs

To: Ali, Katie, Ashley, Morgan, Gracie, Caitlin, Helene and Bob Carrington
From: Nicole
Date: September 20 at 6:29 p.m.
Subject: Re: #JENTERVENTION!!!!!!!

Which Equinox were we meeting at for Jen's intervention again?? SORRY I CAN BE THERE IN 5!!!!!

~ Nic

To: Ali, Katie, Ashley, Morgan, Caitlin, Nicole, Helene and Bob Carrington
From: Gracie
Date: September 20 at 7:07 p.m.
Subject: Re: #JENTERVENTION!!!!!!!

Hey! I've been here an hour, where is everyone?!

~ Gracie

Sep 20, 8:15 PM

Paul

Hey...are you still coming by tonight?

Sep 20, 10:22 PM

Paul

Checking in...

Sep 21, 1:03 AM

Paul

Um am I being ghosted?

To: Katie, Ashley, Morgan, Gracie, Caitlin, Nicole, Helene and Bob Carrington
From: Ali
Date: September 21 at 11:04 a.m.
Subject: Re: #JENTERVENTION!!!!!!!

Hey Ladies + Helene,

Well, last night was very interesting! Since this was all of our first #Jentervention, I hate to monday-morning quarterback this, but I think there's a lot we can learn from this experience.

Pros:
- Great news! It turns out Jen isn't actually addicted to anything, nor does she have an eating disorder. Turns out stevia is basically like Splenda, and waist trainers are basically like Spanx, so it's all good. So this is a huge #WIN!
- The Intervention Specialist including Brad as a surprise guest and him ending up crying and opening up about how he's so sorry he's neglected her with his long hours, and will now consider getting a less-demanding and lower-paying job so that he can be there more for Jen... I mean, wow! Maybe we've brought them closer together. And I'm sure Brad quitting his job will be a good thing for them as a couple? Right? Um.

Cons:
- Jen seemed a bit traumatized, and I had no idea the intervention specialist would conduct the entire intervention in the secret underground sweat lodge at the Equinox. #LessonLearned
- It might have been a bit much when she tied Jen up. Again, this was our first rodeo...
- Brad might be a bit peeved he quit his job prematurely since Jen is not, in fact, addicted to anything....Sorry again!
- The Intervention Specialist is charging $10,000 for the two-hour session, so it's a bit higher than I originally thought. Sorry, Helene!

- Nicole missed the entire #Jentervention and ended up visiting 19 Manhattan Equinoxes before arriving at the right one. Oops.

Anyway, at least we all lost like 5 lbs sweating it out last night! This should be great for the #WeddingDiet...

Love you girls! Drinks soon?

xo,
Ali

"Sorry" —Justin Bieber, Beyonce, Demi Lovato, Elton John

Sep 21, 1:05 PM

Jen

Dear Friend, I cannot tell you what happened last night, but I beg you from the bottom of my heart to forgive me for not being there. For what happened, I feel terrible that you found yourself in a situation that caused you additional pain...The fault is mine. Someday I'll explain everything -- meanwhile, I'm still here. Talk to me.

Paul

Um is that a quote from You've Got Mail? It's my sister's favorite movie. WTF.

To: Ali, Katie, Ashley, Gracie, Caitlin, Nicole, Helene and Bob Carrington
From: Morgan
Date: September 30 at 2:05 p.m.
Subject: Re: #JENTERVENTION!!!!!!!

...It wasn't the first time Halie had planned an intervention for a friend.

"I have a friend who does this, like, for a job," she told me. Indeed, out of all of her friends, Halie did seem the most prepared to handle the elements of an atypical "friendtervention." First, she and her girlfriends, Kristine and Tasha, booked a private room in Planet Fitness

and called in catering from a local Au Bon Pain. The women even invited the girl's mom to join up, though she could not attend.

"It's important to know that your girls are there for you even when you're struggling with an addiction and may not deserve it," Halie concluded.

Hey ladies.

I just read the above in this week's *Times* Styles section (byline: Katherine) and I have some questions....Katie can you call me? In the meantime, can we make sure Jen does NOT read this?

Morgan

To: Katie, Ashley, Morgan, Gracie, Caitlin, Nicole, Helene and Bob Carrington
From: Ali
Date: September 30 at 3:17 p.m.
Subject: Re: #JENTERVENTION!!!!!!!

Hey Ladies!!

OMG KATIE YOU'RE IN PRINT IN THE *NEW YORK TIMES*!!!!!!!!! Congratulations!!!! I am totally free to autograph anyone's copy as "Halie." Lol. I feel famous!

Totally unrelated: I would love to grab coffee if you have some time today! I am thinking of branching out and taking on my own PR clients, and I think my story could be really on-brand and Styles-section worthy! The hook: a Millennial woman, starting her own company, juggling it all -- work, relationships, meddling and overbearing friends' mothers. The story writes itself!

Let me know if you have some time today! Would love to hear more about the latest with Topher also!

I can't believe I have such a big-time famous friend!!!

xo,
Ali

"There's [STILL] a special place in hell for women who don't help other women."
—Madeleine Albright and me

To: Ali, Katie, Ashley, Morgan, Gracie, Caitlin, Nicole
From: Jen
Date: September 30 at 5:08 p.m.
Subject: OMG. Shoes.

Hey Ladies!

Last week was so intense! I guess I appreciate that you all were worried for me and wanted to try to help? But in the future, I'd really appreciate it if you don't hold me against my will at an Equinox secret sweat lodge. Brad went into work to beg for his job back, and his boss accepted his apology! But now he's gonna have to work way more hours to ingratiate himself. :/ Anyway, I'm ready to put this all behind me since we are only THREE MONTHS AWAY from the Wedding of the Millennium (TM). I'm seriously so stressed out, can everyone send me 10 possible rehearsal-dinner shoe options by EOD??

Thanks ladies!!

Love,
Jen

p.s. Saw you had an article in the *Times*, Katie, congrats!!!!! Didn't get a chance to read it cause I have SO much wedding stuff to do, but can't wait to read it soon! :)

october

To: Ali, Katie, Ashley, Morgan, Gracie, Caitlin, Nicole
From: Jen
Date: October 2 at 4:00 p.m.
Subject: wedding odds and ends

Hey all,

Now that I've had some time to process, I just wanted to say thanks for being such good friends. I had a freezing case of cold feet and meeting that chef guy didn't help. I needed a little slap back to reality, and you guys gave me that. Thanks for being there. Nicole, it's okay that you got lost on the way to the gym. It's really the thought that counts.

Anyway, I severed ties with Paul the chef and Brad is none the wiser. (I also changed my email password so he can't see this), and I am just appreciating this moment of like, starting off marriage to Brad on the right foot. :)

I feel more like myself than ever before. Thank you, again, for the humbling experience. That being said...MORE WEDDING DETAILS!

With only a few months to go until #TheBigDay, I am putting together a comprehensive bulleted list of reminders/to-dos/etc.

- Feel healthy! The intervention was a huge reminder that the most important thing is that we all feel healthy and comfortable within our own bodies, instead of trying to adapt to some ideal that society has arbitrarily chosen for us. We are all beautiful and different in our own ways. I will now go to the gym only for the purpose of enjoying the body-soul connection, and encourage you to do the same!
- The bridesmaid dresses: After the Oscar snafu, Nicole came through and designed perfect gowns for us. #ad. Thank you Nicole The Runway! I have each of the gowns at my apartment and some of them require extra beading. My mom hired a local seammaster to bead for $450 a day plus health benefits, so please make sure you come to my apartment to get fitted and then we can ship the dresses to my mom. Thanks Helene!
- Order down the aisle: Ali, I would love it if Morgan could go first down the aisle, and then you second. It's just something we have been talking about lately and it actually makes sense, height-wise. She'll also be matched up with my brother Tristan, whom she has known for like, ever. Morgan, you haven't ever fucked my brother, right? Haha! Jk! Lmk though because that might change things. Thanks for understanding, Al!
- Shoes: You're all responsible for ordering, buying, and then dyeing your shoes. The color is Hollywood and it's a really subdued glitter gold. Amazing. The dye is cheap at $75 a square inch, and you'll totally wear these shoes again. I also recommend getting plastic tarps to lay down all over your bathroom/apartment/wherever you will dye the shoes. It's really hard to get the dye out of carpet and wood. Also please note that the dye takes 4-6 days to fully dry, and I read somewhere you shouldn't inhale the fumes because it can cause post-mature birth, which is when your child isn't born until 55 weeks. Imagine?!

I think that's it!! What am I going to do when this is all over? Kill myself???

Love you all,
Jen

"I do." —me, in 90 days!!!!!!!!!

Helene and Robert Carrington
request the honour of your
presence at the marriage of their daughter

Jennifer Mercer Carrington
to
Bradley Cromwell Wallace

on the thirty-first of December
at five o'clock in the afternoon

The Carrington Estate
Northern Virginia

Black Tie Required.

To: Katie, Jen, Ashley, Morgan, Gracie, Caitlin, Nicole
From: Ali
Date: October 2 at 4:59 p.m.
Subject: Re: wedding odds and ends

Hey Ladies!

We are officially in Q4, and the #THEBIGDAY is soon approaching!!!

Jen's wedding is obviously our #1 priority for the next 3 months. I'm happy to take the lead on organizing and coordinating for Jen's wedding since I'm the (co-)Maid of Honor, but I would be remiss if I didn't mention what an honor it is to be a bridesmaid, and how you all have a ton of responsibilities as well that you REALLY need to get on right now.

#BJPartyof2 Details

1) I'm personally challenging myself to lose 10 lbs, if anyone wants to join me. To paraphrase Sean Parker (SWOON) in *The Social Network*, "5 lbs isn't cool. You know what's cool? 10 lbs." I think we can all do it, and we're stronger together! We could all sync up our Fitbits!

2) REHEARSAL DINNER DRESSES!!!! Thanks for taking the lead on providing the MoH and bridesmaid dresses, Nicole! For the rehearsal dinner, I think it's really important for us to support Jen and have a cohesive, unifying, early days of Destiny's Child type look. I think it would be fun if we all purchase the same dress -- since Jen's eyes are green, I was thinking we could do green cocktail dresses. Can everyone send me some looks by the end of the day?

3) Mindset! Since weddings can be so stressful, plus the holidays bring on seasonal depression, I'm thinking we should just get ahead of it and all aim to be in the most healthy mindset possible. Can everyone either start therapy (either in-person or virtual) or begin an Ayurveda vitamin regimen -- I'm not exactly sure how it works, but I read about it in this week's Goop.

4) Order down the aisle -- I was actually going to ask to go down the aisle second, as I think it's the best spot to stand strategically for photos, so thanks for taking the lead on that. Gracie, you'll be last since you're tallest -- can you make sure to get the wedding shoes in flats, so your height doesn't stand out in our photos? Could you practice slouching, while appearing as if you have good posture? I did some modeling in Greenwich when I was a pre-teen, so I'd be happy to share some tips!

5) Accessories: This is your chance to shine! Please choose jewelry in the gold or diamond arena ONLY. The wedding decorations will all be sparkly, so I'd love to keep it in that ballpark and complement, rather than compete with, the aesthetic.

6) Shoes!!! I LOVE the dye Jen selected. I think we should all choose the same shoes (I already purchased some Stuart Weitzman shoes -- please either get the same ones or a knock-off brand that look exactly like mine). It would also be okay if everyone wore flats and only Jen and I were in heels.

7) +1: I'm assuming I'm getting a +1 to your wedding even though on the invitation it seems that all of us were just invited with our names on the invites and no "and guest" but assuming that's an oversight! Just want to confirm. I went on a date last night with this guy I met at SoulCycle -- and I'd love to invite SoulCycle Boy to the wedding in the next week and get that all tied up. Please let me know as soon as you can!

Please write back ASAP, so I know you got this!!! T-90 days!!!

xo,
Ali

"Things he should never see: Your emotions, your google search history, your eyelashes without two coats of mascara." —*Ice Queens Melt Hearts*

To: Ali, Katie, Jen, Morgan, Gracie, Caitlin, Nicole
From: Ashley
Date: October 2 at 9:09 p.m.
Subject: Re: wedding odds and ends

Hey Ladies!

I just assumed we were invited with +1s, right??! I'll be bringing either my friend Bill (super fun, super gay), or I was going to use your wedding as motivation to lock down a winter boyfriend!

Love, Ashley

ps - Jen, don't read this: What's the protocol for how much you're supposed to spend on a gift if you're a bridesmaid?? Between the Oscar dress, the Nicole The Runway dress, SoPu, engagement presents, etc., I think I've spent about $4k so far, not including all the travel expenses! EEP!

To: Ali, Katie, Jen, Ashley, Morgan, Caitlin, Nicole
From: Gracie
Date: October 3 at 12:20 p.m.
Subject: Re: wedding odds and ends

Hi all!

Just confirming: I am so looking forward to attending the wedding, but I am not able to be a bridesmaid. I told Jen earlier in the summer I wasn't able to be a bridesmaid, and I thought she passed along the message...Also, I would so much rather be able to take photos from the pews of all of you looking amazing! Don't worry -- I won't upload any until everyone confirms. And I'll try to get a variety so you can all put up different Instagrams.

Early congratulations, Jen. Looking forward to the big day.

My love,
Gracie

To: Ali, Katie, Ashley, Morgan, Gracie, Caitlin, Nicole
From: Jen
Date: October 3 at 12:22 p.m.
Subject: Re: wedding odds and ends

Hi Gracie & JMs (Jen'smaids -- cute!),

I'll be the first to admit I've been a bit distracted for the last few months, but this feels like the first I'm hearing of you not being a bridesmaid!! I made Brad include his cousin Tyler just so he could walk you down the aisle -- and I personally CAN'T STAND Tyler -- he has visible tattoos which is SO not part of my #BJPartyOf2 wedding aesthetic!! It would realllllly mean a lot if you could be a BM (bridesmaid!)! Plus it's gonna be so fun to get ready together that morning -- which reminds me, hair/makeup will begin in the bridal suite at 4:00 a.m.!! Everyone's responsible for paying for their own hair and makeup, BUT my mom has generously provided a full breakfast of 0% Greek yogurts and Kind bars for everyone!

Please, please reconsider. It would seriously ruin my wedding if you don't stand up there with me!!!

Love,
Jen

To: Ali, Jen, Ashley, Morgan, Gracie, Caitlin, Nicole
From: Katie
Date: October 3 at 1:48 p.m.
Subject: Re: wedding odds and ends

Hi ladies,

So excited! On board with the 10 lbs weight loss (but to be honest, ever since the breakup with Topher, I've already lost 12. So I guess I'll lose 22 lbs. Silver lining!).

One of the things that hasn't been discussed here is the playlist the band/DJ will be using at the reception. A few requests, since sometimes the song choices dictate whether the party feels like it's for couples or for individuals. Since my breakup with Topher, I would really, so very much appreciate you guys taking me into consideration as we plan the musical aesthetic.

I took the liberty of typing up a few of the notes I've been jotting in my various reporter's notebooks and moleskins, so pardon if it doesn't make a ton of sense (my shorthand could use some work -- journalism!).

- "How Will I Know?" Whitney Houston: Obvious hit, yes. Fun to dance to, yes. But the lyrics make me think of Topher :("There's a boy I know, he's the one I dream of." Ughhhh. Ixnay on the HitneyWay OustonHay. Sorry.
- "Party Rockers" LMFAO: Was once playing in a car that passed me and Topher while we were on a walk. He said, "Love this song."
- "The Way You Look Tonight" my parents' wedding song. At this point it's like, will I even get married?
- "Gangnam Style" Psy: Topher and I both hate that song. It was an inside joke of ours.
- Anything Taylor Swift: Breaks my heart in a thousand pieces if I even just have to hear one note of any song off her several hit albums.
- No Rihanna.
- Anything off of *Lemonade* is a no.
- No "Halo" either.
- "Runaround Sue" is just a bad song so please don't play it (same with "Celebrate good times, come on!")
- No Calvin Harris
- No Chainsmokers
- No "And I think to myself...what a wonderful world."
- No "My Girl" by the Temptations

Okay I think that about covers it for songs. So excited otherwise! Also, Jen, I think I mistakenly checked "veggie" on my RSVP, but I one-hundo want the steak.

Thanks!
Katie

Oct 3, 1:55 PM

Ali

I just wanna say I think it's fucked up that gracie is like "I'm not a bridesmaid!" Do you want me to yell at her or force her to do this? It's up to you, babe, you're the bride

Oct 3, 2:00 PM

Morgan

Totally don't worry about gracie. I think it's great that she'll be taking pics of us looking so amazing...so you can choose which one gets to be the FIRST INSTA of you in your dress! Gonna be great! Can't wait for the big day!

To: Ali, Katie, Jen, Ashley, Morgan, Gracie, Nicole
From: Caitlin
Date: October 3 at 5:13 p.m.
Subject: Re: wedding odds and ends

Hey y'all,

Katie, it's so crazy, I actually ordered the steak by mi-steak! Let's switch plates! Jen, can you have your mom tell the chef to cook my food in sesame oil only, I'm kind of on this cleanse, and it runs through the end of the year.

Going to the chapel and Jen's gonna get maaaaarried.

Caitlin

Download my CaitlinTalk on why white foods are the silent killer!
CaitlinYourLife™

To: Ali, Katie, Ashley, Morgan, Gracie, Caitlin, Nicole
From: Jen
Date: October 6 at 1:11 p.m.
Subject: Re: wedding odds and ends

Hey everyone,

Thinking about doing a Snapchat filter for the big day but also the week before and after. It costs $6/hour (cheap) so 6 bucks x 24 hours x 14 days = ??? Can everyone just Venmo me $100 even? Should cover it.

Excited!
Jen

To: Ali, Katie, Jen, Ashley, Morgan, Gracie, Caitlin
From: Nicole
Date: October 6 at 1:50 p.m.
Subject: Re: wedding odds and ends

Hey Jen and ladies,

I love the idea of the Snapchat filter, but I'm not sure we should have it for 14 days! If the guests already see the filter prior to the wedding it's not as exciting as if they only see it while they're at the reception! Plus it's more cost-efficient for all of us that way.

It's called supply and demand and I learned about it in the business book I'm reading!

Thanks!
Nicole

To: Ali, Katie, Jen, Ashley, Morgan, Gracie, Caitlin, Nicole
From: Helene and Bob Carrington
Date: October 6 at 10:17 p.m.
Subject: RE: FWD: wedding odds and ends

Hi Ladies!

Jen forwarded these emails to me and I have some thoughts.

I believe it would be best if we were all to stay away from "Snap Chatting" Jen's wedding. Bob and I have a bit of an issue with the Spiegels -- it's a boring story, but let's just say John and Melissa Spiegel chose to attend a leukemia benefit the night they promised to attend our tennis-elbow benefit, and we really haven't spoken to them since. I think it would be best to do a social media ban and confiscate all guests' cell phones upon arrival at the wedding. I read that was done for Kate Middleton's wedding and also Jennifer Aniston's. I just think it's classier. We have an excellent photographer from whom you can order as many prints as you like for all your picture needs. :)

Can everyone please purchase and sync up their Fitbits? That could be a fun way to motivate each other!

Warmest,
Helene

CEO of the Carrington Family

To: Ali, Katie, Ashley, Morgan, Gracie, Caitlin, Nicole
From: Jen
Date: October 7 at 8:00 a.m.
Subject: Re: wedding odds and ends

Hey Ladies!

Sorry, Katie, Brad is in charge of the music. It's the one job I gave him, so he'd let Mom and I plan everything else. I think his sister wants to sing some hipster cover of "First Day of My Life" for our first song. Gross.

But!! Good news! Mom and I were able to pull some strings...and we're super close to booking a makeup artist who once did Michelle Obama's makeup!!!! Helene has an in, but I think it would also be really great if we all purchased some makeup from her line as a thank you.

I seriously can't even believe how everything is coming together for this! Only the best for my girls!

Love,
The Future Mrs.!!!!

To: Helene and Bob Carrington
From: Morgan
Date: October 7 at 10:19 a.m.
Subject: Hi!!!

Hi Helene!

Did you mean Louisa Spiegel's parents? If so, right on. I never liked her OR her parents. They were always so basic.

Morgs

To: Ali, Katie, Jen, Ashley, Morgan, Caitlin, Nicole
From: Gracie
Date: October 8 at 11:01 a.m.
Subject: Re: wedding odds and ends

Hi everyone!

Just checking in here. I wanted to let everyone know that I am not going to be able to attend the wedding as a bridesmaid. I have to admit this might be my fault for not really actually reading all of the emails (I see now that there were several attempts at getting me to come in and try on Nicole The Runway dresses as well as some Venmo request for an Oscar de la Renta gown???), but I am just putting here in writing that I will be at the wedding as a guest, and I am looking forward to it.

I hope this doesn't mess anyone up, and I am appreciative in advance of your understanding.

Thank you!
Gracie

To: Ali, Jen, Ashley, Morgan, Gracie, Caitlin, Nicole
From: Katie
Date: October 10 at 3:43 p.m.
Subject: Re: wedding odds and ends

Hi gals,

I don't have a +1, because I am still mourning Topher. Jen, would you please make sure I am not awkwardly seated at a kids' table or like, with random second cousins? Unless they are good looking. I decided I'd rather go stag to the wedding than bring a rando, because I truly am focused on my career this year and I wouldn't want to derail my Pulitzer aspirations. I just rewatched *Spotlight* twice last night and I am INSPIRED. God, 2002 was such an ERA for newspapers, you know? (If you don't know why, lmk, and I can fill you in.)

That being said, I want to make sure my aesthetic that evening is "single by choice," so please talk up my journalistic goals and achievements (editor of high school paper, 2003-2004, go Bulldogs!) to other guests so no one gets the wrong idea about me.

Can't wait for this amazing day! And that's ON THE RECORD! :)

Katie

To: Ali, Katie, Ashley, Morgan, Gracie, Caitlin, Nicole
From: Jen
Date: October 11 at 8:15 p.m.
Subject: Re: wedding odds and ends

Hey,

Just getting around to checking email (been doing cake tastings for the last few days and went OOO) and honestly WTF????? I CAN'T BELIEVE GRACIE IS DOING THIS TO ME!!!!!!

Honestly, I give and I give, and all anyone ever does is take from me!!!! I AM SO DONE. I am seriously rethinking all of my friendships now. I'll be at Equinox if you need me.

~Jen

\#BJ4Ever

To: Ali, Katie, Ashley, Morgan, Gracie, Caitlin, Nicole
From: Jen
Date: October 11 at 8:18 p.m.
Subject: Re: wedding odds and ends

Sorry, thought I was sending this only to Morgs. Didn't realize everyone was on this thread. But also I'm not sorry, since I'm speaking my truth.

Hugs!
~Jen

\#BJ4Ever

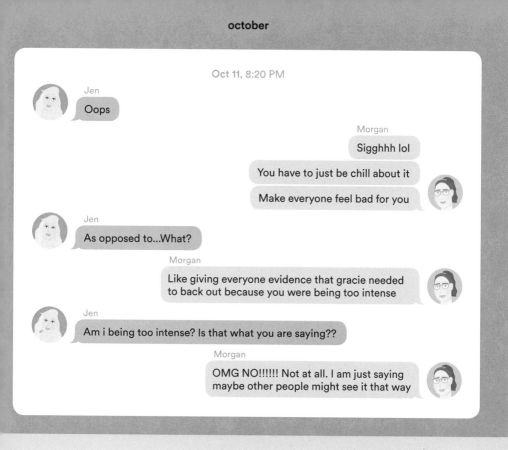

Oct 11, 8:20 PM

Jen
Oops

Morgan
Sigghhh lol

You have to just be chill about it

Make everyone feel bad for you

Jen
As opposed to...What?

Morgan
Like giving everyone evidence that gracie needed to back out because you were being too intense

Jen
Am i being too intense? Is that what you are saying??

Morgan
OMG NO!!!!!! Not at all. I am just saying maybe other people might see it that way

To: Ali, Katie, Jen, Ashley, Morgan, Gracie, Nicole
From: Caitlin
Date: October 13 at 4:01 p.m.
Subject: Re: wedding odds and ends

Hey Ladies!

As you all know, one of the core tenets of CaitlinYourLife is feeling gratitude when the Universe helps you experience what humans may process as "setbacks" but are really the Universe being like, "Just breathe. Feel grateful. Change your intentions. Slay the dragon. Eat some chia. Ok, now I'll totally give you something even better than what you wanted in the first place!"

So! Since Gracie has recused herself from our bridesmaid tribe, and we have an odd number, I think we should ask the most logical, brilliant, innovative, powerful woman we know...someone we could all benefit from being in close proximity to...Sherri Gold! I think she'd be an amazing addition to the group. I would love to swing by and let her know in person!

Jen, what do you think? Also, she's roughly the same size as Gracie, so she can wear her dress.

Let me know!

Love and gratitude and light and forgiveness,
Caitlin

CEO of CaitlinYourLife™
Intention put forth into the Universe: Secure series A funding this month.

To: Ali, Jen, Ashley, Morgan, Gracie, Caitlin, Nicole
From: Katie
Date: October 14 at 2:52 p.m.
Subject: Re: wedding odds and ends

Hi ladies!

Quick edit on your email, Caitlin! Universe doesn't have to be capitalized.

Thanks!
Katie

To: Ali, Katie, Jen, Ashley, Morgan, Gracie, Nicole
From: Caitlin
Date: October 15 at 1:30 a.m.
Subject: Re: wedding odds and ends

I think you're thinking of "the Universe" as a noun, not as an entity. Breathe in. Now breathe out. You're welcome.

xx,
Caitlin

"'You're gonna be okay.' —The Universe" —Caitlin
CEO, CaitlinYourLife™

To: Ali, Jen, Ashley, Morgan, Gracie, Caitlin, Nicole
From: Katie
Date: October 15 at 6:01 a.m.
Subject: Re: wedding odds and ends

Oh interesting!
Katie

Oct 15, 8:01 AM

Morgan

FWIW I think katie is right about universe not needing to be capitalized.

Jen

FWIW I am fucking pissed that Gracie just backed out. She never read the emails???? Like??? What??? There have been like, 6 emails about the wedding since the engagement. 8 TOPS. Gracie just thinks she's above everything including email. Can you imagine if I was a bridezilla???? You guys are lucky I'm so fucking chill.

Morgan

Oh forget it, it's fine, it's totally fine. Everything is fine. Why would you want someone who didn't want to be a part of it? You know?

Jen

I just want to be the center of attention for ONE DAY

To: Ali, Katie, Ashley, Morgan, Gracie, Caitlin, Nicole
From: Jen
Date: October 18 at 11:00 a.m.
Subject: A REMINDER

Hi ladies!

Just a reminder that I could be way fucking worse as a bride.

There have been barely any emails about this wedding, I've been super chill about dresses and bachelorette parties, and I didn't even care when Katie brought her "boyfriend" to MY SoPu weekend.

I feel like you guys aren't appreciating me enough for how calm I am. I told you guys you could wear your hair whatever way you wanted for fuck's sake! How many brides can say that? Seriously how many???

Jesus Christ,
Jen

To: Katie, Jen, Ashley, Morgan, Gracie, Caitlin, Nicole
From: Ali
Date: October 18 at 11:06 a.m.
Subject: Re: A REMINDER

Hey Ladies!

1) Your ONLY priority for the next 2.5 months is Jen's wedding. Not your career, not your family, not even yourself (except for self-care Sundays wherein we SoulCycle).
2) Being a bridesmaid is an HONOR, not a right. I am completely willing to make suggestions about cuts to our roster, as needed.
3) Part of our sacred duties is to make sure Jen is as relaxed and calm as possible. That means dropping everything if she needs us. That means helping to hold her dress while she pees. And *not* just on her wedding day -- on any day.
4) I'm happy to have one-on-one sessions with anyone who doesn't completely understand what it means to be a bridesmaid. It's a sacred office.

Please let me know if you have any questions. I look forward to all of you rising to the occasion.

Best,
Ali

"Sure! Whatever you want!" —WHAT ALL OF US SHOULD BE SAYING TO JEN

To: Ali, Katie, Jen, Ashley, Morgan, Caitlin, Nicole
From: Gracie
Date: October 18 at 11:07 a.m.
Subject: Re: A REMINDER

Hey, Ali, do you think you could take me off these emails? Thanks, Gracie

Oct 18, 11:30 AM

Jen
Do you think ali has gone a bit crazy per her last email??

Morgan
Well lol

No nevermind. Yah she's a little nutto

Jen
What what it's fine just tell me

Morgan
It's just that your latest email, the one before ali's, might also be classified as a bit crazy as well

Jen
Ugh maybe. You think I should talk to ali and calm her down?

Morgan
If you think it would work, sure!

Jen
Lol

What a nightmare. Maybe we just elope.
Actually can you do me a favor?

Morgan
"SURE! WHATEVER YOU WANT!" :-P

Jen
LMAO fuck off

Can you try talking to ali? You know, as the co-maid of honor

Morgan
Hmmmmm yeahhhhh about that. Think I can abdicate that position?

Jen
Morgannnnnnn

Morgan
Jennnnnnnnn

november

To: Ali, Katie, Jen, Ashley, Morgan, Caitlin, Nicole
From: Gracie
Date: November 2 at 11:19 a.m.
Subject: Friendsgiving

Hey all,

I turn 28 (ahh) on November 25th, so I would like to invite everyone to a FRIENDSGIVING/
BIRTHDAY PARTY :)

Come and enjoy my shared rooftop for a potluck dinner with mucho wine! There will be
outdoor heaters but bring a warm coat, and a potluck dish to share with the group. I am
super excited to see everyone! Jen, do you think you can make it? I know with the wedding
just two months away it's probably a really insane time for you, but I promise it will be a
really relaxing night and you'll have fun. Bring Brad, even!

Sat. November 27th, @ 7:00 p.m. -- my apartment.

Thanks!
Gracie

GRACIE'S BIRTHDAY & FRIENDSGIVING!!

i'm turning **28** !!!!

DATE:
November 27th

TIME:
7:00pm to ?!?!

PLACE:
My apartment!

FOOD

- Mulled Wine & Turkey
- POTLUCK
- Vegetarians welcome!

GAMES

- Cards Against Humanity
- BYOG – Bring Your Own GAMES!

To: Katie, Jen, Ashley, Morgan, Gracie, Caitlin, Nicole
From: Ali
Date: November 2 at 2:40 p.m.
Subject: Re: Friendsgiving

Hey ladies,

Omg so cute, Gracie! I love it! You're such an old soul. How about if, instead, we went out for drinks? It can be like #Party4BJ! A second bachelorette party for Jen because you couldn't come to the first one! As the co-maid of honor, I know Jen would be really thrilled if we did this for her. I know how much she missed you in SoPu, girl. Right, Jen? So are we all in?

Itinerary:

November 27
- 6:00 p.m.: Meet up at Caitlin's parents' pied-a-terre in Gramercy Park. They won't care, right, C? I know they are almost never there since your grandma passed away. Sorry about that by the way. May she rest in peace :(but also :) because you probably have some amazing memories and also inherited a good amount of money since you don't have siblings and your dad is estranged from your family. Silver lining!
- 6:15 p.m.: I arrive with the shirts: #BJ4EverGoesBK or #BJ4EverInBK? Either way, Venmo me $17.50 for your shirt. I already ordered when I got Gracie's email. PS -- I only ordered small. Incentives to visit Equinox!
- 6:25 p.m.: Pre-game with Skinnygirl margs and cucumbers.
- 6:45 p.m.: Get cab to Brooklyn.
- ??????? Not sure how long it takes to get there so whenever we get to BK...9:00 pm? Wythe Hotel rooftop. Williamsburg. #RoseInNovember.
- 10:00 p.m.: Champagne toast to Jen and Brad!! Sing "Happy Birthday" to Gracie.
- 10:30 p.m.: More shots! Dancing on the bars.
- 11:00 p.m.: Make sure the DJ plays amazing songs. Get in a fight with him if he doesn't.
- 12:00 a.m.: One day closer to Jen's wedding!
- 1:00 a.m.: Check in to Wythe Hotel (Surprise, Jen!!! We love you!) Everyone Venmo me $65.76 for your share.
- 1:30 a.m.: Order one burger from room service to split (you *can* indulge!)
- 7:00 a.m.: SoulCycle Survivor (60 mins) in Wburg.
- 9:30 a.m.: Take cab back to NYC.
- 12:00 p.m.: Arrive back in NYC?
So excited for this. And happy birthday, Gracie!

XO,
ALI

"You have to go to Brooklyn, it's the law." —Me to the cab driver right now

To: Ali, Katie, Ashley, Morgan, Gracie, Caitlin, Nicole
From: Jen
Date: November 3 at 7:13 a.m.
Subject: Re: Friendsgiving

Hey Ladies!

Omg you girls are too sweet!!! I would absolutely LOVE to attend #BJsInBrooklyn (is it too late to get t-shirts with that hashtag?? Ahhh, I'm such a pain!! Promise to tell me if I turn into bridezilla, ok??), but I have some huge news...

I am having vaginaeoplasty (sp?) to spruce up for the Big Day and to be revirginized for Brad!!! I found a doctor that comes highly recommended via *The Real Housewives* and Yelp. I am having it done on November 25, so I should be recovered by then?? I might have to bring an ice pack and have it covering my vajayjay region all night, but I'm down!

That reminds me, who can come with me to the doctor?? I'll need someone to hold my hand, get my meds, and change my bandages! It's a surprise, so I'm telling Brad I'll be attending a "bride conference," which he totally bought. Sometimes I swear he doesn't even listen when I'm talking!!

Can't wait!! Ahhhh, less than 2 months!!! It's crazy I'll be an old married woman, but my flower will be just like new!!

xo,
Jen

To: Ali, Katie, Jen, Ashley, Gracie, Caitlin, Nicole
From: Morgan
Date: November 3 at 12:28 p.m.
Subject: Re: Friendsgiving

Hey ladies!

Happy early birthday, Gracie :) I always thought it would be fun to have a Thanksgiving birthday because you get to see your family! Exciting!

Jen, I'm happy to accompany you to your vagina Botox whatever. Let me know. I've started volunteering at the ASPCA, so I'll let you know my schedule there.

As for the rest of the night, I'm happy to throw down for whatever.

Also has anyone seen those cute DIY videos for concert tees on Facebook? I'm gonna turn a few of mine into crop tops for Burning Man next year. Anyone interested?

Morgan

To: Katie, Jen, Ashley, Morgan, Gracie, Caitlin, Nicole
From: Ali
Date: November 3 at 3:07 p.m.
Subject: Re: Friendsgiving

Hey ladies!

As much as I'd love to discuss Coachella or Burning People or whatever, let's try to stay focused on Jen's wedding, because that comes first! Not to be a bitch or anything, can everyone Venmo me quickly for t-shirts and hotel rez? I have to pay rent.

Xo,
Ali

"Don't let what others think or say get in your way; their actions reflect on them, not you."
—Suze Orman

To: Katie, Jen, Ashley, Morgan, Gracie, Caitlin, Nicole
From: Ali
Date: November 4 at 8:17 p.m.
Subject: Re: Friendsgiving

Hey ladies!

Quick check in about those Venmos. Can you all shoot me over the money when you get a chance? Preferably within the hour. Thanks!

Ali

"Money can easily ruin friendships." —Monthly newsletter from Samuel, my dad's accountant

To: Katie, Jen, Ashley, Morgan, Gracie, Caitlin, Nicole
From: Ali
Date: November 5 at 10:45 a.m.
Subject: Re: Friendsgiving

Thank you to Caitlin and Ashley! Morgan, Katie, Nicole, Gracie, can you Venmo ASAP?

Thanks!

xo,
Ali

"I use the negativity to fuel the transformation into a better me." —Beyoncé

To: Ali, Katie, Jen, Ashley, Morgan, Caitlin, Nicole
From: Gracie
Date: November 5 at 11:02 a.m.
Subject: Re: Friendsgiving

Hey ladies,

Just circling back here -- so I invite you guys to my birthday party, then Ali, you overhaul it into another bachelorette for Jen, and now somehow I owe you, like, $200?

Gracie

To: Katie, Jen, Ashley, Morgan, Gracie, Caitlin, Nicole
From: Ali
Date: November 5 at 1:07 p.m.
Subject: Re: Friendsgiving

Hey Ladies,

Wow, Gracie. I can't say I'm surprised that you are somehow making your birthday ALL ABOUT YOU. I understand if you don't appreciate the time, energy, love, and googling that goes into a fun night out -- but I for one am sick of being underappreciated! If it weren't for my planning, then where would we even be?? I'll tell you where: somewhere in Brooklyn with a Trader Joe's hummus quartet for 20 people, playing Cards Against the Settlers of Catan, and not having any fun at all. No offense, but your parties suck. And your attitude sucks. And you not being a bridesmaid totally sucks.

This is the Year of Jen, and like CaitlinYourLife tells us: "It's important to speak your truth. And eat your chia seeds." So I'm doing both of those right now. (I just googled Goop recipes for chia pudding -- yum!) Anyway, hope we can come back from this. Or not.

For everyone else: I will see you in Brooklyn. (But please refer to my itinerary on the earlier email since we're meeting in Manhattan first.)

Katie & Gracie, can you PLEASE Venmo me today?? Morgan, I'll see you in small claims court.

xo,
Ali

"Let your smile change the world, but don't let the world change your smile." —something I saw on Pinterest that is now my mantra

To: Ali, Katie, Jen, Ashley, Morgan, Gracie, Caitlin
From: Nicole
Date: November 5 at 3:14 p.m.
Subject: Re: Friendsgiving

Hey Ladies!

While Nicole The Runway is doing AMAZINGLY, I don't have a ton of liquidity right now due to something going on with the Chinese yuan. I'll just make my own T for Jen's night out! Also, if someone can buy me drinks and pay for my share of the Uber, I am willing to compensate them with .00000005% share of Nicole The Runway™.

Please let me know. And please don't mention this to Sherri Gold.

Love!
Nicole

CEO, Nicole The Runway

To: Ali, Katie, Jen, Ashley, Morgan, Gracie, Nicole
From: Caitlin
Date: November 6 at 1:04 a.m.
Subject: Re: Friendsgiving

So excited to party with my girls!!! Quick note to Ali & Gracie: I'm available for conflict mediation. The CaitlinYourLife™ method includes just stripping down (metaphysically, and also physically), walking on fire (insurance pending!), then releasing your negative feelings into the Universe. I can give you all a 2% discount if you tweet/Instagram about it. I'm pretty busy this week, but could be available Monday-Sunday. Let me know!

In love and light,
Caitlin

CEO of CaitlinYourLife™

Nov 6, 1:15 AM

Jen
You need to make up with Gracie!!!! I'm seriously STRESSED!!!!!

Ali
Gracie can make up with me. I'm doing Ice Queens Melt Hearts on her.

Jen
 I am SO not that bride, but this is my wedding year!!!! I can't take the infighting. I need to focus right now on all the wedding details and my upcoming vag surgery!

Ali
I'll think about it. Btw, google Justin Gillieson. Met him last night and he won't stop texting me! He's obsessed. I'm gonna reserve AliGillieson@gmail just in case.

To: Katie, Jen, Ashley, Morgan, Gracie, Caitlin, Nicole
From: Ali
Date: November 6 at 9:45 a.m.
Subject: Re: Friendsgiving

Hey ladies,

Gracie, I appreciate your thoughts on the...I believe you used the word "overhaul"? Thanks for reaching out. I've been reading a lot about how important it is for women to be able to express their feelings within the environment of their closest female friendships, so I completely understand the context. Thanks for making your concerns known. I see you, I hear you.

That being said, I think it's still important that we relish these last few weeks before #BJ4Ever. I will take into consideration that Gracie's birthday is also an important event (albeit, something that happens every year unlike a wedding), and I want to make sure you feel celebrated, Gracie.

Wondering if we could arrange a compromise. Maybe we start out the night doing the potluck but then move on to drinks to celebrate Jen? This is the best deal I can offer on such short notice. Hoping you'll realize this is a petty thing to argue about with your best friends :)

Gals feel free to chime in! Would like to get a run of show sent out 14 days in advance to allow for any edits.

Thanks!
Ali

"I, too, shall rise above this." —Me and a Phoenix

To: Ali, Katie, Jen, Ashley, Morgan, Gracie, Caitlin
From: Nicole
Date: November 7 at 3:08 p.m.
Subject: Re: Friendsgiving

Hey ladies,

Compromise night sounds fine. Are we still thinking Wythe Hotel? Can we potentially move the drinks into the city? I have a few VC meetings in Silicon Valley, CA, the week before, and I'll be flying straight into the helipads on 34th Street. Maybe Murray Hill for drinks? I won't be able to make the potluck part.

Leave word with my assistant at Nicole The Runway if this is kosh. Thanks!

Nicole

P.S. Btw, I always get VC confused with VD, lol! It would be so much easier if VC was an acronym for something so it was easy to remember!

To: Ali, Katie, Jen, Ashley, Gracie, Caitlin, Nicole
From: Morgan
Date: November 8 at 4:03 p.m.
Subject: Re: Friendsgiving

Hey ladies,

Happy early birthday, G! I wish I could make it, but I'm already out of town for Thanksgiving at that point. I'm renting an Airstream with my cousins and heading home that way -- isn't that amazing? We're going to get some records and homemade mason jar yogurt parfaits, and I might even buy a floppy hat for the occasion. It'll be very Madewell x *Country Living*. Make sure you watch my Insta story! Will miss you gals but excited to hear you'll head to Brooklyn! Don't bother with anything in Williamsburg around Thanksgiving -- it's so amateur. Have you heard of Ridgewood? Text me and I'll drop a pin if you're interested.

Morgan

To: Ali, Katie, Jen, Morgan, Gracie, Caitlin, Nicole
From: Ashley
Date: November 10 at 5:42 p.m.
Subject: Re: Friendsgiving

I'm in! My parents are doing Thanksgiving in NYC this year instead of Connecticut! There was apparently some Styles piece that talked about how New Yorkers were trading in a traditional Thanksgiving dinner and going out to eat at five-star restaurants.

My parents really like staying ahead of the curve in Greenwich, so they thought this was a good opportunity to one-up their friends at the country club! I'm coming along for the ride!

The only thing I'm going to need you ladies to take into consideration is the fact that the morning after I am expected at the horse farm to take the annual family Christmas picture. I can't eat anything with sugar, gluten, carbohydrates, oils, or salt 72 hours prior to any photograph. This card goes out to my daddy's entire mailing list at Citibank and there are potential husbands in that pool.

Thanks for understanding! For whoever is spreadsheet'ing who is bringing what, put me down for baby spinach.

Excited!
Ash

"They want three things: to ride front row, green juice, and to be on the cover of *Vogue*."
—a Racked article about the guy who makes SoulCycle tank tops

P.S. Please see last year's card attached here. Cute, right? :) But also, please send critiques so I can improve for this year.

To: Ali, Katie, Jen, Ashley, Morgan, Gracie, Nicole
From: Caitlin
Date: November 11 at 9:07 a.m.
Subject: Re: Friendsgiving

Hey ladies,

I am unable to attend as I'll be on an e-book tour for my new nonfiction novella, *Get Thin and Rich or Die Trying* -- on sale now!

Happy birthday, Gracie!

Caitlin

"You continue to amaze me." —What The Universe would say to me if she could CaitlinYourLife™

To: Ali, Jen, Ashley, Morgan, Gracie, Caitlin, Nicole
From: Katie
Date: November 14 at 11:54 a.m.
Subject: Re: Friendsgiving

Hey gals,

I am in for this if we can keep it more potluck than party -- I am on a tight deadline as I have started freelance plant watering and have several clients that are counting on me for the holiday weekend. It's actually a really busy time for plants, FYI. I don't get a byline or anything but I am allowed to post pics of the plants on Insta.

LMK if anyone needs any freelance watering!

Katie

To: Katie, Jen, Ashley, Morgan, Gracie, Caitlin, Nicole
From: Ali
Date: November 14 at 4:09 p.m.
Subject: Re: Friendsgiving

Hey Ladies,

That is so cute you have a side hustle now, Katie!! Very entrepreneurial of you! Sidebar: Does anyone know if there's an app where you can tell your friends when they owe you money? That would be sooo great to avoid potential "awkwardness" while still not taking a total loss of hundreds of dollars every time you and your friends go out for brunch or plan a girls' night or like a fun Gal-entine's Day or whatnot lol.

This is such an afterthought, but I just realized Surf Lodge Boy is actually an investor in the Wythe Hotel and might be there for Jen's Brooklyn send-off night? What a small world. Ash -- I'll be joining you on a 72-hour detox for the occasion. I'm not sure about my Thanksgiving plans yet (my stepmom is being such a C U Next Thursday), so tell your parents I'm in! (Parents love me, haha. It's a blessing and a curse.) Plus, I know your dad just finished that big addition on your townhouse so there are probably tons of bedrooms avail. No one will even know I'm there! Let me know what I can bring? Maybe like, those cute napkins with the turkey on them? I can't cook so no one should count on me for food! Yay, can't wait! Unless something comes up last minute, and then I'm so sorry but I'll have to skip this year!! ☹

Anyway, I'm sure that after SoulCycling and avoiding all carbs/fats/nightshades/digital media between now and then, he'll be all like, "Omg, Ali, you look amazing! I just...wow. I forgot how beautiful you are!" And I'll be like, "You look soooo familiar. Remind me where I know you from again?" And he'll be like, "It wasn't over. It still isn't over!" And then we'll make out!

Caitlin, can you resched your tour so you can just Skype in?? I know that everyone appreciates how epically important this night is.

I look forward to you all exceeding my expectations.

xo,
Ali

To: Ali
From: Morgan
Date: November 14 at 4:27 p.m.
Subject: Re: Friendsgiving

Hey Al, quick sidebar, are you mad at me? You asked Caitlin to reschedule her tour but you didn't ask me to reschedule my plans. Do you not want me at the Gracie/Bachelorette #2? Are you upset we're co-MoHs? Are you trying to edge me out? I'm on my period...

To: Katie, Jen, Ashley, Morgan, Gracie, Caitlin, Nicole
From: Ali
Date: November 14 at 5:02 p.m.
Subject: Re: Friendsgiving

Hey Ladies!

First off, Morgan, I'm not upset with you at all! I actually am *relieved* that we are both co-MoHs. I was going to suggest it to Jen! I have so much on my plate -- I'm probably going to get a huge promotion at work, things are heating up with Surf Lodge Boy (he just accepted my LinkedIn request!!!!), and I'm trying very hard to practice work/life balance, which is why I've been stress-crying in the bathroom at work instead of at my desk.

I have an easy workaround for this -- can everyone please text me when they're PMS'ing and I'll add it to our shared google calendar? So far only Nicole and I are on it -- btw: Nicole, your period is super irregular!! Are you still using those birth control pills you bought online from Turkmenistan???

Everyone's in for the Brooklyn night, right? If I don't hear, I assume it's a go! SO excited!!!!

Ali

"You are only as strong the weakest woman you know." —My spinning instructor, Layla

Nov 14, 5:26 PM

Morgan

Hey! Okay good to know...but I didn't email everyone when I sent that to you...so now everyone knows I thought you were mad...That was supposed to be a private convo.

Ali

Sorry! Ever since I saw the James Frey episode of Oprah, it's made me really obsessed with full disclosure and honesty. Should have just texted you. Love ya.

Morgan

Lol.

To: Ali, Katie, Ashley, Morgan, Gracie, Caitlin, Nicole
From: Jen
Date: November 17 at 10:56 a.m.
Subject: Re: Friendsgiving

Hey Ladies,

Since it's November, I would just like to take a moment to say what I am most thankful for this year:

- Brad: I thought I knew what love was...until I met my partner in crime, Brad. I'm just so excited to be his wife and grow old together! All I can say, ladies, is that to feel and experience love like this is COMPLETELY worth the wait! In a way, I think that when you're truly ready to meet The One he'll just show up. It always happens the moment you stop looking for it! It's just so relaxing to wake up every morning with someone who completely adores me and makes me feel totally secure. Since you girls haven't met your Forever Person yet, trust me, it's just because you're not ready for it, and you haven't called him into your life yet! LOL I'm sounding like Caitlin, I'm just so happy and AT PEACE. I wish that all of you girls can experience a love like this one day!

- Helene: I'm so lucky to have a mom that is more like a friend! Helene always has my back -- from paying my rent to providing all of us with Equinox memberships (reminder: they all expire on my wedding day!).

- The 7 women I could never live without who have been my spiritual guides and there for me every step of the way this past year: Maya, Olivia, Samantha, Stacey, Rhiannon,

Julie, and Bevin!! Not only are they my SoulCycle teachers, they are my close friends. I can't imagine life without them!

Your turn! Tell me what you're most thankful for!!

Also -- Morgs + Ali, can you both accompany me to my vag reconstruction/rejuvenation procedure?! I'm sending Ubers for you both! We have to be at the hospital at 4:00 a.m.! I'll spring for coffee!!

Love, Jen

To: Ali, Katie, Jen, Ashley, Morgan, Caitlin, Nicole
From: Gracie
Date: November 17 at 5:02 p.m.
Subject: Re: Friendsgiving

Hey Ladies,

To respond to your prompt Jen, I'd like to say that this year I am really grateful to my therapist, Dr. Judy. Dr. Judy and I have spent a lot of time talking about "boundaries" and the choices we make in our adult lives about who to surround ourselves with. Without getting too into it, I've found that I've been sort of repeating some of the dynamics from my childhood -- things like having a self-involved mom and being the youngest where I was often overlooked and just went along with what was best for the group as a whole. Anyway, as Dr. Judy and I have discussed -- this time in my life is about breaking familiar patterns and focusing on myself and my needs right now. As Dr. Judy said, it's about giving birth to myself, or to the person I'm becoming. To be honest, I didn't totally follow that analogy and kept getting distracted by picturing myself giving birth to an adult version of myself.

But anyway...I think it's best if I take a break from our friend group right now. I have really treasured all the time we've spent together, but I think I need to spend some time on my own/with my boyfriend/with my other friends. The way that my birthday invite went down this year was a huge eye-opener for me. I've tried to pull back a bit, but I think it's time I faced something I've known all along. It's become very obvious that my needs and feelings, even celebrating my own birthday, will never be the priority in this particular group of friends. I have no bad feelings here -- I just think this is the best move for me right now.

I'll still be attending Jen's wedding as a guest, and can't wait to celebrate Jen and Brad's big day. I won't feel awkward at all seeing any of you, and hope you feel the same. I just think it's best if we take some space for now. You can remove me from these future threads.

With love,
Gracie

Nov 17, 5:13 PM

Morgan
OMG Gracie's email!!!! Should I call her??

Jen
I know! :(

I think we should give her some space for now...Bevin always says, "Given space and time, we can renew ourselves."

Morgan
Yeah, about you calling out the 7 women in your life you're most thankful for....

Jen
What?

Morgan
....

Jen
You're confirmed for my vag surgery right??

Morgan
You don't wanna ask Bevin instead??

Jen
Well that would be inappropriate! Right? Hmm.

To: Ali, Katie, Ashley, Morgan, Caitlin, Nicole
From: Jen
Date: November 18 at 9:42 a.m.
Subject: Re: Friendsgiving

Hi ladies,

Like you all probably did, I scheduled an emergency six-hour therapy session with my doctor after reading Gracie's email.

After emerging from that session feeling renewed and energized, I have a few things I want to say to the group.

It doesn't feel good to be victimized for my own happiness.

As much as I really love Gracie and think she brings a level of chill to the spectrum we have here, between all of us, I am hurt by her accusations.

From here on out, I think we should give Gracie some space and no longer CC her on our emails. Because of this, I'm calling off my second bachelorette party. I don't want anyone to think I'm an "attention whore" as Gracie so clearly called me between the lines of her email.

I wish I was in the mood for being thankful. But I'm just so sad. I'm sorry if I am guilty of making this last year all about me. What I am truly guilty of is just being in love. And being happy.

One day I hope to not be burned at the stake for that.

My best,
Jen

To: Katie, Jen, Ashley, Morgan, Caitlin, Nicole
From: Ali
Date: November 18 at 2:43 p.m.
Subject: Re: Friendsgiving

Hey Ladies,

I'll never forget where I was the moment I read Gracie's email. I had just popped into Equinox because I needed to feel tranquil/I was out of lotion and wanted to use some of their Kiehl's. While I'm surprised by the severity of her accusations and low-key character assassination, I think our best course of action is to move on without her. Jen, if you don't want her at your wedding now, I completely support that decision. Maybe Helene should hire security just in case? You and Brad are so happy together, it's not surprising that people are being derailed by it.

I think the best course of action here is to just stay strong. I also charged an "oh hey, where do I know you from again? Yeah, I just look this effortlessly fierce all the time" dress for running into Surf Lodge Boy that I really can't quite afford. I think the important thing here is to not let Gracie win here. We must remain strong in times like these and continue on with our plans. Can I count on my squad??

xo,
Ali

"A good plan violently executed right now is far better than a perfect plan executed next week." —General George S. Patton

To: Ali, Jen, Ashley, Morgan, Caitlin, Nicole
From: Katie
Date: November 19 at 9:12 a.m.
Subject: Re: Friendsgiving

Hey ladies,

This could actually be an amazing story. Like *Spotlight* meets *Mean Girls* meets *Working Girl* meets *The Newsroom* meets *Bridesmaids*. Can I quote these emails on the record?

Lmk, Katie

Nov 27, 7:15 PM

Jen

Hey Ladies! Just had the vag rejuvenation done!! Who wants to see pics??

Nicole

Did they give you extra Vicodin?? Can I have some??

Morgan

If you send pics of your vag, our friendship is over

Ali

Hey! I'm at the Wythe Hotel, where is everyone????

Nicole

I'm at Brother Jimmy's right now!! Come!!!!

Morgan

I am off the grid in an Airstream! Just texting you guys back to let you know I am off the grid

Caitlin

Do they have gluten-free options there?? Can someone ask a waiter??

Ali

I thought you were on an e-book tour, Caitlin??

Caitlin

I am, I just like to know

To: Katie, Jen, Ashley, Morgan, Caitlin, Nicole
From: Ali
Date: November 28 at 7:46 a.m.
Subject: Re: Friendsgiving

Hey Ladies,

So good news/bad news.

Bad news first: I ended up running into Surf Lodge Boy! Unfortunately he was 100% making out with this girl. I obviously took a photo of her and did a reverse search on google images, and I think she's one of the random Bush cousins, but on the Billy Bush side of the family. Say la v!

Which brings me to my good news....I ended up running into one of my dad's friends who just got divorced! At first I was all like, "Oh, hey, Ken. What are you doing here?" But then we got to talking, and he's such a great guy! He's thinking of getting an apartment in the city, which obviously I would help him decorate. I feel so Monica when she dated Richard!!! It's just nice to be with a guy who's really mature! And his youngest is almost in college, and then we'd have so much time to spend together! Can you guys see me as a stepmom?! What are baby boomers into?? Should I get him something from the SkyMall catalog for Christmas?? I'm literally in his bed right now!! He's been on a conference call for the last hour! Cute! Can you all google "Sloan Cabot" -- that's his soon-to-be ex-wife. Please let me know if I'm prettier than her! I know I'm like 20 years younger, but I think she has a Silda Wall Spitzer–type elegance. It's so funny, this time next year we could be planning MY wedding!!!

Jen, I can bring him as my +1 right??

xo,
Ali

"Sorry, this has never happened before." —Ken to me mid-lovemaking last night! I'm assuming he's talking about feeling intense emotions!! SWOON!!!

december

To: Ali, Katie, Ashley, Morgan, Caitlin, Nicole
From: Jen
Date: December 1 at 12:02 a.m.
Subject: My wedding month!!!

To the tune of "Here Comes the Bride"
Dun dun da da...dun DUN da daaaaa...

Hi ladies!

AHHHH! Only 30 sleeps until I am signed, sealed, delivered into the loving arms of my one and only, Bradley! I cannot believe it is already December. This last year literally both flew by and has also crawled along. I have been waiting and dreaming of this day not just since our perfect engagement when he presented me with my beautiful diamond and asked me to "hang out forever" (just like Lamar and Khloe when they got engaged!), but since I was a kid. Morgan knows this, as she planned my playground wedding in the third grade.

And now, here we are. Insane.

I just wanted to check in with some itineraries, details, calorie counts, dress codes, spin schedules, tanning bed recs, weather projections, et al.

You will notice Gracie is not included on the email, because you'll recall she seems to be too overwhelmed by us (???) and called me a selfish bitch in between the lines of her last notice to us. Anyway, similar to how Danielle Staub set an empty place at the table for Dina Manzo even though Dina RSVP'd that she couldn't make it to Danielle's luncheon celebrating her daughter's cover of a trade magazine, I am letting you all know that Gracie isn't on this email and that was all her doing.

Onto the important things!

30-day diets:
Please follow THIS LINK to take you to a curated Pinterest page full of weight-loss tips that only require 3-4 weeks to see amazing results. Be warned, if you haven't been proactively trying to lose weight, do not expect a major loss. We can discuss your lack of planning off thread.

These diets are meant to knock out the last 10-20 lbs. Text me with any Qs. I can vouch personally for the lettuce and yogurt diet as well as the "200-calorie Monday" tip sheet. I don't want any complaints about not being able to indulge in holiday food. Get over it. You can do that next year.

The shoes:
Just to check this off my list, can you all send me a Snapchat showing me that you have purchased and dyed your shoes the correct color? EOD would be great.

The dresses:
Nicole is transporting all of your gowns to my mother's house the day before the rehearsal dinner. You will do last-minute fittings there. To incentivize you, the bridesmaid who has to get the most taken in during that fitting will win a $20 gift certificate to Drybar. Let the Hunger Games begin! LOL!

Rehearsal and rehearsal dinner:
The info for this is in your wedding invites but please note, no +1s are allowed at either event. Thank you!

Day of wedding:
Please be at my parents' at 4:00 a.m. on New Year's Eve, aka 12/31, aka my wedding day. Makeup will start at 4:30 a.m. sharp. Come with a clean, exfoliated face and wet, just-washed hair. I know it will be cold to go outside at 4:00 a.m. with wet hair, but this is really the only way we can make this work. Beauty is pain!!

Am I forgetting anything??
JEN

"A bride is many things. But above all, she is perfect." —me

To: Ali, Katie, Jen, Morgan, Caitlin, Nicole
From: Ashley
Date: December 1 at 9:00 a.m.
Subject: Re: My wedding month!!!

Hi ladies,

So excited for the wedding :) Jen, I wanted to let you know that even though I RSVP'd with a +1, my date, Colin Wilford III, will be unable to make it. Apparently his family does a big New Year's regatta in the South of France every year, and his secretary double-booked him. He said he would normally skip a family event but his grandfather is extremely sick so he wants to spend more time with him in case the will gets an edit pre-death. He's gunning for the family's Rhode Island estate as well as a few homes up and down the coast.

I am definitely down for 200-cal Mondays if anyone wants to buddy up? And I Insta-storied my shoes to you.

Thank you for understanding about me going solo! I hope it doesn't mess up the seating?? I am still so excited either way!

XO,
Ashley

To: Katie, Jen, Ashley, Morgan, Caitlin, Nicole
From: Ali
Date: December 2 at 3:45 p.m.
Subject: Re: My wedding month!!!

Hello #BJLadies!

Thanks for kicking off this thread, Jen! This year has absolutely been the best of times (losing 19 lbs!, getting semi-name-checked in the *New York Times* Styles section, and meeting Ken Baby Boomer <3) and the worst of times (gaining 18.5 lbs :(, the Valentine's Day letdown/super-exciting day for Jen, and meeting Surf Lodge Boy/Tribeca Tristan/Jorts Guy/some guy in my phone as "Dan Harvard Hedge Fund? -- TOXIC DON'T PICK UP!!" Does anyone remember who that is??). Totally unrelated, but Ken has a son in college that I'm like 99.9999% attracted to. I think I'm prob just projecting my white-hot attraction for Ken onto a younger, way more virile, non-dad-bod, funnier, and more-fun-to-hang-out-with package. Such #StepmomProbs, right? Lol.

A few action items for Jen's wedding. Please let me know your status by EOH (end of hour).

1) Diet -- Nic, are you still performing those at-home colonics?? Or was that before Nicole The Runway took off? Can we bring it back for old time's sake? I'm trying to save $$$ this month. I'm anticipating Ken asking me to St. Bart's over Christmas, and I'll obviously need new clothes! Ash -- can you send me some Pinterest options that are like Greenwich in the streets/Darien in the sheets.

2) Shoes! I bought some new sparkly Stuart Weitzmans at a sample sale!!!! I figure since I'm the MoH, it's cool if I wear something to stand out a bit. Since our dresses are all uniform (luv you, Nic/Helene!) I'll be expressing myself via my footwear and cleavage. Everyone else should send over their dyed shoes to Jen today and CC me so I can cross it off my list. Confirming you all went with a low heel no higher than ¼ inch, right?

3) +1s: Totally get no one being able to bring a +1 unless they were in a serious relationship at the time the invites were sent out. I understand if the bridesmaid squad is disappointed, but I totally think that's a fair decision. Just so there's no drama and surprises, I plan on inviting Ken as soon as he invites me to St. Bart's. In fairness, I've known him my entire life since I used to babysit his kids!

4) HAIR! I think it would be really fun if all the bridesmaids did low buns! I am so jealous, I wish I could pull it off. I'll be doing my hair in a beachy wave with extensions, but I seriously wish I could do a low bun instead! You girls are so lucky. I found a blowout artist that once worked on an updo for Blake Lively, so I'll join you ladies for mimosa time!!

5) Nails! Since I'm not sure if they have manicurists in Virginia, can everyone please show up for the weekend with their nails already done? I'm pretty open about what style/color, but I think we should all do a gel French manicure, so as to not take away

attention from Jen. Morgan, I know "nail art" is really big in Brooklyn, so I made an appointment for you to join me at this nail place on the Upper East Side. Fun fact: Nancy Reagan used to have her nails done there too! I'll try to find a Groupon for this place, but I'm not sure if I'll have any luck. You get what you pay for! ;)

6) Jewelry -- All bridesmaids, please purchase earrings (studs only) and bracelets in the gold arena.

7) Rehearsal dinner attire -- Since this is both New Year's Eve Eve and also Virginia, please plan to wear a green cocktail dress and pearls that pay homage to both Jen and Brad's heritage as white Protestant Southerners. I'll update everyone with more specifics later, but this gives you a ballpark to plan for.

8) Prezzies! Can everyone please text me offline and let me know what they are planning to purchase for Brad and Jen as a gift? I have some fun ideas that are off registry! ;)

9) Father-daughter dance! I think you should do "Butterfly Kisses"!!!!!

That's all I can think of for now! Let me know if anyone has any questions! This is going to be the most amazing weekend ever!!!!

Love!!!
Ali

"If you're a bird, I'm a bird." —*The Notebook*

Fun! Hope you girls like these! Note: The above three low-buns are the only approved & sanctioned hair options. YAY!

To: Ali, Katie, Jen, Ashley, Morgan, Caitlin
From: Nicole
Date: December 3 at 4:47 p.m.
Subject: Re: My wedding month!!!

Hey Ladies!

So excited for #BJ4Ever!!! The Nicole The Runway dresses should be in v. shortly!

I'm a bit cash-poor, equity-rich right now -- this is like right after when Steve Jobs invented the Lisa computer right before he invented the iPod. I expect the first round of seed funding to go through in Q1, but the good news is, I am down to barter for old time's sake!

If someone wants to buy my shoes/gold jewelry/manicure, I'd be happy to either gift them with one colonic courtesy of yours truly! OR a 1% share of Nicole The Runway!! LMK if I can crash with someone in VA! Totally unrelated: does anyone know if Jen's uncle Ted will be staying at the Westin also? He seems like a Starwood guy ;)

For a present I am going to gift Jen & Brad a coupon book good for one share of Nicole The Runway when we go public and one couples massage done by me. I downloaded a podcast on how to massage, so it should be pretty intuitive.

So excited for #FirstComesBJThenComesMarriage!!!

x,
Nic!

CEO, Nicole The Runway

To: Ali, Katie, Jen, Ashley, Morgan, Nicole
From: Caitlin
Date: December 4 at 12:05 p.m.
Subject: Re: My wedding month!!!

Dear Friends,

I know the holidays can be a very stressful time -- people tend to take stock of where they are in life vs. where they thought they might be. That disconnect can be really painful.

Let's break down the word "dis-con-nect":

Dis: According to Urban Dictionary, the word "dis" means: to disrespect someone. Example: "When you dis Dre, you dis yourself." (Dr. Dre)
Con: According to Google, the word "con" means: to persuade (someone) to do or believe something, typically by use of a deception.
Nect: ...This actually doesn't mean anything. See above.

I have been there, and I can help. I am here to offer you a limited-time special CaitlinYourLifeHolidayIntervention™. This includes:

- Two affirmation texts per day. (iMessage only. Texting rates apply and will be an additional charge.)
- Special holistic holiday "recipes." Sample: Caitlin's Egg Nog™: Mix one egg white with one part water and a smidge of nutmeg. Serve in a mason jar!
- CaitlinYourLife™ Guide to New Year's Goals. You will receive the password to my Medium post on the best way to set goals for the new year that you will actually keep!

I am also available to do Instagram consultations. I will peruse your Instagram feed and offer you my honest, expert opinion on how you can better build your brand to align with your goals and soul's purpose.

The price for all of this is usually $1,020, but I am offering a special Friends & Family discount so the cost is just $1,000.

Don't feel strife. CaitlinYourLife.

In light,
Caitlin

CEO, CaitlinYourLife™

To: Ali, Katie, Ashley, Morgan, Caitlin, Nicole
From: Jen
Date: December 4 at 12:40 p.m.
Subject: Re: My wedding month!!!

Hey Ladies!

Caitlin, can you please stop spamming us with CaitlinYourLife stuff here?? Or can you at least email us off thread? This is my WEDDING THREAD to be used for serious wedding business only! I just don't want us all to needlessly spam each other's inboxes :)

For +1s, since my parents are inviting so many relatives/fellow board members (they're on like a dozen boards each, ha) -- unforch we really need to limit who can bring a +1. Since you all are my special girls though, we came up with the following guidelines. Just don't tell any of the other guests! :)

You are allowed to bring a +1 if your +1 meets the following criteria:

- Both Brad and I have met him on at least 3 separate occasions.
- You have been in an exclusive relationship for at least 12 consecutive calendar months.
- I have never hooked up with him at any point. (I'm defining "hooking up" as going by the spirit of the law versus the letter of the law. Please text me for individual clarifications, and I'll let you know if I count it as a hookup or not. Ahh, college was fun!)
- Your +1 willingly calls you his "girlfriend" and has defined your relationship on Facebook and has at least 3 Instagram portraits of you.

Can everyone please confirm they've purchased their shoes/accessories??

Btw, our apartment is bursting at the seams with all the registry presents we've been receiving. Can I store some KitchenAid mixers at someone's place?? We keep getting them!

So excited/so stressed!!!

Love, Jen

To: Nicole
BCC: Everyone Nicole Knows
From: Nicole
Date: December 7 at 3:00 p.m.
Subject: An important message from NICOLE THE RUNWAY

Dear Friends and Family and Exes of NICOLE THE RUNWAY,

This holiday season, it's important to remember community members in need. We want to remind you all that starting a business as a woman is extremely difficult, and Nicole The Runway has fallen on hard times this Christmas season. If you can find it in your hearts, we have set up a GoFundMe for our intrepid SHE-E-O, Nicole, to help lift this burden.

Your tax-deductible donation will ensure Nicole can still live a normal, happy life as a 20-something in the Big Apple. We are seeking $25,000 to cover the high costs of rent, cocktails, Ubers, and haute couture.

Thank you for your generosity this holiday season, and may your days be merry and bright.

Your friends at Nicole The Runway

To: Ali, Katie, Ashley, Morgan, Caitlin, Nicole
From: Jen
Date: December 7 at 8:00 p.m.
Subject: Re: My wedding month!!!

Hi all!

Can I put someone on hashtag duty #hashtagduty for the night of? You just have to basically follow everyone at the wedding on Insta and make sure their photos are tagged appropriately.

LMK! Would mean so much to me! And I promise it's way cooler than being stuck on the guestbook like Miranda in that episode of *Sex and the City* where Carrie's speech is a poem.

xo,
Jen

To: Ali, Katie, Ashley, Morgan, Caitlin, Nicole
From: Jen
Date: December 7 at 8:50 p.m.
Subject: Re: My wedding month!!!

I just got a few photos of the shoes and everything is wrong, wrong, wrong. Can everyone hop on a conference call right now?

Thanks,
J

To: Ali, Katie, Ashley, Morgan, Caitlin, Nicole
From: Jen
Date: December 7 at 8:51 p.m.
Subject: Re: My wedding month!!!

Please answer my emails!!!

Jen

To: Ali, Katie, Ashley, Morgan, Caitlin, Nicole
From: Jen
Date: December 7 at 8:52 p.m.
Subject: Re: My wedding month!!!

Dial in is 1-802-555-6453 ID: 2914662109578246824. Then #. Then #27. Then hold until you hear the prompt.

I am waiting!!
J

To: Ali, Katie, Jen, Ashley, Morgan, Caitlin
From: Nicole
Date: December 9 at 8:15 a.m.
Subject: Re: My wedding month!!!

Hey Ladies!

So sorry for the delay, I just saw this email! I'm on the call now -- where is everyone??

Gotta jump off -- can someone send over notes?

Btw, I'm putting this out there into the Universe: I am now available for speaking engagements. Tech events, women conventions, or even financial institutions (KA-CHING!). Do any of you know who books the speakers for: Lehman Brothers, Bear Stearns, or Washington Mutual??

Love,
Nicole

CEO, Nicole The Runway

To: Ali, Katie, Ashley, Morgan, Caitlin, Nicole
From: Jen
Date: December 9 at 8:45 a.m.
Subject: Re: My wedding month!!!

Hey Ladies,

No prob that you all couldn't join my fire-drill conference call two days ago -- though in the future, please always respond to my emails within 5 minutes, just so I know you're alive, lol! Truly, this is unacceptable!

Unfortunately none of you have purchased the shoes I asked for MONTHS ago. I'm not really sure what happened, but PLEASE PLEASE if the inventory ran out, or you weren't able to purchase EXACTLY what I asked for, just let me know so I can make other arrangements! Brad and I didn't invite 3/5s of his uncles for the express reason that I don't want anything to go wrong or be a surprise on my BIG DAY, so it's really important we just have complete transparency and nonstop communication as issues arise.

I was able to source another pair of shoes I like (WHEW!). I tried to find something that would look good on everyone and that wasn't too pricey! I found Stuart Weitzman Swarovski-encrusted peep-toe d'orsay 2" heels. They are currently on sale for $175 (plus tax and shipping, which is prob like $5). Please purchase the OVERNIGHT shipping option. If I don't hear from everyone in the next hour, I am purchasing them for everyone myself and will invoice you on Venmo. That's a last resort since I don't know everyone's shoe size, so I will just pick a size 7, which everyone can squeeze into for one night. I NEED everyone to confirm with me ASAP about this, I just don't have the bandwidth for another crisis.

Love,
Jen

To: Katie, Jen, Ashley, Morgan, Caitlin, Nicole
From: Ali
Date: December 10 at 9:09 a.m.
Subject: Re: My wedding month!!!

Hey Ladies!

Sorry, just saw this. Cute shoes! You can order mine in a size 7.5, and we'll call it even for your copy of *Ice Queens Melt Hearts* + the deposit for last Valentine's. Thanks, hon!

Btw, I'm totally available to both Maid of Honor and also officiate your wedding. According to Facebook, Surf Lodge Boy's ex-gf from junior year of college just officiated at her friend's wedding, and honestly, I think I'd be way better at it than she was. I've never met her, but I feel like I know her completely from all her Facebook posts that are semi-public.

If Helene is still insisting on a church wedding (no disrespect, but so '80s), I can probably get ordained as a Catholic priest online. Let me know!

xo,
Ali

"Back to back mtgs. Miss u 2. —Sent from a BlackBerry." —Ken's text to me this morning! It's all going according to plan.

To: Ali, Jen, Ashley, Morgan, Caitlin, Nicole
From: Katie
Date: December 10 at 1:29 p.m.
Subject: Re: My wedding month!!!

Hey Ladies!

Just circling back on the +1 situation. I had my coworker send me a photo from her floor seats at the Knicks, which I then Instagrammed to make it seem like I was there, and Topher liked it this morning. I've just been so busy with my life, and totally forgot it was Topher's favorite team. Anyway, since your wedding will also literally be our anniversary, I'm assuming it's okay to bring Topher as my +1. Plus, being invited to a wedding without a +1 is just cruel. And cheap. And discriminatory.

Thanks in advance!
Katie

To: Ali, Katie, Jen, Ashley, Caitlin, Nicole
From: Morgan
Date: December 12 at 4:34 p.m.
Subject: Re: My wedding month!!!

Hey all!

Just catching up on all of this. Everything sounds good. Excited for the big day. Jen approved my shoes (thanks, girl!) so I am feeling pretty set and happy to help anyone who may feel otherwise. I got my shoes vintage at this super cute sixth-hand store in Ridgewood, and I think they have an extra pair in a size 9. Does that work for anyone? I can pick up tonight on my way to get my hair cut. Finally biting the bullet and getting a pixie cut.

Will send you pics (aka PIX...get it?)!
Morgan

To: Ali, Katie, Ashley, Morgan, Caitlin, Nicole
From: Jen
Date: December 12 at 4:35 p.m.
Subject: Re: My wedding month!!!

MORGAN, CALL ME AS SOON AS YOU GET THIS. PLEASE DON'T CUT YOUR HAIR. I AM CALLING YOU RIGHT NOW, PICK UP.
JEN

To: Ali, Katie, Ashley, Morgan, Caitlin, Nicole
From: Jen
Date: December 12 at 4:40 p.m.
Subject: Re: My wedding month!!!

MORGAN PLEASE PICK UP THE PHONE OR CALL ME BACK

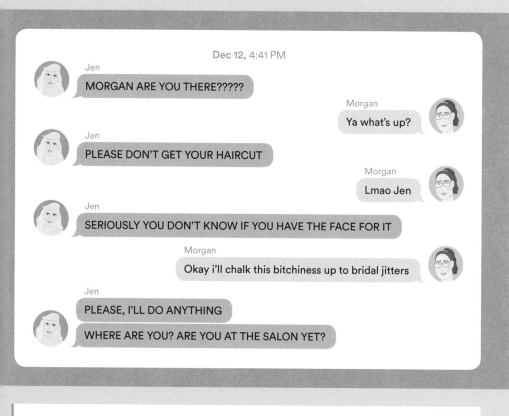

To: Ali, Jen, Ashley, Morgan, Caitlin, Nicole
From: Katie
Date: December 12 at 6:22 p.m.
Subject: Re: My wedding month!!!

Update. Topher is "busy" (which as we all know is an extreme move from the *Why Men Love Bitches* artillery that I respect even if it is vice versa). And I was like, no problem! You're my, like, third choice, haha. Problem is now I can't show up without a +1 and he has to be hot, rich, and higher up than director level in a big-name bank. Send me names and numbers, girls!

Katie

To: Ali, Katie, Jen, Ashley, Morgan, Caitlin, Nicole
From: Helene and Bob Carrington
Date: December 12 at 6:40 p.m.
Subject: FIND MORGAN

Hi Ladies,

Trying to get through to Morgan before her hair appointment. Can someone try her office/cell/home phone/neighbors/super/landlord? Trying to take this off Jen's to-do list. Thanks!

Helene

CEO of the Carrington Family

To: Ali, Katie, Jen, Ashley, Morgan, Caitlin
From: Nicole
Date: December 12 at 6:43 p.m.
Subject: Re: My wedding month!!!

Morgan, stop what you're doing!!!!!!!! Remember that cautionary tale where there was a girl who was totally cute with normal girl hair and then she got a pixie cut and everyone hated her for it??! See: *Felicity*, season 2. Where are you?? I'm literally googling "hair salon in Brooklyn" and calling each one. WRITE ME BACK!!!!!!!!!!!!!!

~Nicole

To: Katie, Jen, Ashley, Morgan, Caitlin, Nicole
From: Ali
Date: December 12 at 6:47 p.m.
Subject: Re: My wedding month!!!

Hey Ladies!

Crisis averted! I went into your phones during SoPu and gave myself access on your Find

My Friends app, so I know where you all are at all times. Before you all get upset with me, remember what Tom Hanks said in *You've Got Mail*, "It's not personal, it's business."

Because of my ingenuity, I was able to track Morgan down at some salon in Bushdick or Bushwick or whatever it's called -- and told her that according to the maid of honor/bridesmaid social contract, none of us can change our looks in the slightest without the bride's approval.

Things that are allowed:
• Losing 5 lbs
• Whitening your teeth

Things that are NOT allowed:
• Cutting or coloring your hair in ANY way unless Jen has given her approval (which must be asked for at least 10 business days in advance)
• Wearing a nail polish in any shade besides the designated color -- it will look really bad in photos and stand out!
• NO TATTOOS OF ANY KIND (Morgan's dolphin tramp stamp and Nicole's star foot tattoo are the TWO exceptions and will be grandfathered in).

I look forward to your continued cooperation.

Does anyone want to go in on a juice cleanse with me? According to a viral facebook post, doing a juice cleanse with a friend gives you a 14% chance of losing an extra pound!!

Love!
Ali

"Sometimes divorce isn't just for romantic relationships." —The Friend Cleanse: How to Rid Your Life of Toxic People in Just Twelve Hours

To: Katie, Ashley, Morgan, Caitlin, Nicole, Patrick, Daniel, Sandip, Trevor, Lachlan, Ken
From: Ali
Date: December 15 at 10:00 p.m.
Subject: WEDDING DANCE FOR BRAD AND JEN

Hey Ladies & Gentleman, Bridesmaids & Groomsmen,

I know we're all looking forward to #BJ4Ever #GiveMeThatBJ! I wanted to write to everyone because I had a really fun idea! I think we should all plan a choreographed dance to surprise the future Mrs. and Mr. on their big day!

It should be really easy and low-key. Let me know who is in!

Song: Something fun like "Single Ladies" or "I've Had the Time of My Life" or "Walking on Sunshine"!

Rehearsals: The choreographer for *Hamilton* is willing to choreograph our dance!!!!!!! There will be 2 eight-hour rehearsals that NO ONE can miss. They're scheduled for the following days:
December 24, 3:00 p.m.-11:00 p.m.
December 25, 10:00 a.m.-6:00 p.m.

Price: Only $500/person -- this is a steal, because this experience is literally priceless!

Please write back and let me know who is in! Remember: this is a top secret surprise!!!

x,
Ali

Maid of Honor, #BJ4Ever

To: Ali, Katie, Ashley, Morgan, Caitlin, Nicole, Daniel, Sandip, Trevor, Lachlan, Ken
From: Patrick
Date: December 15 at 10:19 p.m.
Subject: Re: WEDDING DANCE FOR BRAD AND JEN

Can't, sorry. --patrick

To: Ali, Katie, Ashley, Morgan, Caitlin, Nicole, Daniel, Sandip, Patrick, Lachlan, Ken
From: Trevor
Date: December 15 at 10:25 p.m.
Subject: Re: WEDDING DANCE FOR BRAD AND JEN

Out of town for holidays. See everyone on 12-31.
Trevor

To: Ashley, Caitlin, Nicole, Katie, Morgan, Ali, Daniel, Trevor, Patrick, Lachlan, Ken
From: Sandip
Date: December 15 at 10:34 p.m.
Subject: Re: WEDDING DANCE FOR BRAD AND JEN

Not free those nights. Sorry, all. ~S

To: Ali, Katie, Ashley, Morgan, Nicole, Patrick, Daniel, Sandip, Trevor, Lachlan, Ken
From: Caitlin
Date: December 16 at 7:30 a.m.
Subject: Re: WEDDING DANCE FOR BRAD AND JEN

Hey ladies and dudes,

Happy to do a dance for sure! It's so vintage 2009, and I think Jen will really love it. One small problem with the schedule: this year Christmas falls on the 25th which means Christmas Eve falls on the 24th. I know this may bring conflict for me as my family celebrates the holiday, so I wanna make sure to put that out there early on.

Ali, are there any other days you think might work for the *Hamilton* guy?

In the meantime, check out my blog about #cleanholidayeating. I think you'll all really enjoy it! I included some of my favorite exclusive tips like: drink water instead of eating food, as well as instructions for my "smell, don't eat!" methodology. Guys, make sure you click! My tips do not see gender!

All best,
Caitlin

Disclaimer: Caitlin and CaitlinYourLife owns the copyright to the hashtag #cleanholidayeating. Any infringement upon this will be punishable to the full extent of the law, and would also be really bad karma.

To: Ali, Ashley, Morgan, Caitlin, Nicole
From: Katie
Date: December 19 at 7:30 a.m.
Subject: DO NOT FWD TO JEN OR BRAD! IS GRACIE ENGAGED?

Hey Ladies,

Quick Q, did anyone see Gracie's latest Insta? I still follow (for intel, obv!). I so don't care at all, but her last post said Ryan surprised her with the last-min weekend trip, and then she's been quiet since then. You don't think he proposed to her, do you?? I just don't know if I can handle anyone else's happiness right now. It's really hard not to take it personally.

Katie

Dec 19, 9:15 AM

Ali

It would be so effing insane if Gracie got engaged during your wedding year.

Jen

Honestly, I am not even thinking about it right now. It's fine. I am in a good place.

Ali

Well I'm not. Should I ask Ken if one of his retired cop friends can do a private investigation? Should I casually text G to see if she divulges? I'll take screenshots!

Jen

Ali, I don't care! It's fine! I am trying to be zen Jen and you're taking it to another level. Wait actually...maybe yes on the screenshots.

Dec 20, 4:35 PM

Jen

Since the wedding is so soon I am moving to texts so that we can be in touch immediately. That being said, does everyone have their shoes individually wrapped in tissue paper and in their original bags? Please do not fuck around with these when you pack

Katie
Yep!!! :) :)

Ashley
I do!!!!!

Caitlin
Yes yayyy!

Nicole
Obvi girl <3

Ali

I actually reminded everyone about this the other day so I am so glad to hear everyone is taking me seriously

Jen

Morgan, you there?

Morgan
Yes, sorry! Garment bag, check! Love u!

Katie
SOOOOOOO EXCITED

Ashley
CANNOT WAIT

Caitlin
CANNOT WAIT MORE

Dec 20, 11:02 PM

Nicole
Does anyone have a hairdryer they are definitely bringing to the wedding? Mine hasn't been the same since SoPu

Ashley
I can bring one

Katie
Me

Morgan
I have one

Caitlin
I can bring mine

Nicole
Great! Thanks gals

Dec 20, 11:50 PM

Jen
My mom wants to know if anyone wants to give a toast at the rehearsal dinner

Ali
Me!

Did she say I could also give one at the wedding?

I'd like to do both

You there?

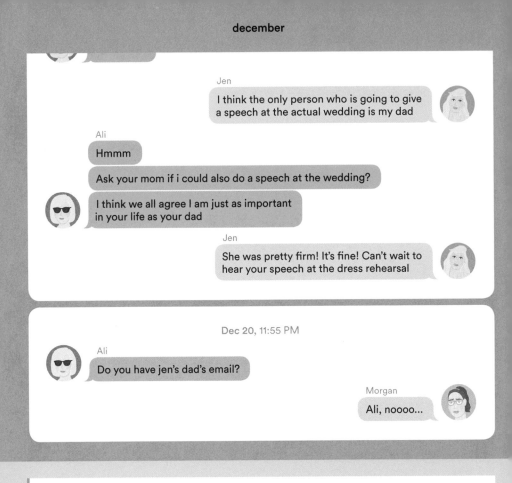

Jen

I think the only person who is going to give a speech at the actual wedding is my dad

Ali

Hmmm

Ask your mom if i could also do a speech at the wedding?

I think we all agree I am just as important in your life as your dad

Jen

She was pretty firm! It's fine! Can't wait to hear your speech at the dress rehearsal

Dec 20, 11:55 PM

Ali

Do you have jen's dad's email?

Morgan

Ali, noooo...

To: Jen
From: Kelly
Date: December 21 at 8:01 a.m.
Subject: Your wedding and some news...

Hey girl,

I hate to do this in an email but I wasn't sure if it was too early to call. My husband's father passed away unexpectedly last night, and we're going to have to extend our trip home for the holidays into the new year for obviously bittersweet reasons.

I am so sorry to have to miss your wedding, and I was so looking forward to you meeting John! Not to mention seeing everyone from back home again and, of course, your parents...I really hate that we have to do this and for such sad reasons.

I wish you the most beautiful day ever and a lifetime of love. Hopefully we can try to plan a weekend or something in the next year (before kids, okay?!). Love you, girl. Congratulations, and Merry Christmas.

All best,
Kelly

To: Katie, Ali, Morgan, Nicole, Ashley, Caitlin
From: Jen
Date: December 21 at 9:48 a.m.
Subject: FWD: Your wedding and some news…

hey ladies,

okay well this fucking sucks (see attached email). my friend from high school, kelly, can't make it anymore because her father-in-law is dead as of last night. i know I'm being harsh, but i am just super stressed out. sorry this is so messy i am literally typing with one hand not looking at the phone while getting a facial.

unforch i had put kelly and her husband john at a table with my extremely evangelical cousin anna and will need a diplomatic replacement by EOD. does anyone have the b list invite spreadsheet handy? i need either a republican or…okay i need a republican.

is one week before a new year's eve wedding too late to try to pass off an invite as intentional? please let me know, i'll be out of this facial by 10:30am.

Jen

If you want know my current emotional state, please refer to the hit song "Torn" by Natalie Imbruglia, as seen on TRL circa 1997

To: Jen, Nicole, Ali, Katie, Ashley, Caitlin
From: Morgan
Date: December 21 at 10:06 a.m.
Subject: Re: FWD: Your wedding and some news…

Oh no, Kelly Mittson's father-in-law? That's really sad. I'll have to reach out. Jen, should we send her flowers? I probably haven't talked to her since 11th grade, but I would feel bad if I didn't acknowledge this loss, and she knew I knew because I was in this wedding!

Morgan

To: Morgan, Nicole, Ali, Katie, Ashley, Caitlin
From: Jen
Date: December 21 at 11:11 a.m.
Subject: Re: FWD: Your wedding and some news...

Morgan, great idea. Who should get an invite now -- who will both not care that they're b-list and also definitely come AND be nice to my weird cousin?

~J

To: Morgan, Nicole, Jen, Katie, Ashley, Caitlin
From: Ali
Date: December 21 at 12:04 p.m.
Subject: Re: FWD: Your wedding and some news...

Hey Ladies,

This is actually a blessing in disguise! Not your friend's father-in-law dying. That's really sad. Especially around the holidays. But it's a good reminder to us, the living, to not take any single moment for granted. As Caitlin's Instagram motto constantly reminds us: All we have is this moment.

This is our chance to infuse your wedding with some last-minute diversity. I'm thinking less country club Virginia types and more beach club Hamptons types! Also, FYI, Ken can't make your wedding. He didn't invite me for the holidays, which is totally cool because I was looking for a reason to break up with him anyway. I know I've said this a million times before, but I really truly am going to use this time to focus on myself and make my life as great as it can be. That said, we need to be really strategic in who we invite.

Tier B Dream List
- Tracy M: She runs a secret supper club for ultra-successful entrepreneurial young women. I heard a rumor that one of her cocktail parties was where a cycling aficionado and a musician met one another and came up with the idea of cycling in dark rooms to loud music. Iconic. It might help if you ask her to officiate the wedding, so it seems less weird you're inviting her so last minute. I'd be happy to make an intro. Her website has a "contact me" form on it.

- Cheryl V: She's the scion to this French cheese family. The moment certain types of unpasteurized cheeses become legal in the US, anyone who invests with them now will be overnight billionaires. My dad's friend has an in at the FDA, I really think this could be the moment to strike!

- Surf Lodge Boy: He really likes you and Brad! Remember that time we bumped into each other in Union Square? After you both walked away, I asked what he thought of you and he said, "They seem cool." Would be so funny if we ended up together and then your wedding is the first of a lifetime of double dates together!

- Barbour Jacket Boy (I think his name is Charles?): We hooked up after your bridal shower -- can Helene ask your country club manager for the names and addresses of men under 35 who own a Barbour jacket and also talk about golf as they reach climax?

Let me know! Happy to put out feelers! I can start inviting people via text!

xo, Ali

To: Morgan, Nicole, Jen, Katie, Ashley, Ali
From: Caitlin
Date: December 21 at 3:25 p.m.
Subject: Re: FWD: Your wedding and some news...

Hey Ladies,

I'm so sorry to hear of your friend Kelly's father-in-law's journey into the next spiritual plane. If I can be of assistance during this difficult time, please feel free to pass along my mantra specifically designed to help with the grieving process:

"Death is simply your soul telling the Universe TTYL." (™ CaitlinYourLife)

How about you invite Sherri Gold?! I have some ideas I'd love to bounce off of her.

The light in me acknowledges the light in you,

Caitlin

Founder, CaitlinYourLife™

To: Jen, Morgan, Ali, Katie, Ashley, Caitlin
From: Nicole
Date: December 23 at 3:27 p.m.
Subject: Re: FWD: Your wedding and some news...

Hey Ladies!

Everything's totally cool, but if it's all right I prefer we don't invite Sherri Gold until my lawyer tells me we can be in contact again, once litigation ends. We can invite my lawyer actually! He's a 1L at this online law school, and since I can't exactly pay his hourly fee right now, it would be cool to pay him via other means (i.e. the raw bar station during your cocktail hour -- he LOVES shrimp!).

Who's down to carpool to VA together?? Whoever is the first to volunteer to let me crash in their hotel room gets 5 shares of Nicole The Runway!!!

xo,
Nicole

To: Nicole, Morgan, Ali, Katie, Ashley, Caitlin
From: Jen
Date: December 23 at 7:46 p.m.
Subject: Re: FWD: Your wedding and some news...

Hey ladies,

I have it figured out. I'm going to send a last-minute invite to my favorite Soul instructor, Moon. Moon is a 5-year veteran of the company and loves organic yogurt, eastern grains, Buddhism as an aesthetic (though Moon is agnostic, she believes we are all gods inside), henna, sustainable farming, and, of course, Kelly Clarkson. Weirdly enough, she is NOT a vegetarian, so we won't have to shift Kelly and John's double beef entree order and, therefore, we save money (I'm so into finance!).

Before anyone freaks, I want to get in front of the story (that should be a familiar turn of phrase, Katie!) and let you know I am inviting Moon, her husband, Bartholemew, and their two sons, Ranger and Park. I know I didn't allow any of you +1s but I feel like since it's somewhat last minute AND the holidays, she may be more inclined to come if I invite her family.

So the way this will work is Caitlin and Ashley will take Kelly and John's seats at table 18, and, if they RSVP yes, Moon, Bart, Ranger, and Park will join us at the bridal table. I feel that having children really close to me for such an important milestone will help project my own fertility for the future of my family. Moon would say that's me "finding my light." You guys are going to love her. Especially you, Caitlin! You both love blogs and kale.

Hope this all makes sense! I am so zany. Tomorrow is Christmas Eve, wow! Hope everyone enjoys their time with their families, but please remember you're on call :)

Love and Light,
Jen (almost a bride)

To: Nicole, Morgan, Ali, Jen, Ashley, Caitlin
From: Katie
Date: December 23 at 9:11 p.m.
Subject: Re: FWD: Your wedding and some news...

Okay, I feel like this is almost more confusing now! But it's your wedding, Jen, and I won't cry (even though I want to!). If you're asking why I'm crying, it's because I just watched *When Harry Met Sally* and the part when Meg Ryan is dragging a Christmas tree across the Upper West Side by herself because Harry won't allow himself to confront his own feelings is hitting a little too close to home this holiday season. It's so fucking relatable for a vintage film! All I want to do is listen to James Taylor and kill myself. :(This is not a cry for help, but it is. Should I try pitching a breakup piece somewhere? Caitlin, can you send me some contacts?

Also, Jen, if Moon and her children and husband can't come, do you think I should just invite Topher's friend Pete? Like, "to send a message" to Topher? LMK...about to send him a LinkedIn message.

Katie

To: Katie, Morgan, Ali, Jen, Ashley, Caitlin
From: Nicole
Date: December 23 at 11:08 p.m.
Subject: Re: FWD: Your wedding and some news...

Hey ladies,

Last minute emergency. I lost one of my shoes. I had it, and now I don't. I think my mom's dog ate it. She just adopted him from one of those rescue vans that's like an ice cream truck but it's puppies, and they drive into your community and you feel guilty until you take like, 6 of them home. Anyway, she just took in a pup named Roscoe, and he's sort of a disaster. Apparently he had a really traumatic life, and his owner only had him to try to get Instagram famous, and when it didn't work out she ditched him at a puppy daycare. Like never came back to get him. The whole thing is so sad, but I am still missing a shoe. Any ideas?

Should Nicole The Runway make shoes?? I prob cannot get a prototype before Christmas day, but I could get an old shoe and decorate it or paint it? Please advise. Anyone who helps me gets half a share of Nicole The Runway!

Nicole

"I'm an acquired taste. If you don't like me, acquire some taste!" —Ramona Singer

To: Ali, Katie, Ashley, Morgan, Caitlin, Nicole
From: Jen
Date: December 31 at 1:04 a.m.
Subject: MY WEDDING IS TODAY

It's the day of the wedding y'all!

I have taken 4 Ritalins, and there is no way I am sleeping tonight! Thanks, gals, for making my rehearsal night an evening to remember! I will even forgive you, Nicole, for wearing white! Even though are you fucking serious? Good thing you're my BM, or I would be seriously worried you'd be showing up tomorrow in bridal.

Anyway tonight was so amazing. Did you guys like the food? Did you like the wine? Did you think the lighting scheme worked well? Did you notice when my Great Aunt Helene (my mother's named after her) passed out at the table and my cousins had to carry her back up to her hotel room? Or were you having too much fun to care? Did you think the speeches were good? Did you have a favorite? The whole night just flashed before me. Here's hoping I can really take tomorrow in and appreciate every moment.

That being said, it's now past midnight and you all will be arriving for hair and makeup in mere hours. Did you all do face masks before going to bed to keep down the puffiness? Is anyone else awake and want to go on a run to shed 1 last lb? Haha, but really -- anyone????

Jen

"I do!" —Me in 16 hours

To: Katie, Jen, Ashley, Morgan, Caitlin, Nicole
From: Ali
Date: December 31 at 3:54 a.m.
Subject: Re: MY WEDDING IS TODAY

Ahhh good morning, gals!

About to head out to meet everyone for hair and makeup. The sun should be up soon (2-3 hours). So fun! I have already done a YouTube fitness video in my hotel room and paced around enough to rack up 35,000 steps on my Fitbit!

Jen, happy happy wedding day, girl. I am so thrilled to stand by your side today as one of the most important people in your life and watch you marry the man of your dreams. Brad is SO lucky to have you, and I know I speak for everyone when I say that all of the diets, SoulCycles, acupuncture, Botox injections, STDs, STIs, DUIs, and UTIs were worth it. This is YOUR DAY, so enjoy.

Because you asked me for the text of my speech last night I put it in here:

J *is for* jenerous. E *is for* elegant. N *is for* never *a bad friend. Jen.*

Jen, we've been friends for so long, and it's almost sort of unbelievable that I am standing here today as you get ready to marry your soulmate. You are a sister, friend, granddaughter, daughter, niece, cousin, and Protestant. You are a public-relations maven, a social-media guru, and an interior-design whisperer. You are so unique and amazing, and I am so proud of you.

Now. Not many people know this about Jen, but there was a time we didn't think we'd make it to this most blessed day. See, our friend Brad over there was playing super hard to get from 2009 onward, and a lot of us were like, Jen, you can do better, and honestly, a lot of people have said his dick isn't even that big! (Pause for laughter!!!) We never confirmed...no blushing, you two! (Pause for more laughter!!!) But as the years went on, we saw something of Brad's that was truly humongous. His heart. (Pause for AWWW!!!)

There were definitely moments on life's rocky shore that tested the commitments of Brad and Jen, like when Jen's ex-boyfriend Gchatted her two summers ago and asked to meet for a secret two-martini lunch, or when Brad faked a business trip and pretended he didn't remember Valentine's Day (pause for AWWWW, as everyone knows this is how he proposed!), and also the few Christmases where Brad didn't really buy Jen anything good, but IN THE END...Brad's huge, beating, throbbing heart proved to be perfectly Jen-sized. I know that when I get married in probably 9-18 months' time, I will be standing at the altar wearing a beautiful couture gown, surrounded by friends, family, and expensive flowers, 12-20 lbs lighter than I am today, and hoping that the love I share with my fiancé is half as amazing as yours, Jen.

So raise a glass, everyone, to a beautiful couple, and may you always laugh, cry, celebrate, and dance like nobody's watching. As David Matthews once said, "Celebrate we will, because life is short, but sweet, for certain."

Love you guys. Cheers!

By the way, is your dad's friend Robert (I think?) single? He had a bare ring finger but just making sure. Hoping we get sync'd up tonight on the dance floor! Anyway just let me know his deal whenever you get a chance today! Btw, I just want to say before today gets crazy -- I love you girls!!! It's our first wedding!!!! Who's next??

xo,
Ali

"Love actually is all around." —Hugh Grant, *Love Actually* <3

To: Ali, Katie, Ashley, Morgan, Caitlin, Nicole
From: Jen
Date: December 31 at 4:00 a.m.
Subject: Re: MY WEDDING IS TODAY

Hey Ladies!

I can't believe I get to marry my best friend today!!!! Really quick, last night I got some last-minute texts that some people can't make it now (so rude!!) -- but since we're already paying for the headcount, I'd like to invite some people from my Tier D list. Do you think they'll know they were a last-min invite?? Maybe we can all play it off like how celebrities invite friends over for a last minute party and then surprise them with a wedding (see: Jennifer Aniston & Justin Theroux / Julia Roberts & Danny Moder). Do you think everyone could keep that secret?

Anyway, just texted you all my Tier D list. Please let me know when the guests are confirmed. It's only a 5-hour train ride from New York, so please contact my Tier D right away, so they have time.

Thanks, girls!!!

Is everyone on their way?! You're all supposed to be here right now!!! I'll call all of you now to make sure you didn't oversleep...

Love,
Jen

A-List   B-List   C-List

Mr. and Mrs. Jonathan Smith
42 Hamilton Court
Cos Cob, CT 06807

Lisa Parker
24 25 Park ave
New York, NY 11210

Kaila M. & Guest
c/o Soul Cycle
103 Warren St
New York, NY 10282

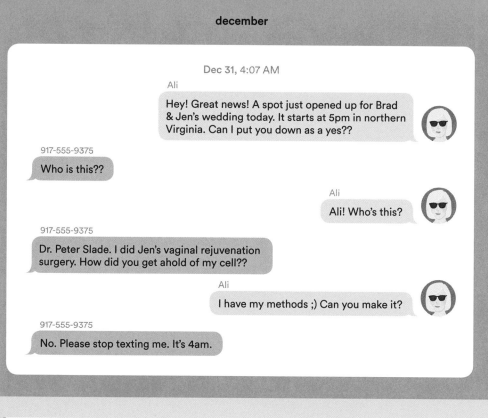

Dec 31, 4:07 AM

Ali

Hey! Great news! A spot just opened up for Brad & Jen's wedding today. It starts at 5pm in northern Virginia. Can I put you down as a yes??

917-555-9375

Who is this??

Ali

Ali! Who's this?

917-555-9375

Dr. Peter Slade. I did Jen's vaginal rejuvenation surgery. How did you get ahold of my cell??

Ali

I have my methods ;) Can you make it?

917-555-9375

No. Please stop texting me. It's 4am.

To: Ali, Katie, Jen, Ashley, Morgan, Caitlin
From: NicoleCEONicoleTheRunway@gmail.com
Date: December 31 at 4:50 a.m.
Subject: Re: MY WEDDING IS TODAY

Hey Ladies!

Sorry for the last minute notice, but I have some conf calls for Nicole The Runway this morning, so I'm going to just do a YouTube tutorial on wedding hair. See you all soon, can't wait!!

x,
Nic

CEO, Nicole The Runway

To: Ali, Katie, Jen, Ashley, Morgan, Nicole, Helene and Bob Carrington
From: Caitlin
Date: December 31 at 12:34 p.m.
Subject: Re: MY WEDDING IS TODAY

Hi Helene + Ladies,

Just confirming the vegan, lampshade-free, non-protein, non-GMO meal I requested on my RSVP card? I'm sure you're super busy right now, but please confirm this when you get a sec!

So excited!!

Namaste,
Caitlin

CaitlinYourLife™
Author of the e-pamphlet How Your Soul Can Thrive During Toxic Weddings!
Boring legalese: How Your Soul Can Thrive During Toxic Weddings! is a work of fiction. Names, characters, quirks, country clubs, mothers, exes, places, events and incidents are either the products of the author's imagination or used in a fictitious manner. Any resemblance to actual persons, living or dead, or actual events is purely coincidental.

To: Jen, Ali, Katie, Ashley, Morgan, Caitlin, Nicole
From: Gracie
Date: December 31 at 2:15 p.m.
Subject: Happy wedding day!!!

Hey Jen + Girls,

I want to wish you the best wedding day ever!!!! What a perfect day!

It's the last day of the year (I know it's cheesy, but I've been taking stock), and I just wanted to say I'm so lucky to have you all in my life. I know we drive each other nuts sometimes, but I'm still so glad we're friends (You make my life much more fun. And crazy.). I've missed you all the last few weeks. Anyway, I know you're probably running around right now, just wanted to say love you guys. Can't wait to see you all walking down the aisle later!

Love,
Gracie

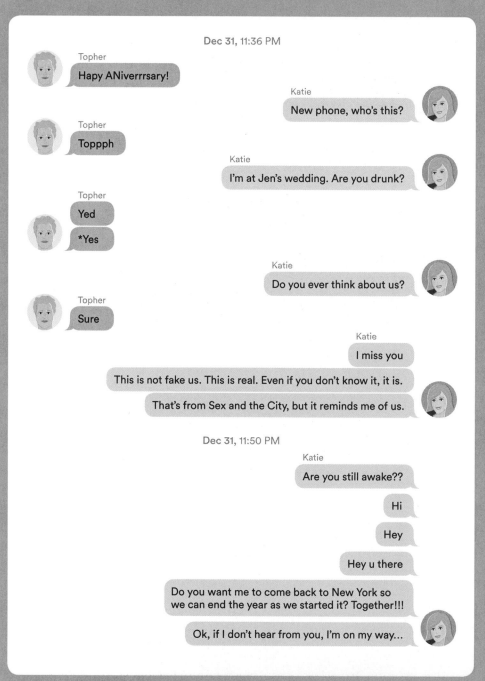

epilogue

To : Ali, Katie, Jennifer, Ashley, Morgan, Gracie, Caitlin, Nicole
From: MrsWallace1231@gmail.com
Date: January 1 at 6:19 a.m.
Subject: Re: Hey! :)

Hey Ladies,

Happy New Year!!!

Mrs. Brad here. Haha! Before we jet-set out for the Maldives (Google Image it, you'll recognize it as the iconic Microsoft screensaver background), I wanted to say thank you all so much for making the most magical night in history as magical as it was.

From the dresses, to the music, to the cake, to my father's 20-minute long speech complete with photo montage, to the champagne toasts, to the sparkler finish, it was an amazing night. It was so amazing that I am overlooking the fact that my cousin Kayla wore white, that the DJ played "Gangnam Style" even though I specifically sent an email being like, no "Gangnam Style!" and Brad passed out literally the second we got back to the room.

I'm looking at Brad sleeping/snoring next to me and I feel so happy and thankful for everything that has led me to this moment. Since it's a new year now and I'm a new woman, instead of doing resolutions, I want to do Thanksolutions, which is something I just made up which means to list out what you're thankful for. (Caitlin -- if you'd like me to give a CaitlinTalk on this word/movement I just made up, I'm avail! I just realized I have no long-term plans after we get back from our honeymoon!)

My Thanksolutions:

Morgan: You're the best friend a girl could ever have. Thank you for keeping me sane this year and dealing with all my quirks! And you thought I'd be a bridezilla! Thank you for not cutting your hair, or getting a new tattoo, and for holding my dress when I went to the bathroom last night. Will totally return the favor someday.

Ali: Thank you for organizing The Year of Jen!!! You looked beautiful last night! Looks like you hit it off with my cousin Lachlan! He's so great. His only red flag is that he's been so focused on his career, but told his sister over Christmas he's ready to meet someone, so his light is on! Get it. I gave him your number, so please send me screenshots and lemme know how this goes! (If this goes well, this means we will be cousins and Helene will be your aunt-in-law!)

Katie: You were so fun on the dance floor last night! I noticed you kept requesting songs that weren't on my approved list, but I'm totally cool with that! I saw you were on your phone a bunch too, so thank you for being on #hashtag duty, even though you weren't technically assigned. You're the best. Since you're currently heading back to New York to canoodle with Topher, I'm sorry you won't get to enjoy the omelette bar featuring the chef from Per Se :((p.s. Happy Anniversary! What if you and Topher are next??!)

Nicole: Thank you again for saving the day with Nicole The Runway!! My parents' friends Helen and Ira were complimenting the dresses, and I think once the lawyers figure out the alleged insider trading scandal, they said they are interested in investing in NTR!

Caitlin: I noticed you missed my first dance -- were you in the bathroom?? Totally cool, just wanted to make sure you're okay. Thanks for being there during my mini-meltdown when the makeup artist messed up my smoky eye. Your talk really helped me stay in the moment. Whenever I got overwhelmed during the night, I kept reminding myself to Caitlin My Life and be in the moment.

Ashley: Thank you for being such a calm presence yesterday! I saw you talking to Brad's groomsman Jeff. He lives in Darien! Did you guys talk about Connecticut stuff??? Please tell me everything. Brad is still sleeping.

Gracie: Your email yesterday was so sweet! I had so much fun on the dance floor with you! Thanks again for running up to the altar and bringing me tissues when I sobbed mid-way through Brad's vows! You saved my smoky eye, and in fact, my wedding!

Did anyone take any good pics? I believe you all were told to save your Insta stories to your camera rolls. Can you upload them to a Dropbox?

Seriously, I couldn't have done any of this without all of you! From being there at my Surprise Gal-entine's Engagement Gala -- to our summer nights in Montauk -- to traveling the globe and experiencing the SoPu McDonald's bathroom together -- to the triggering "friend-tervention" you forced me to attend against my will -- to the GREATEST NIGHT OF MY LIFE when I got to marry my best friend (!!!!!) you ladies have been there for me every step of the way! I couldn't have done any of this without you.

Here's to the best year yet! I really, truly hope you all find your perfect bliss, your perfect blowout, and your perfect Brads!!!

Brad, sorry, I mean MY HUSBAND is *still* sleeping next to me right now.

Who wants to get together to meet me before our Official Wedding Goodbye Brunch at the country club? Let's meet for a post-mortem where we go over MY DAY in detail and I can veto any wedding photos. I'll be in the lobby restaurant in 20! If no one responds to this, I'll assume you're all joining me!!

xoxox,
Brad's Wife!!!

---

* I recently got married, so please note my new email address!

To: Ali, Katie, Jen, Ashley, Morgan, Caitlin, Nicole
From: Gracie
Date: January 5 at 12:00 p.m.
Subject: Hey! :)

Hey ladies!

I wanted to wait a few days until after Jen's wedding to share some news with you all....
I AM ENGAGED!!!!! Ryan proposed to me in mid-December up in Vermont!!! It was just the
two of us, and it was really low-key and perfect. He proposed in our room at the
bed and breakfast where we were staying. We wanted to keep it between us for a few
weeks and enjoy the holidays/Jen's wedding, and then tell everyone after.

I'm so excited and over the moon! I've always pictured going down to the courthouse
and having a nice lunch after, but now that we're engaged, I actually *want* to have
a wedding! Trust me -- no one is more surprised than me! I was thinking something in
Brooklyn, maybe at an event space, or in a backyard (that's somehow big enough for
all our family and friends).

Anyway, there are a million details I need to plan, and it's as overwhelming as everyone
always says it is. I wanted to share the good news, and also see if maybe you all would be
down to meet and help me actually plan this thing?

I promise I won't be a bridezilla -- I'm just honestly feeling really overwhelmed. My cousins
and book club friends are no help with this kind of thing. (One suggested we plan a potluck-
themed wedding. Seriously! Ali, I thought of you!) And you guys are the best.

What do you guys think of a book-themed wedding, though? Are mason jars in or out?

Would everyone want to meet for brunch on Saturday? We can do it at my place and have
mimosas! How's noon for everyone? If you can't make it, no worries! If you can, just let me
know this week so I have a headcount and can make sure I have enough food and drinks!
Just reply all and we'll figure it out!

So excited!!!

Love,
Gracie

acknowledgments

We are incredibly thankful to have developed and grown *Hey Ladies!* surrounded by the support and tireless dedication of the following people who made this possible. Thank you to our unbelievably supportive agent Kate McKean, who guided us from our very first email and without whom we would probably still be talking about workshopping a Hey Ladies! musical. We are so grateful to our editor Samantha Weiner at Abrams Books, who saw how this story should be told even before we did and whose intelligence, humor, and encouraging notes in the margins kept us going throughout the process. Thank you to Danielle Young and everyone at Abrams Books for being a complete joy to work with, and to Carolyn Bahar for her beautiful illustrations and for bringing the ladies to life on the page.

Thank you to Nicole Cliffe, Daniel Mallory Ortberg, and Nicole Chung for giving us a home on the greatest website of all time, *The Toast*. And a huge thank you to the *Toast* community for being the most supportive and kindest place on the internet, and for inspiring us.

From Michelle:
Thank you to Deidre Moore, for being the best friend and the best reader, and for always being honest. An extra big thanks to my friends Sarah Tannenbaum-Dvir and Allie Ostrow-Sills—there's no one I would have rather gone through my Hey Ladies! years with than you two. Thank you to Davina Harilela for all our talks, Anjali Khosla for being the most encouraging boss I've ever had (and an even better friend), and Kate Brown for everything. Thank you to Bryan Rucker, Chris Honorio, Saida Cooper, and Shalin Agarwal. Also, sincere thanks to Nora Ephron and Rob Reiner for making a seriously perfect movie.

It's my greatest luck that I get to walk through life with my two best friends, my sisters Cheryl Vawdrey and Tracy Markowitz. Thank you Cheryl for always leading by example and showing us what kind of life we could have if we worked really hard and had a little chutzpah. Thank you Tracy for always being in my corner, always picking up the phone, and always making me laugh until my stomach hurt. Thank you to André Vawdrey for being the best big brother and sorry for stealing all your jokes! Thank you to Francesca and Henry Vawdrey for bringing so much happiness into my life. And finally, thank you to my parents, Diane and Eddie Markowitz. I literally could not have done this without you. Thank you for encouraging me, for giving me my sense of humor, and most of all, thank you for always believing in me.

And to Caroline—thank you for sending that first direct message, and for being my collaborator and friend. There's no one else I would have rather taken this journey with.

From Caroline:

Thank you mom for your unending support, friendship, and love and for always being awake when I call you in the morning. Thank you dad for passing along a love of storytelling, for editing my homework in 4th grade even though I didn't want you to, and for knowing I would someday write a book. I love you guys. Thank you to my favorite people, my siblings Ben and Lucy. You can't pick your family but you can pick your friends and I choose you two either way. Thank you to Charlotte Alter and Cara Eswein for reading the book at its earliest stages and cheering the ladies on, and to my dear Kaitlynn Murphy, who let me read twenty pages out loud as we drove down the coast of California. I am lucky to have a life full of talented friends whose words and art and work inspire me every day. This book exists because you all dove in first and showed me it can be done. Thank you!

To Dan Nosowitz, who pretended to believe me when I swore I wouldn't write Hey Ladies!-style emails the second we got engaged and didn't call off the wedding when I did. I appreciate it, and I love you.

And to Michelle Markowitz, who was once an internet stranger but is now a friend: With the birth of this baby we are now bonded for life. I am so glad we did this!

about the authors

MICHELLE MARKOWITZ has written for *The Toast*, Fast Company, *New York* magazine, the *New York Times*, and *The Hairpin*, and her videos have been featured on *Today*, MTV, *Jezebel*, and more. She lives in New York.

CAROLINE MOSS has written for *The Toast*, the *New York Times*, *New York* magazine, *Cosmopolitan*, *Racked*, *The Hairpin*, and more. She lives in New York.

Editor: Samantha Weiner
Designer: Danielle Young
Production Manager: Kathleen Gaffney

Library of Congress Control Number: 2017949403

ISBN: 978-1-4197-2913-3
eISBN: 978-1-68335-237-2

Printed and bound in the United States
10 9 8 7 6 5 4 3

Abrams Image books are available at special discounts when purchased
in quantity for premiums and promotions as well as fundraising or educational
use. Special editions can also be created to specification. For details, contact
specialsales@abramsbooks.com or the address below.

ABRAMS The Art of Books
195 Broadway, New York, NY 10007
abramsbooks.com